Blind Love

by Leon M A Edwards

New Generation Publishing

*I would like to dedicate this book to
Andrea and Alina for leaving me to it, to write.
Thank God for giving me the confidence to start writing
and the ability to write a story.*

CHAPTER ONE

Crash Boom Bang

It is late October and it has been raining since six o'clock in the evening. It has calmed down a bit now and it is drizzling. The dried-on oil on the road has been diluted by the rain and so the roads are a bit slippery.

There is a woman who is in her early thirties, black, slim and about five foot six. Her skin complexion is mahogany brown and she is naturally pretty with European features. She looks a little like Halle Berry but she has long hair going just below her shoulder. She wears it down all the time. She is a lonely child with her father, a lawyer and her mother, a doctor. Her parents are Guyanese who came over to America in the early seventies. She was born here in Los Angeles.

Her father has his own practice and employs about twenty staff. He struggled to find employment, when he first came over so he decided to find his own work. He began doing pro-bono work to gain experience and improve his resume. As a result, he gained a reputation and started to receive money for his work. Over the years, he grew his clients and started to make real money. He looks a bit like Danny Glover with the same similar physique. He is six-foot-tall with a crew cut and grey hair with a slight bald patch on his crown. He is now a wealthy man who lives with his wife in a cul-de-sac with a handful of luxury mansions next to the Bel Air Country Club. He has an authoritative personality and a serious nature. The neighbours keep to themselves except for one neighbour who holds four barbecues a year to represent the four seasons. They invite the neighbours every year but none of them come along.

Her mother is a paediatric doctor dealing with children that have acute illnesses that cannot be diagnosed as easily. She qualified as a nurse first before deciding to train as a doctor. She studied at night school and spent five years getting her qualification. She grafted hard for it. She is now a senior doctor at the Children's Hospital of Los Angeles. She looks a bit like Rochelle Aytes in her fifties. She is elegant and reserved. She always wants the best for her daughter as she is her only child. Helen became a doctor because of her mother.

Her parents live in a road called Groverton Place which is one of the wealthy parts of Los Angeles. The houses on the right as you drive into Groverton Place, back on to a lake. You can access the lake from your back garden, if you lived in one of those five houses. Her parents are well-off due to her dad having a business working as a lawyer in the corporate world.

Their daughter had a good upbringing with plenty of friends at school. She was a little chubby at elementary school but as she grew up she took part in sports. She naturally toned up taking part in netball and being a cheerleader. As she reached her teens, she started to attract boys and all the boys in her class wanted to date her. She was fortunate that she did not suffer bullying for being black.

She decided to become a doctor like her mom but specialised in Cardiothoracic Surgery. She is currently in a long-term relationship with someone who she met at university. They have been together for twelve years and she is totally in love with him.

They share an apartment together in Westwood of Los Angeles. She is a six-minute drive from her work. They met at one of the summer balls and he was her first and so she has not been with anyone else. All her previous boyfriends were at school and she concentrated on her studies at college and the first three years of her four-year university degree.

Her boyfriend is a regional manager and his work involves travelling around the States. In the last two years, he has been mostly working away for weeks at a time. She copes by choosing to work night shifts while he goes away and then changes to day shifts when he is home. It is not always possible for her to swap her nights for days all the time and so it has caused some friction between them.

Her boyfriend has been distant from her for a few weeks and she has her suspicions. They have not made love for six months and neither has tried to be intimate due to ships in the night. She has become suspicious when she unintentionally saw a text come through on his phone when it was on the sofa arm and she was sat next to him reading a magazine. She could see the message in the corner of her eye while looking at the pictures of the magazine. She could not help but divert her eyes to the message. The message showed a female name as the sender and the text was mid-conversation about how she enjoyed their night out. She was shocked by the content of the message but it was too vague to conclude that it was more than friendship. She had not heard of the name before but it would be highly likely a work colleague.

She saw the text a couple of weeks ago and so she has let it fester inside her ever since. She has not had a chance to bring it up in conversation, due to him working away and herself working night shifts. She has been trying to keep tabs of his whereabouts outside of his work. She has not seen his phone since that day and so she cannot confirm her suspicion. She spoke about the text to a male colleague and he suggested to her to track his cellular phone. He explained to her how to set it up and by using her phone on his. She then started to monitor his phone to see where it went and had been. She decided to follow him when he was next home and she was on a shift. In her head, it was likely that he would do something when she was doing a night shift, with plenty of time to be home before she arrived back by eight o'clock in the morning.

So, when she went to work on a Thursday night shift, she kept her phone poised to see if the phone leaves their apartment. In between seeing her patients, she would anxiously open the phone app to see if the phone had left the apartment. She already had her excuse for leaving her shift unexpectedly. Her male colleague, who suggested the idea of the tracking his phone, was happy to cover for her. She started her shift at six o'clock and only an hour has gone by. She hears her phone make a noise and quickly checks it while looking at a patient's note at the end of their bed. The phone app tells her that the phone is on the move. She stops everything and rushes to her male colleague to let him know.

She has to run to her locker in the staff changing room to change into her own clothes and grab her car keys. She then gets in her car in the multi-storey car park and drives in the direction of where the phone is on the app's built-in map. She assumes that he will be staying where ever it is the phone is travelling to. Luckily it is still in Westwood and so she does not have to travel far to catch up.

She is playing with her keys to start the car and then fighting to get the key into the ignition. As she travels to the location, her heart starts to have palpitations with the nervousness and last-minute dash. She feels herself sweating a bit around her neck and hair. The annoying thing about the app is that it does not say how far in measurements of time. It just measures in distance and living in Los Angeles, that can vary depending on the time of day. While she is driving, she starts to wonder what she looks like. She pictures a black girl, a white girl, looks, height and size. She imagines them kissing or being in bed together. She feels sick about the thought of them kissing. She is not worried if they are having sex because the sex is mechanical. The kissing is personal and intimate. It is passionate and in your personal space.

It is around eight o'clock in the evening and dark.

Her boyfriend and the woman are going out for dinner at a posh restaurant on Westwood boulevard road, called the "Flair Persian Cuisine". Her boyfriend is dressed in a dark blue two-piece work suit. The woman is dressed in a gun metal two-piece suit as well, with a white blouse that has a frilly design along the front of her buttons.

They park in the restaurant patron car park and go inside the venue while giggling together like two little school kids. Their table is at the front window of the restaurant, so you can see them clearly from the sidewalk and road.

She comes along in her car following the couple to the restaurant. She was caught at the traffic lights and so is a few minutes behind the couple. She passes the restaurant almost missing their car in the car park. As she drives passed their parked car, she breaks suddenly. She looks in her rear-view mirror post-breaking. She briefly panics that there could have been a car behind her. Luckily there is no a car behind her or tailgating her, for that matter. When it is safe to do so, she makes a U-turn in the road. She is able to turn the car in one attempt.

She then parks parallel to the restaurant on the other side of the road. She realises that they are sat at the window which makes it easy for her to watch them. She does not know whether to go inside the restaurant and sit at the bar. Or sit at one of the tables and order a side dish, so she can hide behind a menu card and spy on them. She decides to stay in her car so she can see them without being noticed. Because it is night time, they cannot see who is in the car if they were to look over. The restaurant has dim lights and so she can make them out clearly.

Her boyfriend and the woman are Caucasian. He has short dark brown hair and she has light brown hair that is shoulder length. They are both slim athletic like and he is slightly taller than her. They are both very attractive.

They are engrossed in conversation, laughing and smiling in the right places. This is the first time she has ever stalked anyone and she feels disgusting doing it but she needs to see that they are together. All they have done so far is laugh and smile. They have not held hands or kissed each other. They look like they are best friends going out for a friendly dinner. The woman in the restaurant with her boyfriend has no heavy makeup on and they both look like they are wearing the same clothes that they went to work in earlier today.

She looks at her watch to see how long she has been sitting in her car, watching them in the restaurant. It is eight thirty now and so she sighs as it has only been half an hour. She feels that it has been longer.

She feels famished as she watches their meal arrive at their table. She remembers seeing a cafe when she did her U-turn in the road earlier. She looks in her left wing mirror and rear-view mirror to see if their lights are on. The Mary and Robbs Westwood Cafe is still open. She decides to get a roll and a latte coffee.

As she goes to open her car door, she realises that they may notice her so she looks in her car for any kind of item that will distort her appearance. She remembers she has an umbrella and even though it is not raining, she opens it up before she comes out of the car. There is no one around for her to feel silly under an umbrella when it is not raining any more.

The man behind the counter takes her mozzarella and tomato panini that she chose, from the shelf and her coffee order. He is in no hurry to make her latte. The man is dilly-dallying about replenishing the coffee bean container and then heating up the milk. It feels like he has been twenty minutes.

She checks her watch wondering what time their food arrived and guessing what stage they are at finishing their meal. It is eight forty-five now as she gets her coffee, with her heated panini. She struggles holding the panini and umbrella in one hand and the latte in the other. When she gets to her car, she has to put the latte on the roof, then search for her car keys. She has to think about which pocket she put her keys in. When she remembers, she is anxious to get in her car and settle in. Once she opens the door, she quickly puts her food and drink in her car and relaxes.

She looks over at the couple in the window to see that they are still there. She then bites into her roll and gives a huge sigh as she savours her bite. After she has swallowed her first bite, she takes a sip of her latte. She does not take her eyes off the couple when taking her first bite and sip.

The couple are still sat having their meal, still smiling and engrossed in conversation. She wonders what they could be talking about. They are not being intimate or touching each other inappropriately. She is more concerned about what they may do intimately, when her boyfriend takes her back to her place.

It is now coming up to ten o'clock. Eventually they have finished their meal and desserts and are about to pay for the bill. She wonders who is going to pay for the bill. If they are friends, they will split the bill and if it is a date then he will pay and she expects her to be affectionate towards him as a way of saying thank you. She waits patiently for the outcome. The male waiter walks up to them with the card machine to take payment. Just a few seconds to wait to see who pays the bill. They both look at each other while the waiter shows the payment card.

She is disappointed when he pays for the meal and she goes in for a kiss on the lips. She starts to shed a tear when her suspicion is confirmed. She waits to see them drive back to her place.

When she sees them leaving the restaurant to go back to the car, she frantically gets her car started so she is ready to follow them.

After they leave, she follows them along West Wood Boulevard Road towards West Wood Village. They turn right into Rochester Avenue and travel through six crossroads until they almost reach Fairburn Elementary School. They turn into the fifth house on the left, almost opposite the school. She stops a couple of houses back until she thinks they have gone inside. She then parks opposite the house. She sees lights on downstairs which she assumes is the hallway. The light upstairs comes on before the downstairs lights are switched off. She notices them in the top window of one of the bedrooms. She can see a silhouette of their bodies entwining, behind net curtains and she assumes what she can see is kissing. She starts to cry as she sees in the window how together they are. She is hurt seeing them kiss passionately. The next thing is that there is an assumption that they are taking their clothes off, as that is what it looks like. She continues to observe them despite being adversely affected by their behaviour. Eventually they walk away from the window and the lights are turned off.

She sits in her car still sobbing, with her head rested on her forearms over the steering wheel. Her shoulders are shuddering as she uncontrollably cries.

Her suspicions are proven right and she wanted to be wrong. She blames herself for working too many long shifts to progress her career, and for what? She has no boyfriend any more to share it with. She was hoping that her gut feeling was messing with her head. After about half an hour trying to stop herself from crying any longer, she turns the car round to drive back to West Wood Boulevard Road. She does not want to go back to their place at Westwood Riviera Apartments where they share a flat, in Wellworth Avenue. She does not want to be round his scent, clothes, joint furniture and pictures of him. Also, their road is parallel to Rochester Avenue. She thinks to herself that they must have bumped into each other at one of the eatery places along West Wood Boulevard Road as both roads branch off from it.

It is about eleven o'clock when she decides to leave. She wants to go to her parents' and spend the night there and think about what she is going to do the next day. As she approaches West Wood Boulevard, the traffic lights are still red. She is still crying and finding it hard to see through her tears. It has started to rain hard again since she passed three of the six crossroads. She puts on her windscreen wipers, reacting to the rainfall. She is oblivious that the traffic lights are still red and drives through them. The roads are quiet at this time of night and no cars have driven across.

When she drives through the red light, a truck is approaching the same intersection. It is his right of way as the traffic lights on his side are still green. The truck is coming from her right of the crossroad. The truck has a heavy long base trailer which makes it hard for the truck to slow down quickly. It is even harder in the rain when the rain water has created the dried-on oil spillage and embedded rubber to turn slippery. The truck driver is not aware of her driving into the crossroads as he is concentrating on his sat nav to see whether he should be turning or going straight over.

The truck driver is not from around here and so he does not know the roads very well. It is only her and the truck driver in this part of town tonight.

While the truck driver concentrates on his sat nav, Helen drives through the red light. He glimpses up above his dashboard through the windscreen wipers and pouring rain, to check that there is no car or person suddenly appearing in the road. His reaction is too slow when he sees in the corner of his eyes, while looking back at the sat nav, her travelling in his drive path. He does not have enough distance between him and her car to break and allow the truck to come to a natural standstill. The roads are also slippery as a result of the rain.

The truck slams into the passenger door with such force, the car flips on its side and rolls over a few times, while the truck is struggling to stop. The car rolls on its side about four times.

During the car rolling, her head hits the door window causing her head to bleed instantly and crack the window. The impact causes her to black out straightaway. Her body becomes lifeless and floppy. Luckily, she is wearing her seat belt. As the car rolls four times along West Wood Boulevard Road, her floppy arms sway about in the confined space of her car. Her body literally rolls with the car as her body is not stiff. After the car stops rolling, it ends up on the driver's side. The chassis by the petrol tank catches fire from the impact.

The car is crumpled all over with the paint work flaking off in the creases. All the windows are cracked but intact. You cannot see how she is, as the front windscreen is too shattered to see through. She is bleeding quite heavily from the side of her head from hitting the door window. The truck is barely scratched and dented. The driver has only suffered a slight cut on his forehead when he hit the steering wheel on impact. The trailer swung out to his left as he slammed on his brakes hard, almost taking out one of the street lights. Luckily, there were no parked cars or any other traffic on the road. It is still raining but has slowed down. Her car chassis is still on fire.

The truck driver frantically feels for his cellular phone under his seat on the foot well, so he can call for an ambulance. She is still lying lifeless in the car. The commotion has attracted local shop owners and their customers to see what the noise was about.

A few minutes later, sirens from a distance can be heard which are not in response to the truck driver as it has taken him a while to find his cellular phone. It must have been one of the owners or customers.

The police arrive first in two separate cars with two police officers in each car. Once they get out of their cars and assess the accident, they are aware of the situation and try to free the woman from her car before the car potentially explodes. Two police officers use their rain coats to smash the windscreen in, while one of the other two police officers use their rain coat to put out the fire on the car's chassis. After about five minutes, the fire brigade arrives and uses their mechanical metal cutter to get the roof of the car removed. It is easier to get her out.

The ambulance arrives last, waiting for the go ahead of the firemen to get her on a stretcher and rush her to hospital.

After about ten minutes spent cutting the roof off the car, they gently move her out of the car seat and on to the stretcher. Once they secure her head in a cervical collar neck brace and her body is tied down, they put her in the back of the ambulance and then set off with lights flashing and siren noise blaring. She is still unconscious.

The paramedic sitting in the back of the ambulance with her, on the way to the hospital, puts pads on her skin by her heart for an electrocardiogram reading, also known as ECG. This is to monitor her heart rate pattern as she is non-responsive. The paramedic then puts an intravenous Cannula in the back of her hand to allow access for administration of fluids such as medications and blood, via her veins. Once the intravenous cannula is put through the back of her hand, he gets a syringe bottle of isotonic crystalloids fluid. He uses a syringe to suck out the fluid and then injects it into her hand via the cannula

During the journey to the nearest hospital, Ronald Reagan UCLA Medical Centre, about five minutes away, her heart gives out. The paramedic picks up on it as the ECG gives a loud single-pitch noise. The paramedic prepares to do an emergency cardiopulmonary resuscitation, also known as CPR, to get her heart started.

In a nimble way, he places one hand on her forehead and uses two fingers under her chin, then tilts her head back and lifts her chin. He then goes to start CPR and tells his partner what is happening as he starts chest compressions, before mouth to mouth resuscitation after twenty compressions. The driver acknowledges him and radios into the hospital to ask for a trauma and resuscitation team to be ready when they arrive.

He starts giving her chest compressions on her breastbone thirty times before pinching her nose and breathing in her mouth. He breathes in her mouth twice before repeating the chest compressions another thirty times. There is no response from her and so he keeps going so her brain is still receiving oxygen and being pumped around her body. The ambulance is only a couple of minutes away now and so the paramedic does not have to keep going for that much longer before the doctors and nurses can take over in the emergency room.

When they arrive, the paramedic that looked after her hands over their clinical notes. The notes include her age of thirty-two, the time of incident which is estimated at around ten past ten, cause of injury being a car accident and obvious signs of injury is trauma to the head. The notes also include the isotonic crystalloids solution and vital signs such as her body temperature, rate of breathing and blood pressure before she cardiac arrested.

She looks lifeless on the stretcher as she is moved from the ambulance to the hospital crash trolley.

The on-call female doctor greets them along with a male nurse. The crash team that includes an Anaesthetist and surgeon are on standby in response to the paramedic driver radioing ahead of arrival. The doctor and nurse recognise her straight away as one of their colleagues. They make her a priority and rush her to the crash team. The nurse continues CPR while wheeling her there.

When they arrive in the room, the crash team already have the defibrillator charged up. The nurse takes two pads from another nurse, holding them, and places them on her chest. The nurse shouts out "clear" to avoid anyone from getting an electric shock from the defibrillator.

The doctor uses her stethoscope to listen for a heartbeat. The nurse then shouts out "clear" again to shock the heart. The doctor checks for a heart rhythm again. They wait for the defibrillator to warm up again. The nurse then tries a third time to get the heart to pump again. The doctor checks her heart.

The crash team, the doctor and the nurse in unison give a huge sigh of relief. The doctor then notices a dark patch on her stomach and orders an emergency surgery for internal bleeding.

She is in operation for two hours to stop the internal bleed. After the surgery, she is moved to the intensive care unit. She is in a coma and is monitored every hour.

Her close friend checks to see that there is no change before calling her parents. She does not tell them the severity of her condition. She wants to tell them when they arrive at the hospital. She does not call her boyfriend as he is not put down as next of kin on hospital personnel records.

Her parents are naturally asleep when they get a call on their landline. It takes them a while to stir from their sleep to pick up the phone. They hastily get out of bed, change into casual clothes and rush out of the house. They are only an eight-minute drive away from Ronald Reagan UCLA Medical centre. They try calling the landline of their daughter's apartment, but there is no answer. They leave a message on the answer machine. They do not know her boyfriend's cellular number.

A friend and her supervisor, Doctor Faye is sat by her bedside as she waits for her parents to arrive. Doctor Faye is concerned that she will not wake up from her injuries. Doctor Faye wonders how she will tell her parents about her condition. How do you tell someone that their child is in a life or death critical condition? Doctor Faye is also worried how they will react when they hear the news.

Doctor is a homely mom with big bones. She is black with straightened hair down to her shoulder. She has been happily married for thirty years. She is in her fifties and she has three grown up children.

When her parents arrive, they go straight to reception to ask where their daughter is. The woman at the reception desk asks for her name so she can locate her. Once she is able to, she tells them to take the lift to the third floor and follow signs for intensive care unit. When they find the ward, they are greeted by her work colleague.

The doctor assumes that they are her parents. "Are you Mr and Mrs Simms?"

Her dad answers. "Please call me Bill and my wife, Martha. What has happened?"

She nervously explains. "My name is Doctor Faye. I am a close colleague and her boss."

Her mom Martha Simms stands over her bed and starts to get teary-eyed. Her dad Bill Simms walks over and hugs her shoulder. He looks at his daughter as well.

Doctor Faye continues with a sympathetic face. "Helen suffered internal bleeding."

Bill asks her with a worried look. "She will be fine, right?"

Doctor Faye looks down briefly and with a concerning look says. "She had to be resuscitated in the ambulance on the way here. We believe that she was not breathing for about ten minutes. We do not know what the severity will be."

Martha has faith in God that she will be okay. "She is a fighter. She will wake up."

Doctor Faye sighs. "We have put her in an induced coma. She has a swelling in the brain which is putting pressure on her frontal lobe. It is likely to cause temporal blindness. She will not be able to bear the pain now and so we need to allow the swelling to go down."

Bill looks at Martha and gives her a hug as she starts to cry in his chest. Doctor Faye looks on, thinking the worst.

CHAPTER TWO

Intertwine

I start to think back to when I was child and I was six years of age. I knew Helen from when we both went to Warner Avenue Elementary School. She was a little chubby back then, when I first saw her from afar. I did not find it an issue whatsoever. Back then, how you looked in Los Angeles was not the be all and end all. It would never have dissuaded me from liking her if appearance mattered. I would be in the same class in something like geography and she would be at the front of the class. I would choose to sit at the back of the class to her right. I would just find myself staring at her and wondering what soap she smelt of or what it would be like to kiss her on the cheek. I had a crush on her throughout the whole of elementary school, high school, as well as university. I daren't go up to her. I was happy to just enjoy the warm feeling of having an attraction towards her.

I would daydream about going on a date with her, to the park or going to an ice cream parlour. I would pay for her whipped ice cream and she would kiss me on the cheek to as a way of saying thanks. We would then go on a long bike ride around the block or through the local park.

The teacher sometimes caught me staring into space and they would joke with the other kids. I would just laugh it off. I would lie saying I was thinking of a film or thinking about what the teacher said earlier in the class. Helen would never turn around to join in with the teacher and the rest of the kids.

Some of the boys had cottoned on and teased me. But I always denied it. Helen never picked up on it and she never was drawn in by the attention of my teasing. She had her friends to play skip rope and skip games drawn on the concrete with chalk.

We did not live in the same neighbourhood and so I would not have a chance to bump into her, outside of school.

We were in the same class for all subjects, even though we did not introduce ourselves or cross paths in conversation. In elementary school, the boys hung out together and the girls hung out with each other. We were too young to form any feelings like that and so I did not like her in that way back then.

At the time, my understanding was that she lived about five minutes' drive away and I lived about twenty minutes' drive away from South Fir Avenue. There are two roads with the same name. We were in the road between Lime Street and West Hillcrest Boulevard. Not the South Fir Avenue between West Hillcrest Boulevard and West Buckthorn Street. I went to the elementary school at Warner Avenue because my mother worked there as a teacher and we had the fortuity of going to that school. All my brothers and sisters went to Warner Avenue Elementary School as well.

As I was growing up through the years of Warner Avenue Elementary School, I noticed quite early on that I was not like most kids. My learning ability was not as quick as the other boys in school and felt myself falling backwards in learning. I knew what the subjects were about but I could not grasp them that well. As a result, I suffered mental bullying and this made me keep to myself. By the time I finished elementary school, I was mentally scarred for life. My life at school was to stay at home until it was time to go to school. I never socialised with any kids because I was scared they would treat me the same as the boys at school did. Helen did not notice me as a result but I noticed her. She eventually lost the slight chubbiness and blossomed into a cute girl. All the boys liked her as we grew up, suddenly realising why girls were put on earth. I did not stalk Helen but I always looked at her whenever she was in my line of sight in between lessons.

When I was at school, I hid myself in the library during breaks and lunchtime. I felt that the library was my haven. The guys who always picked on me never used the library as a hangout. As I spent more time in the library, I gradually started showing an interest in the books I saw in there. I had a fascination with fictional books, touching on adventure, romance, and science fiction. I found myself critiquing the books, thinking to myself I could write a better story or detail the plot more interestingly. I also fell in love with going to the movies to get out of the house but not having to hang around areas where other kids were. I loved the stories they portrayed in the films and again critiquing the plots and how the scenes were used for the plots. I found reading and watching films was my saviour.

The bullying did not stop until I finished middle school. Helen went to the same Emerson middle school as me. She had become a swan and joined the cheerleader squad, dating footballers and I was not in the picture. Because I was in the bottom class for everything, I never saw her in my classes again.

I would go for walks by myself, through Grevillea Park. I would mull over how I would take my own life. I would dream up ideas that did not involve any pain and would be quick. I wanted it to guarantee success rather than have the embarrassment that everyone knows now. I had no interest in writing any goodbye letters. For all I knew, everyone else had their own wellbeing and their own little bubble. They would not notice little old me one day not being around. They would probably not notice until graduation day when they would have to read out the register. I also thought about how to hide my body so it could never be found; not even a person walking their dog would not find me. I would spend hours mulling over it.

There would be times when I suddenly wanted to achieve something like buy a skateboard. I would put my ideas of killing myself, on hold until I bought my skateboard. This happened a lot, like waiting to see if I would make it to university and then complete university. It would then be to wait till I found out if I would find a graduate job.

As I matured and became aware of my geographical surroundings, I realised that Helen lived in Groverton Place in Westwood. She was nineteen minutes' drive away from where I lived. She never ventured out my way as she had no connection in my part of town.

I quickly found where the library was in middle school and found the library much better than Elementary School with the facility they had here. The range of fictional books were more interesting even though I continued to critique them. The bullying never went away and I started to have suicidal thoughts again. Hiding in the library was not enough anymore. I became a hermit even to my family and I never left my bedroom. Eventually I began to cry myself to sleep quietly so no one could hear me. I thought the only way to cope was to start writing my own stories, writing my own experiences into fictional characters and stories. By the time I finished middle school, I had written over ten stories, with word counts of almost one hundred thousand per book. My mom found them one day and read a couple of them. I caught her in my bedroom crying as she read them. I felt embarrassed and just wanted the ground to swallow me up. I thought my mom would have a meltdown finding out what I had been secretly hiding. Instead, she said I should publish them and educate people about bullying.

She also asked what I wanted to do with my life. I said I wanted to find out if I could achieve what my brother and sisters have: go to university. So, she helped me do that, using my stories that I had written and also the grades I had achieved. I went on to high school to improve my grades in English and maths to study at university. I wanted to study English to help improve my story writing as well as looking to become an English teacher.

I was still dealing with my suicidal thoughts each time I had a setback whether it be girls, coursework or exams.

Helen went to the same school as me which was Marymount High School. She was only a minute's drive away and I was twenty-three minutes' drive away. I found out that she was studying science and biology and wanted to become a doctor or at least work in the medical profession. I thought at one time she noticed me when she waved in my direction. I waved at her with a smile, not believing that she finally saw me but it ended up being a girl standing behind me. I felt so embarrassed wondering what she was thinking, about me.

I noticed that Helen walked to school and I ended up following her home to see where she lived. She took a route walking over the Bel Air Country Club golf course. I thought it was a bit strange. Why she was walking through a golf course to get home? I made sure I was a good forty or so feet away so she would not feel I was stalking her. As I follow her, I come across a lake that was a part of the golf course. I was amazed by it. I wished that we lived near a lake. It looked tranquil. I continued to follow her along the lake and suddenly realised that her house backed on to the golf course, as I saw the top half of houses behind a large hedge row acting as a boundary for the golf club and the residents. I watch her open her fence door to her back garden and panicked that she would turn around and see me as she shut the gate behind her. Luckily, she did not.

I only followed her home once after that. I fell in love with the lake and ended up going there regularly at weekends and sometimes in the week. I started taking notice of the other houses I could see from the lake and one particular house grabbed me. I loved the look of it. It was not Helen's house. It was next door to her parents. I felt that I wanted to live there. I did not have any ambition to make a million to live there, I just wanted to live there. I ended up finding a favourite spot along the lake and I could sit there for hours. I visualised myself sitting here and walking back to the house. Now and again I would catch Helen walking along past the lake and I would quickly hide behind the tree, where my favourite spot was. She was totally oblivious of me being there. I was sad that I could not see her bedroom from the golf course. The hedge was over ten feet tall and the leaves obscured the view. It was one of the reasons why I liked it so much there.

As and when people asked me what I wanted to do when I finished high school, I told them that at some point I would become a teacher and publish a book. I base my books on characters that face problems and suffer through life but come out of the other side.

The response I would get back would be a mockery. No one believed in what I was saying. I was glad that people did not believe in me as it would set the path I ended up travelling on. Don't get me wrong, it hurts that no one believes in your ability and your dreams. It almost sent me over the edge but someone would speak to me and I would like to say it was God. Not one person apart from my family believed that I would get into university and study English to become an English teacher and a famous author. I was not interested in whether I could live off the money selling books, it was just that achievement was one of my dreams.

I ended up channelling the pain into my writing and creating fresh story plots and fictional characters to pour out my feelings. I found it was a way of releasing the pain I was going through and it was times like these that I wish I had a girlfriend. I think I was desperate to find a girlfriend so she could be my shelter and my strength.

I prayed every day that I would find a girlfriend that I could cry into her arms and talk about my issues. But God never answered my prayer. I did not hate him and I hoped one day that he would show me the reason why. So, I continued my life in a lonely existence and channelled myself in my studies and wished the days, months and years went by so I could get into publishing my books and be a teacher.

The more I was asked what I was going to do when I finished school, the more I convinced myself that I definitely wanted to become a teacher and focused on becoming a head teacher eventually, of my own school. Then I would re-educate people that you don't laugh at people's dreams. You give the child every reassurance that they will do okay, regardless of their abilities. Tell the parents that there is no such thing as failure. Failure is created by humans, not God. If you do not achieve your goal, then all it means is that the method you chose was not the right one. Go back to the drawing board and work out why that path did not work out. Then find the path that will help you get what you want to achieve.

I ended up going to university to study English, thanks to my mom encouraging me. I still did not publish my stories as I did not have any confidence and I felt embarrassed publishing my bad experiences at school. I went to the same university as Helen which I only found out by noticing her there. I assume she would go to Harvard as she was very bright. But I guess she did not want to leave home. We both went to the University of California. For her it was only another minute drive and a twenty-minute drive for me. I hardly saw her at uni.

I was still having suicidal thoughts, especially where I knew no one as I did not make friends during school. As per usual, I kept to myself and lived in the library in between lessons. I found that I eventually moved out of first gear and accelerated at university. I revisited my stories that I had written and began to type them up on my new laptop that I brought with my student loan, in between coursework. My subjects were not exam-based and so I had time to both study and write up my stories. I made improvements where I felt I could and left things alone where I was happy with the original stories.

After my first year at university, I never saw Helen again. Our paths never seemed to cross. I think her studies were too intense as she did not seem to be around much on campus. I thought about her more as I never saw her. I eventually lost knowledge of her boyfriends and social life, as a result. She still did not notice me.

I did have copious daydreams of being her boyfriend and being seen at various social events with her. Wondering what it felt like to be in a relationship, any relationship. I eventually started having daydreams of having sex with Helen. Visualising what sex positions, we would have. Wondering what it would be like to feel her, touch her hair, find out how she smelt. I tried to think how her boyfriend's felt when they slept with her.

She was my first crush and only crush. I did not meet or see another girl to have a crush on. I did not seem to find any other girl as fanciable as Helen.

I did wish that I would meet someone that I could fancy. But I never did. How I wished I could. I struggled to picture myself with any other girl I saw on campus. There were plenty of girls that were very attractive, but they did not have any spark for me to fancy them.

Even if I found another girl to fancy, I would not have done anything about it. I would over-analyse that girl like did with Helen, putting loads of building blocks between us. It was an excuse as to why I did not ask a girl out. Like I did with Helen, I would look at what guys the girl would chat to and put myself beneath them.

My bullying had a detrimental knock-on my confidence. I would find it easier to kill myself rather than ask a girl out. I would rather choose death than face a rejection from a girl. I would still be around after the rejection by a girl, to face the embarrassment.

But I could not pluck up the courage to end my life. So, I chose my studies as a way to avoid my dilemma. Studying did not judge me, make me feel worthless or magnify my lack of confidence. My studies did not let me down. My studies never left me and they were always there the next day. My studies were my comfort to try to make my life bearable for living. The more I felt hurt, the more I studied hard. As a result, my grades excelled.

During my spare time, I spent it burying myself in my story writing, to avoid my loneliness. I found that it distracted me from my real life. It also acted like a therapy for me.

Even though I lived twenty minutes away from University, living at home would not have been a good idea. It would have magnified my feelings of worthlessness and low self-esteem. It felt weird as my parents were not far away. I struggled to click with the other students on my course. I felt that they were better than me.

Even though I earned my place on the course, I felt I should not have been picked. All the people on the course found their new group of friends quickly. I would just make idle chatter to get along but I did not feel that I was gelling with them.

When my degree was coming to an end, I had about twelve stories completed on my laptop and backed them up on an external hard drive and cloud. I did not want to lose them.

I went straight into work not believing that my stories would be published. I did not go into teaching in the end. By the time I had graduated, I fell out of love with wanting to teach. I had no idea what I really wanted. I joined a couple of recruitment agencies and looked at what they had to offer me with the degree I achieved. The agencies pushed me into writing and editing. The work that seemed to come up most often was underwriting.

I was offered a job in an insurance company and they were impressed with what I studied at university and, having knowledge of story writing, they took me on. They trained me as an underwriter. The job involved my insurance company taken on a risk on behalf of the customer. The customer did not want to lose his own money correcting an error like flooding or being sued for an accident. I would be asked to assess the risk and then prepare the document for the customer to accept the agreement. You did not need to be a lawyer as it was assessing risk. The company had a template and it involved editing it to suit the type of insurance agreement. There was a steep learning curve in the first couple of years which kept me busy. But once I reached that curve, the work was no longer challenging and became monotonous for me.

Once I found the work easy I was able to tailor the insurance agreement more specifically to the requirement. After a few years of doing this I no longer felt fulfilled. The underwriting document templates became too easy and quick to edit and I could do it in my sleep. I started to become depressed and suicidal again. I felt my life was a failure because I was not being challenged. I felt that this was it. Was this as good as it got? I looked at my brothers and sisters and they looked like they had become more successful than me.

I found myself writing again and thinking of fresh stories to make into novels. I spent the evenings and weekends, including my lunch hour, writing my stories. At this time, it became more easier to self-publish and so I went down that route. That way I could never face rejection as I was in control of my own destiny. I started getting my stories from my school days published by saving up my employment income and as soon as I saved enough money, I would publish. I did my own editing with the degree I gained and also saved money by the same process.

I was still worried that I would not get anywhere doing my own self-publishing, but I had nothing to lose. I was in a job that I found boring in the end as it did not challenge me. The work itself was nothing wrong, but it did not suit me. I did not have a second plan if it did not work out. I was putting my life all into one basket.

The worst-case scenario would be to take my own life still. At least I would have known that I did the best to try to find something that would make me happy and worth sticking around.

When I started looking for publishing companies, I found it a minefield as there were so many. I ended up dwindling the choices by what they had to say about themselves.

I was worried that this was my only chance of finding happiness.

When I felt that I had found the right publisher, I looked at their fees for affordability. While I was looking into the publishing company, I started having doubts in myself. As I was perusing the company's website, I started to get nervous, wondering if I would actually get my books published and if anyone would be interested in buying them. I almost decided not to go ahead with it as I was depending my happiness on this. Because this was a dream for me, I was scared that I would fail. Then I revert back to wanting to take my own life.

I never told anyone at work or any of my family because, if it never amounted to anything, I would not have to explain myself. Nothing would have changed.

After about five months of emailing my manuscript and waiting for a couple of months for it to be published, I became nervous again. This would confirm if I was to stay as an underwriter or work full-time as an author. I started to question if I had used the right book as my first publish or whether it did not matter as I had plans to publish all of them. The sale was really slow at first and I ended producing a page on social media and a page on a business website. I linked this with my own website to tell readers a bit about myself and get the book more focused.

I was able to quit my full-time job after I managed to get two books published. I was nervous handing in my notice thinking that my book income would drop but I had enough money saved up to find another job if the sales dropped abruptly. My boss did not believe me when I told him it was because of my book.

He thought I was being premature. I had to give him a picture of the previous month's royalty cheque. He almost fainted when he saw it.

I gave all my ex-colleagues a copy of my book for free. I then wrote full time and never looked back. As a result, I found that I did not have to be around anyone. I did not have to answer to anyone or be sociable. I kept to myself at my parents' home while preparing all my remaining books to be published. I found peace with myself and was content. I started to think about Helen again and wondered where she was now and if she was with a long-term boyfriend or married now with a baby on the way. One of my books describes a character like her. I have had no reason since finishing high school to be near her house. I never crossed paths with Helen when I was working in the city, at the insurance company. I never saw any of the people from Warner Avenue Elementary School, Marymount High School or the University of California. I rarely ventured out of the house unless it was being taken out for lunch or dinner with the self-publishing company or doing errands.

An agent headhunted me and thought it was a wind-up. He ended up trying to impress me by offering free meals and basketball tickets. I had thought he was a stalker and gay. I checked him out just to make sure. I made sure I avoided going to the toilet the same time as him. I eventually agreed once I realised he was not after my butt and promised me fortune and wealth. I just took it with a pinch of salt. Apart from him, I never saw anyone else, except for my family.

This is why I now live my life as a recluse. The only people who see me is my family. No one knows who I am or that I exist. I am a famous writer but no one knows that I am that famous writer in Los Angeles. I did not put a picture of myself on social media, the business social website or my own website. Because I am a recluse, I am not put in a position to reveal my profession or have to tell people that I am author.

If you have ever been bullied, experienced depression, had a mental illness or a disability, then it is likely you have been drawn into reading one of my books. My fictional books, I am told, have helped a lot of people come to terms with their issues and accept who they are. That has made me feel a reason to live.

My real name is on my books and on my website, so if people were interested in finding out about me they could. I did not want to become famous. I just wanted to write my books and sell them, without the other crap that may come with it. All I cared about was putting a smile on my readers' faces and giving them a feel good story to read.

When I was on my third book to publish, I had an overwhelming feeling of being complete. I felt I found my purpose in life. My confidence started to grow and I felt reassured that I was good at something. I was never confident in any of my other areas of my life.

I had set up a forum for people to leave a message or opinions of the contents of my books. The majority were nice and I found myself having conversations with my readers. It was nice to hear that I was not alone with my bad childhood experiences. I could relate to them and the experience was overwhelming. However, it did not help me have closure and I felt something was missing or empty.

By the time I published all twelve books, I was collectively selling a million books a year globally. During this time, I was writing new stories based on what was happening around the world at the time. I also wrote a second and third series on one or two of my original stories.

Some of the chapters I wrote were tough to write. The reason is because I had to use my own experience to describe the characters' feelings. It caused me to have my own pain surface, pain I thought I had moved on from. It also made me have suicidal thoughts. I eventually decided to go for counselling. I knew that if I had not made myself go, I would have taken my own life.

None of my family knew that I was going through this. I did not want to tell them because I did not want sympathy.

When I felt I was eventually successful, I was sad and depressed as I had no one to share my happiness with. I did not have Helen.

By the time I was thirty-three, I became a millionaire. I went to my parents one day and told them that I wanted to move the whole family into a single house. I paid the mortgage on my parents' house and sold their house. I decided to buy a house that backed on to a lake, so I could spend time at my favourite spot.

CHAPTER THREE

Family Ties

We all now live in a fifteen-bedroom house. I do not see our house as a mansion. We each have our own bedroom, including my nieces and nephews. We have lived in the cul-de-sac for almost five years now. I bought it and put it in my parents' name. When we first moved in, my family organised a barbecue in the autumn to invite uncles, aunts and first cousins. It was not my suggestion. So, I chose to hide in the solarium that I paid for. It was for my parents to grow their flowers and a place to relax. I decided to use it to stay away from everyone.

After our first barbecue they thought it would be a good idea to hold four a year. Each barbecue party is in winter, spring, summer as well as autumn. I was not thrilled with the idea of feeling over crowded in my own house. During each party, I would hide away in the solarium with a bottle of my favourite wine and a wine glass. I found a good spot that allowed me to oversee the party in the garden.

I am the youngest of five siblings in our family. My eldest is my sister Natalya, who has just turned fifty years of age. Second eldest is my other sister Mercedes, who is forty-eight years of age. Third eldest is my brother Chevalier, who is forty-five years of age. Fourth eldest brother Xavier, who is forty-three years of age. Finally, there is me, Harvey, thirty-three. I cannot seem to meet anyone with my catch-22. I do not want to be around people but I crave companionship.

I feel the world is turning and I am standing, watching the world go by. I am reminded every morning at breakfast. I sit at the table looking around being reminded that I do not have a family of my own. It resonates, like the first time you go to the dentist.

We live in a quiet neighbourhood that backs on to a golf club. The house is big enough to house four families and my parents. My brother and sisters are all married with children. I am the only one who is not married and do not have any children.

Natalya is married to Michael Swan and they have two children. Their children are named Monica, twenty years of age and Lucy, eighteen years of age.

Natalya is about five foot six and slim. She wears a long flowing weave, down past her shoulder. Her natural hair is an afro that is relaxed but is long as her neck. She wears suits where the jacket matches the skirt. Her suit patterns range from patch quilt cordial style fabric to solid colours in nylon stroke cotton. She carries a dark brown leather handbag that is a third the size of a briefcase. She has large, circular sunglasses that she wears when driving. Her personality is feisty. She always has something to moan about.

Her husband Michael is in employment as a construction worker, project managing new build residential homes. He works for one of the household names. He is six-foot-tall and slim with slight muscular definition. His hair is an old-fashioned flat top. His personality is opposite to his wife. He is chilled out and does not let people get to him. He has to always rein her in if he feels she has spoken out of turn.

Mercedes is married to Montel Freeman and they have two children. They are Alina, seventeen and Andrea, nineteen.

Mercedes is similar height to her sister with short straightened afro hair to the base of her neck. She is slightly plump and wears suit trousers with a suit blazer and blouse to work. She does not bother with a briefcase or anything similar. Her personality is full of sunshine and bubbly-ness. She sees the best in everything.

Montel works at a high street bank as a bank manager.

He is slightly plump as well and the same height as Mercedes. He wears three-piece suits to work. His personality is as if he is downtrodden. He will moan about how his day was with work colleagues and customers. She will have something nice to talk about but he will find fault but he will do anything for her.

Chevalier is married to Melissa and they have one child. His name is Carlton, aged sixteen.

Chevalier is tall at six foot six and slim with a chunky build. He wears dark smart blue jeans to work with a double cufflink shirt and no tie. His work is writing bespoke software for medium to large businesses. He also contracts for agencies working in various industries. His personality is cautious and pessimistic. He always questions people's motives.

Melissa is six-foot-tall and slim with a booty on her. Her hair is afro and she corn rows it, tying it at the base of her neck. She works as an administrator for an insurance company. Her personality is calm and placid. She works to live rather than lives to work. She does not need to work and so she chooses to work to be around other people. Her hours are fixed and her day-to-day is routine.

Xavier is married to Christine and they have two children. They are Simon, aged six and a new born named Alexandra, aged three months.

Xavier is about six-foot-tall and slim. He has his hair completely shaved off. He cuts his own hair with an electric hair cutter. He is an IT supporter. He looks after servers that hold companies' emails, documents and employees' details. He also contracts as well as run the business with his older brother. His personality is laid back as well. His attitude is *things will be done tomorrow, except for work*.

Christine is five foot five with straightened afro hair, that she wears up most of the time. She works as a paralegal in the head office of a motor company. She also helps out as and when at her husband's business. Her personality is *things have to be done now*. She is regimental and would rather get things done herself rather than wait for Xavier.

I am five foot six with a bit of a belly. My face is round and I have a scraggly beard that is kept trimmed. I have my head completely bald so people cannot recognise me, if anyone knows that I wrote the books. My personality is that I am shy and reserved. I only feel comfortable with people I know well enough. I cannot naturally make conversations with strangers. I have to wait for the person to say something first. I still do not have a girlfriend. I am not looking but I think about a relationship a lot. I spot a lot of women that I fancy, but never have the confidence to find out if they are single and whether they would go out with me. I am not into stealing other men's partners or having an affair or fling. Writing some of my books about affairs is enough to put me off. I wear fashionable jeans with fashionable flip fops without socks. My jeans are boot cut as I feel straight jeans make my belly stand out. I like to wear polo shirts untucked. I am not into jackets. If it is chilly, I will wear fashionable cardigans. I hate suits and so you will never see me in one.

The eighteen of us use up thirteen of the fifteen bedrooms. The two remaining bedrooms are for guests or family to stay over. Parents and children have their own rooms, including Alexandra.

Monica, Lucy and Andrea are at university, while Alina and Carlton are at high school. Simon is at elementary school. They all study in Los Angeles and so still live at home. They are run-of-the-mill kids with no hang-ups or issues. They all get along with their grandmother's influence.

Their grandmother is a typical, strong black woman who rules with an iron rod. When the kids were younger and misbehaving, they would be sent to her. Nowadays their grandmother busies herself cooking, with a hired maid.

Their granddad is quiet and reserved. He lets his wife sort out any family issues. He is happy to watch his sports in their own living room that was allocated in one of the rooms downstairs.

Both my parents are retired. As I mentioned before, my mom is a retired teacher and my dad is a retired postman. He delivered the post in and around Bel Air. My parents came over from Guyana in the late sixties when America were opening the floodgates for people to help meet labour demand. Mom originally came over as a chef but wanted to change career. She went to night school and dad was in the army at first and transferred to America.

My dad is of Portuguese descent and my mom is Guyanese. Both my parents were born in Guyana and grew up there. They left Guyana when they were both in their late teens. They did not meet each other until they came to America.

My dad's name is Cadwell. He has dark white skin and slim. His hair is straight and combed into a side parting. It is almost white with some of his original black hair. He is frail now and so potters around in the solarium as well as watching the sports channel is his own room in the downstairs of the house.

He just wants a simple life and does not want for anything. I check to see if he is okay and if he needs anything weekly.

My mom's name is Lyra and she is a tiny bit overweight that has come on over the years. She has a pear-shaped frame. She is old school and has no idea about technology. She is happy reading the newspaper and reading her Bible. Now and again she would read a book, but none of my ones. She used to rule with an iron rod but now we are all grown up, she is mellow and butter would not melt.

She bakes cakes on a weekly basis, which all of us have. I would cut a piece and have it with half and half milk in my coffee. It is the best part of writing my books. She makes traditional Guyanese black cake. It is really nice. At Christmas, she would make it with rum. I import Guyanese rum so the black cake is genuine. It is one of the privileges of being wealthy.

I wanted to be able to give back to our parents for what they did for us. Both my parents worked hard to help send us to university so I wanted to show our appreciation by making sure they do not have to lift a finger. We have a maid who sorts out my parents' laundry. We have a chef who cooks and prepares cold food for breakfast and dinner. Finally, we have a gardener who keeps the grass short and the hedges tidy.

My two brothers are techie geeks, providing software suites such as email accounts, servers, website support and information technology consultancy as well as contracting work. They work at 5900 Wilshire Building. They have their business on the twenty-fifth floor. Their office windows face the part of the city that overlooks the US Tower Building. I helped them to set up the business financially in order to get the infrastructure in place, including servers and mainframes. I had visions of where they could be in the future. They made their own success and have plans for their own children to get involved in the business. They were able to repay me the money I gave them. They felt that they could afford to and did not want to be dependent. I used the money to help out a few local charities including a refurbished children's ward at the Children's Hospital of Los Angeles and Ronald Reagan UCLA Medical Centre.

My sisters found an interest in interior design. This was Natalya's idea and Mercedes chose to assist her with the bookkeeping. Over the number of years, Mercedes eventually ended up dealing with preparing the accounts and taxes, as well as sales invoices and chasing money. The business did not use any of my money. The two set up the business and made it a success all by themselves.

Both my brothers and sisters have their own office and so the home is a family home. I am the only person who works from home now and again. I have a room downstairs that is made into a makeshift library. I put a desk inside the room and a sofa and when I cannot be bothered to leave the house, I will go in there.

Everyone eats breakfast between seven and half past eight in the morning. It is Wednesday and as per usual, I can hear everyone downstairs having breakfast.

I am lying in bed still and I look over at the clock to see what time it is. It is just after quarter past eight. I get out of bed and put on my pyjamas so I am presentable. I sleep in just my underwear. As I walk downstairs, the noise of indistinct chatter at the table in the kitchen becomes louder. I walk in and pour myself a readymade filtered coffee and carry it to the table. Natalya glances over. "You finally got out of bed. The food is almost gone." I look at her with a blank expression pouring milk into my coffee.

Xavier finishes his last piece of toast. "Are you coming into today or staying at home? I can give you a lift."

I am not fully awake. "Huh… no. I have to be somewhere. So, I will drive in."

Chevalier is curious. "Is that your agent?"

I look fazed. "I have a few errands so I am going to sort them out first. Then get to work."

Mercedes is looking at interior design magazine and says. "When are you going to change that car? It is getting old now."

My mom gets up with her plate to take to the sink. "Leave him alone. He will change it when it is time."

I watch the chef bring my breakfast over. "That car was in *BEVERLY HILLS COP*. It is a classic."

Xavier puts his two cents' worth. "A shitty blue Chevy. You're the only millionaire I know who drives, ha ha ha, a shitty blue Chevy. All the other cars out there are Land

Rovers, Mercedes and Audi's. Even your nieces and nephews don't drive shitty cars."

I tuck into my breakfast and sip my coffee, ignoring the banter. I start to think about my meeting with John, my shrink, this morning. I have to be there for ten o'clock. Everyone starts to leave the table and go to work. Mom and Dad go to their living room to settle for the day. It is just me and the chef left in the kitchen.

I chose the time I wanted to see John, but I wish my day was not so busy. I would have preferred to have seen him in the evening. I have been seeing him for the past year. I have one-to-one sessions with John once a month. So far, I have told him about my childhood, being a recluse and he has encouraged me to join a social club, to start interacting with other people.

John is in his early fifties. He is married and they have a teenage daughter together. He was originally in a band during the eighties. He played bass and then he tried out being a driving instructor.

When one of his learner drivers was panicking before a test he made her pull up on to the sidewalk and get out of the car. He asked her what was getting her worked up. After they chatted, she passed her driving test. He realised what his vocation was.

He had a makeshift office built in his back garden, so he could work from home. The building is made out of brickwork.

His home is a typical white picket fence with a sidewalk leading up to a porch. There is a side gate to the garden.

The building has a tiled pitch roof. As you walk through the door, there is a waiting area with a seat. Then there is a second door to his office.

I get to my meeting at John's house a few minutes before ten o'clock. I am wondering, while I am sat outside his office, what we are going to talk about today. All I have to say is that I have been offered a television dramatization of one of my books. My agent contacted me last week mentioning it. He told me that the television company plans to have an open meeting to discuss the idea. My understanding is that they will ask me if it is okay and if so, they will want the rights to my work. I told him that I will need a couple of months before I can head over to discuss the possibility.

Money is not what motivates me and I do not just jump any opportunity that comes my way. I have had Hollywood producers come to me time and time again. I would ask to see what they have done in the past and not be impressed with their finished piece once they converted the book to film. It has put me off the idea. The money side would go up each time but I refuse on principle. I am content with my life and I do not feel that I need to try to prove myself by going into another venture business.

I have a couple of minutes left, so I now find myself looking around to see if I notice anything different from the last time I came. Nope, nothing has seemed to have been added or taken away or damaged.

Now I am thinking about what we talked about last month and the compact disk he gave me to listen to. I must have listened to that disk ten times in between writing and sorting out my errands. I listen to the compact disk when I feel I want a lie down and not necessarily go to sleep. I would listen on my hard leather couch I have in my downstairs makeshift library. It has my desk in there and a laptop. Nothing on my desk, except for a notepad that I use for sudden conversations or descriptions for my current writing or future writing. I just doodle rough notes to make me remember. It also helps to clear my head so I can focus on the now.

I hear the door suddenly open and see a woman coming out with John opening the door for her. She is a tiny bit overweight, not that it is an issue for me but merely an observation. She is wearing a white dress with a bird's eye view of red, open roses. She is wearing a pair of black stiletto shoes. She gives me a brief smile as she turns to John to thank him and say that she will see him in two weeks' time. I smile back at her in reply, acknowledging that she smiled at me. I watch her walk out of the door into his garden. I then recall that it is my time. John looks excited to see me. Guess that he wants to know what I have been up to since I last saw him.

John sits in his chair as I walk past in front of him to sit on a sofa that faces him. I look around again to take in what is in his office. Behind John is a white shelf, five tiers high, full to the brim with books on psychology. Some of the books are on Buddhism theory, others on psychologist theories on the brains and souls of humans. Each book is a mixture of black, white, gold, blue and red. A multi-colour montage. His chair is black and leather and bolt upright. It reminds me of the English show, *Mastermind*. To his left is a low coffee table with an incense burner and a statue of Buddha, like you would find in a tourist shop in Thailand. On my right is a dark brown cabinet at shoulder height when I am sat down. On top of the cabinet is a compact disk recorder with a microphone and a miniature coffee maker that can make latte, cappuccino or espresso by putting in a pod. He offers me one every time I come in. Depending on how I feel, I say yes. There is also a traditional green lamp like you see in law firms or posh libraries.

The carpet is dark grey and the sofa I sit on is green soft suede fabric with dark brown frame. I seem to like sitting with my legs off the floor, crossed. It makes me feel like a kid again and makes me more relaxed. I say yes to the coffee and as always, a latte, no sugar. It does not eat into my therapy session.

John makes conversation as he puts a pod in the machine and waits for it to do its thing. "So, how have you been?"

I look up at him with no expression. "Fine."

John looks at me with a jolly smile. "Describe 'fine'. One to ten without thinking about it."

My mind goes blank and I just blurt out. "Six?"

John gives me the finished latte. "Oh, so what is up? I thought it would more of an eight. Last time you were a lot chirpier."

I think about the question. "I feel nothing has changed since I last saw you. I feel I have a few issues ironed out but I still feel like me. The old one."

He gives me a frown of concern. "I feel we have come on in leaps and bounds. When you first came in, you were like you had a black dark cloud over your head. Now I see someone who looks like they have shifted that cloud. Have you been listening to the CD recording?"

I am honest with him. "I must have listened to it at ten times. I listen to it mostly when I am lying on my couch in either the office or at home. I rest my eyes as I am listening, almost falling asleep."

John smiles. "Great. That is what you are supposed to do. Just lie there and let your thoughts leave your mind and just listen to my voice. Don't try to hang on to every word. Just listen while you relax. Trust me, it works."

I look at him in disbelief. "Okay. Well I am doing what you ask me. If it is meant to be working, I have no idea."

John changes the conversation now. "So, I checked my notes on what we have talked about so far. We have not talked about your parents yet, or any brothers or sisters. How many brothers or sisters do you have?"

I look up, think about it and then look at him. "I have two older sisters. They are Natalya, the eldest and Mercedes, the second eldest. I have two older brothers who are next oldest. They are Chevalier, the third eldest and Xavier."

John looks surprised. "Wow, who came up with the names?"

I have no idea. "I would assume my mom. She wears the trousers out of Mom and Dad. He just lets her deal with the problems and he just sits in the background."

John asks if my family know that I come here. "So, do

any of your family know you come here?"

I have not told anyone. "No. Should I have told them?"

John quickly replies. "No. You don't have to tell anyone. It is only if you want to. They don't need to know. So, how do you get on with them?"

I start off with my older sister. "Natalya was too old to hang around with. She would go out with her friends while I was stuck indoors going to bed by six o'clock. She thinks that she rules us all being the older sister. But we ignore her. She has an interior design business that she fell into when she finished a degree in fashion. I guess the two things sort of go hand in hand. Mercedes is a book keeper and helped out my sister keeping track of the spending and money coming in. She started to learn about sales tax and income tax. She now deals with all the finances. It is both their business. Chevalier is in IT support so he looks after servers and makes sure that they run. If they crash, then he has to hurry to get it back on line. Xavier does software programming. He makes software to do whatever the customer is looking for."

John asks about nephews and nieces. "So, do have any children?'

I think about how many I have. "There are seven of them. Three of them are at university now. They are Monica, Lucy and Andrea. Two are at college and they are Alina and Carlton. Simon is at elementary school and there is the baby who is three months. She is Alexandra."

John is just sat there taking it in. "Wow, a large family. Do they live near you, or different states?"

I look down, becoming coy. "We all live in one house."

John face goes into shock. "What! Seriously? Are you like one of those Indian families that all live in one house? How big is the house?"

I feel embarrassed. "Fairly big."

John pries some more. "Four, five bed?"

I avoid the question. "Big enough."

John reads me. "No problem. So, you all live together. What is that like?"

I think back, reminiscing. "Okay. I was left to it. They thought I was spoilt. Got away with everything."

John asks me what it was like. "Did you feel isolated?"

I search my feelings. "I think I was a mistake."

John is curious. "What makes you think that?"

I am uncomfortable as I say. "I am not involved in family issues. I don't feel I am a part of the family. I feel adopted. I feel I don't look like them in appearance."

John looks at me with a sincere look. "Have you spoken to your siblings about this?"

I shake my head. "No."

John looks like he has further questions. "Do you feel more left out because they have children?"

I pause to think about it. "Yes and no. If I had met someone already, they would not be right for me. I was not in a good place. Not that I am now. But I would have attracted the wrong person."

John agrees. "You would have only met someone depressive who would have dragged you down."

I finish my latte and put the cup on the coffee table. I wonder what else he is going to ask me.

I jump in. "How did you meet your wife?"

John does not hold back. "I met her at a bar. She was on a table next to me, with her girlfriends. I spilt her drink by mistake and I bought her another one."

I am curious. "When did you realise that she was the one?"

I see John's mind thinking back. "A couple of months in."

I am intrigued. "How did you propose?"

John is pleased to tell me. "We drove to Lake Tahoe and we rented a cabin. It was by a lake. The weather was sunny with patches of cloud. You could see the reflection of the cloud on the still lake. We were sat on the edge, with a bottle of champagne pulled out of the water. It was nice and chilled. We had two flutes. She did not know I had the bottle of champagne tied to the edge of the lake from the night before. Proposed in the morning before breakfast."

I am jealous. "That is how I would like to propose. If only I could meet someone."

John is positive. "You will meet someone."

I am fascinated. "I always wanted to go to Lake Tahoe."

John is encouraging. "You should go. It is a nice place."

I remember seeing it in a film. "I saw it once in *City of Angels*. I didn't know it existed before then. I wanted to go there. But I had no one to take. One day I will go there."

John changes direction. "How about meeting someone now?"

I am stunned. "Have not thought about it."

John becomes enthusiastic. "I want you to try and meet someone. It does not need to be serious. I want you to go on as many dates as possible. No sleeping together. Just take them out and ask lots of questions about them."

I get panicky. "How do I do that? It is not my character to go up to a girl."

John suggests. "Go online, go to a speed dating event or an organised meet and greet. I want to hear how you get on next month."

I feel backed into a corner and nervously say. "Okay. I won't promise anything."

John gets his diary out. "So, when do you want to meet up?"

I think of what plans I have for work. "Wednesday again would be good."

John asks. "Same time?"

I just agree. "Yeah."

John tinkers with his recording machine. "Right, I am going to do a recording to give you some confidence to go on a date. I want you to listen to it as much as you can, before you go on your next date."

I move about on the sofa to lie back on it. He asks me to close my eyes as per usual. He then plays a soothing piece of music. The music he plays has harps and a voice humming notes. It sounds like angels. He then talks out loud into his voice recording machine on to a compact disk.

I almost nod off. The recording normally lasts about thirty minutes.

I drive to the office thinking about what my shrink asked me to do. I do not feel great about it. I would rather go with someone but I do not know anyone. I am hoping the CD will give me confidence to go out there on a date.

CHAPTER FOUR

Spring Party Time

It is the last Friday of March, the following year. I am now thirty-three and a full-time author with over fifteen books under my wing.

It is coming up to seven o'clock in the evening. I am in my office, in my brother's company, sat at my desk in the process of finishing my twentieth novel.

I am struggling to work out how I want my story to end. I am in a quandary and have three different endings in my head and I am trying to decide which one suits the story and the characters. Each one is plausible and as good as the others. As I sit there deciding, I start to look out of the window at the skyline all lit up. I find myself staring into space, making myself detract from my writing.

I am now pondering on my offer made to me by my agent to go to Atlantic City to have a series book I wrote a few years ago made into a television show. The books are a five part series based on a character that goes on adventures. My agent is trying to create a deal and he called early today to get my say so. I told him to go ahead as I have no reason to stay in the city.

I have not told my family yet. Not till I make my mind up. It could be the beginning of turning all my novels into television programmes, even a film. He has given me time to the end of summer to decide. He wants to get my current novel I am finishing to print first and to focus on that before going on to Atlantic City. I plan on spending the summer relaxing and doing activities I like catching up on.

I am not fazed by the idea, as fame does not interest me. I started writing because I had an uninteresting life where I was bullied at school. My way of dealing with the bullying was to escape through my writing. I would write various stories about taking care of my bullies in my mind. Over time, I would write short stories to fill my void in friendship until I went on to college to major in English. After I finished college, I got a graduate job and it confirmed to me that writing was my passion. I wrote my first book while at my graduate job and was quite successful, so I took the leap and did not look back.

I used my job to fund my story writing until my books were making me enough money. If it was not for using my stories to escape my day-to-day life, I would not be here today.

My obsession with writing made me write a proper novel. It got published and then I was paid in advance to write another. It allowed me to give up my work and write full time.

The genres of books that I write are romantic, crime, murder mystery and adventure. I write fiction with real stories but elaborate on them. I let my imagination take me anywhere. I write stories about love, sadness, bullying and what people are afraid to talk about. I think people like my books because I am not afraid to wear my heart on my sleeve and people can relate to my stories. They are not pornographic or mushy. Of course, there is sex involved; aren't all books like that? I write for adults and find it easier. I always struggled with writing children's books and so never got in that domain.

My publisher has given me a deadline to finish the book by the end of next week. I am keen to finish this book by the end of this weekend so I can chill out sooner. I also want to be freed up to promote the book as well as go to meetings on the potential television series. I am told that the deal could be worth several million over the next five years or so of producing them. It could also turn into a film. I already have plans to start another book in late autumn which I have been mulling over for the last year. My stories come from hearing other people's misfortunes and watching films that trigger my imagination. I enjoy writing as it helps me to hide from my real life and my utter loneliness. It has also helped me to pay for the family home and the custom I am used to. I used some of my money to help kick start my two brothers' business which is now a flourishing success and as a result, they give me an office to help me write my novels as a thank you.

I stand up from my desk leaving my laptop on and walk around my desk and stand by the window that is glass from floor to ceiling. I lean against the window pane with my right shoulder and look out down below at street level. I observe the people in the form of silhouettes walking in-between the street lamps. I can just make out couples and families going about their daily lives that look more interesting than mine. I always think that people's lives are more interesting than mine. It is what helps me create my stories and characters. I envy the people because they are living their lives. I, on the other hand, am living inside my stories, writing novels of how I would like to live.

The weather outside is showing signs of summer with the sun setting in the distance and clear blue skies early on. It is close to seven twenty p.m. and I have our seasonal barbecue tonight. We fund it and our invites can bring food and drink if they want which we give to the food bank for the poor. We want for nothing. I have a tradition of going to the bar to grab my favourite bottle of red wine, before heading towards the solarium. This is where I spend the evening observing the guests, preparing for my next character for my next story.

I am trying to finish the book before I go to the barbecue. I don't like getting to the barbecue early. I look back at my laptop, making my mind up on which ending to go with. I look at my watch and accept the realisation that I will not have time to write the ending tonight. I will have to do it from home over the weekend. I can access my story from home on our secured iCloud. My brothers set it up for me. It saves the hassle of carrying a laptop around. I have a laptop at home and a tablet to carry around with me on the road. I can afford to use a dongle to connect to the internet. I use software for writing my stories that converts them into a manuscript. The software also corrects my grammar, as well as spelling so I can just focus on my plot and continuity. It also helps out my publisher to get it to print sooner.

It is time for me go home. My car is in the underground car park of the building. I drive a Nova 1972 blue Chevy like the car in *BEVERLY HILLS COP* and also in *THE MAN WITH THE GOLDEN GUN*. I had restored it and it was a car I had in college. I had the interior redone as well. It helps keep my feet on the ground and reminds me of where I came from. My siblings take the mickey as I can afford any car I want but I don't want any other car. I love driving my car on a hot summer day around quiet out of town roads as it helps me to imagine what to write and the life I think I want in the future. The car also gives me the persona that I am not wealthy. So, girls will like me for who I am. They will not have an insight to how rich I am.

No one knows what I do for a living as I do not brag or tell anyone unless they ask. My books are not advertised in the mainstream. I only use the social media and relevant book websites as well as my own website for networking business. My books are sold worldwide via my publisher.

When I drive up to the house, I notice the driveway is filled with cars and the entrance to the garage on the right side of the house is blocked by the cars. I am annoyed as I wanted to park my car in my space of the ten-row garage that we park all our own cars in. I have to park somewhere I can find a space. I park up next to a BMW, Mercedes and Porsche with my basic car. Once I park up, I go into the front door using my own key. As I open the door, the music is instantly loud with people standing everywhere chatting noisily to one another. I cannot see any of my siblings and the guests do not recognise me as one of the members of the family. The partygoers do not acknowledge me as they see me as another guest they do not know. I politely squeeze through the people to get to the back of the house to the garden. There is a long hallway that divides the house between the living room on the left and the kitchen and dining room on the right. The hallway leads directly from the lobby area of the house that you could call the reception area. The reception area is twenty feet wide by ten feet for people to congregate and be welcomed into the house. The flooring is solid light brown oak throughout the house, including the second floor. It is varnished and polished to a high finish that liquid and food cannot penetrate. The house is worth about four million dollars.

Once I get through to the back of the garden, I see the outdoor bar with a couple of hired staff from a catering company serving the drinks that we bought for the guests. I walk up to the bar asking for my two-hundred-dollar bottle of wine, I asked to be hidden behind the bar for only me to drink. It is a wine I enjoy and only buy four times a year for the barbecue. I have a routine of grabbing a wine glass from the barman and walking to the conservatory to sit in the same corner that faces the garden.

The garden conservatory is made out of a three foot high brickwork with the remaining building made of glass held together by black coated steel joinery holding the glass panes together. The roof is a dome shape and the building is rectangular, fifty feet by twenty feet. It is filled with flowers like roses, jasmine, waterlily, zinnia, tulip and so on. The interior brick wall of the conservatory has a lip-like shelf made of concrete that goes around the perimeter. You can sit on it like a seat. I sit in corner of the conservatory that faces the garden where the barbecue is set, with white garden tables and chairs. The grass is thick and luscious green that is looked after by the gardener we hire. I sit on the lip of the wall, with my favourite bottle of red wine resting on it.

I start my people watching. I am a recluse and find it hard to mingle with people, especially people I do not know. The characters I notice in the garden standing, sitting, merry, completely drunk, I make mental notes of. I like to add these nameless people to my story writing. I do not have a habit of using real people's flaws, intimate embarrassing stories or tragedies in my books. Friends of the family have asked me to in the past but it is not my character. I would rather write about my own tragedy, knowing that I am happy to do that. I don't write anything down on paper as I find I get buried in copious amounts of paper and struggle to get them in chronological order, to put finger to keyboard. So, I mull over stories in my head then just write it out.

While I am sitting there by myself, I get a phone call on my Cellular phone.

I look at the screen to see who it is, focusing hard. "Hello?"

It is my agent and he sounds chirpy as ever, with a loud brash voice. "Hi. Great news. This royalty is better than ever. Guess how much?"

I am unenthusiastic as money does not motivate me. "Have no idea."

He is still chirpy. "You cleared two million. Well, after my commission. It will hit your account… now."

I am too merry to show any excitement. "Just checking it now. Yep, I see it. I will see you in a few weeks."

He sounds disappointed as I was not excited as him and sighs. "Ah, okay. See you in a few weeks. If you need anything, just call."

He hangs up and I go back to people watching. I notice a man walking towards the barbecue. He is tall with a cane in a white suit. He is black with a white grey beard with freckle of black still showing through. He has given me an idea for my next action novel. I think to myself, *'I can see him being the bad guy and the most dangerous villain. The plot can be based in Africa, no, New York. I may have to mull over it for a while. Ah, a nice tidy woman who is Chinese and slender. She can be the best assassin in the world and work for the beaded black dude. His right hand man. And finally, a superhero. Where can I find a superhero? And there, another man who will be that hero. He is Asian with typical features and I can imagine him in a combat gear as an agent.'* I will see about writing that novel after my next one which I have already sketched out in my head.

This is my life. This is what I do. It is my way of battling my demons. I have eventually started seeing a shrink. I decided to finally deal with my demons when I was going to take my own life before Christmas. I dove into my last novel to distract my thoughts. I spent hours on end writing, to block the thoughts from my head. I have only had five sessions so far and my family do not know that I am feeling this way and that I am getting professional help.

I am lonely and have been a recluse all my life. I do not have any friends as I do not trust anyone and so I spend my life between the office and the house. If I want to be alone, I take a walk to the lake from my back garden and spend hours at my favourite spot. It is my tranquillity. I will take my tablet with me and type for hours. No one goes there and so it is my hiding place.

Time has gone by quickly as per usual and I am ready to go to bed as it is close to ten o'clock. I finish the last bit of wine in the bottle by necking the bottle instead of pouring it out. I stand up and stumble a bit. I compose myself and walk out of the conservatory and back into the house. I sneak through the crowd of people in the house and go to walk upstairs. The guests and extended family are not allowed to go upstairs and so they stop at the bottom of the stairs. I go straight to my bedroom and start to get ready for bed. I can hear the faint noise of the guests chatting through the bedroom floor.

My clothes are a standard pair of chinos with a plain t-shirt and fashionable cardigan. I wear sketches shoes that suit my trousers. I am about to start undressing when I hear a knock on the door.

One of my brothers speaks up. "Harvey? You there?"

I go quiet thinking he will go away.

My brother knocks again and speaks louder. "Harvey! Someone wants to speak to you. I know you are in there. I saw you were not in the conservatory. It is ten o'clock. I know your routine."

I close my eyes and clench up thinking I don't want to be bothered. I eventually own up to being in my bedroom.

I sigh. "Okay. I will be there down in a sec. I am in the middle of…" *'Think. Think.'* "I am just brushing my teeth. Tell him… her… I will be right down."

There is quietness, then. "Yep. I will tell him to meet you in the chill out room."

I sigh again. "Yeah. Do that."

I begrudgingly put my cardigan back on and like a school boy that is not allowed to buy a sweet, trudge out of my bedroom and down the stairs. As I go downstairs, I suddenly notice the guests looking at me as if I am weird looking. I think they recognise me as the writer from my books. They seem like new guests that we have not had before. I just walk past them to the chill out room.

The chill out room is like a smoke room that you go to after dinner but it has a snooker table, sofa and a bookshelf full of all the books I have written and other books my family have bought along the way. As I go in, the man is standing by the window look outside at all the cars in the driveway. I quietly walk in so I do not disturb him and go over to the drinks cabinet to pour out a glass of premium rum I import from Guyana. He hears me, as he is startled and turns to me. I look at him as if I have been caught in the cookie jar.

The man reminds me of Earl Jones with similar build and features. He is slender though but not by much. He has his arms behind him and stands tall with his head in the air. He has a posture of a headmaster in authority. Here we go.

I start off the conversation nervously. "Would you like a drink? It the best premium rum in the world. It is from Guyana."

His stern face turns into a smile. "Yes. Can you put in a bit more? A bit more. That's it."

After I fill his glass to the brim, I pass it over, trying not to spill it. "Mr Simms, what can I do for you? I believe you live next door. From what I can remember."

He relaxes his posture. "Call me Bill. I have a favour to ask."

I look at him with a worried look. "How can I help you Mr… Bill? What can I do for you?"

Bill suddenly notices the books on the shelf and is distracted. "You wrote all these books."

I go to sit down keeping my eye on him. "Yes. They are all the originals I get from the publishers, each time they go to print."

Bill never knew I wrote them. "You wrote all these. They must have taken you ages."

I look at my glass. "Since I was about sixteen. I finally started getting them published when I finished uni."

Bill is open-mouthed. "I think I read one of your books. It was about a lawyer and reminded me of…"

I keep looking at my glass and wondering if he has cottoned on yet. I used him as one of the characters in one of my books. I studied his mannerism and researched on his firm using his website and any articles online.

Bill looks at me with a slightly open mouth. "You based that book on me. Accurately. You have a talent, Mr Spade."

I explain myself. "I wanted to write a book on a tragedy and no one wanted to help. I thought you would be a good person to base it on. I just wanted to use your persona and completely create a fabrication. The character was all of you but the story was totally from my head."

He looks at me in awe. "You are good. How did you

study me when you have never been to my house and never seen me at work?"

I tell him how. "I observe. I do not need to interact. If I do, I get to realise they are not what I imagined. So, I just look. It is easier reading about people. I hope you are not offended."

Bill looks complimented. "How did you research on the law?"

I smile. "I watched a lot of films and television shows on courtroom dramas and took notes."

Bill smiles. "If you want to do another book on the law, you can follow me around."

I smile. "Thanks. I will take you up on that."

I feel Bill wants to talk shop now. "Mr Spade–"

I correct him this time. "Please call me Harvey. I don't speak on ceremonial grounds. You wanted to see me?"

He remembers the reason why he came here. "I asked a few people before you, but their lives are too busy. They all said you. You came highly recommended."

I am baffled. "I do not have any friends. Who told you about me?"

Bill recites the names. "I looked at my daughter's yearbook. So, Tom, a car mechanic now. Mike, a computer geek. He works for your company. Charles, a lawyer. He asked me for a job. And Pete, a pet shop owner. I told them I looked them up in the yearbook and internet. They each said you."

I am still waiting in anticipation. "So, why were you looking up people in a yearbook?"

Bill takes a swig of his drink. "It is my daughter. Something happened five months ago in October. We almost lost her but she is a fighter."

I know who she is. "Why doesn't Bob take care of her. He is her boyfriend. I thought he would want to be near her, since she had the car accident."

Bill looks at his glass in embarrassment. "He is always away. It is to do with his work." He suddenly realises that Harvey knew it was a car accident. "How do you know

Helen was in a car accident?"

I read it on social media. "I notice things. So how is she now?"

Bill explains the situation. "She has pressure on the brain. It was caused by the car accident. She was in a coma for a week. She did actually die for about ten minutes. Luckily her heart was pumped to circulate the air around her body and so her brain did not starve of oxygen. However, she cannot remember the accident or why she was driving that night. She does not remember certain things. So, I thought an old school buddy would help."

I think out loud. "A salesman. He can speak to his people. Take compassionate leave. Work from home."

Bill grumbles. "Tell me about it. He doesn't want to deal with the situation so I need to find someone I can rely on."

I show my understanding by nodding. "I guess they know that I am single and have time on my hands. They have family and in are demanding work."

Bill looks up at me, right at my eyes. "I need someone who can spend days at a time with her. Not just the evening and weekends. I can pay you."

I stand up and walk around the furniture, circulating him. "I don't need the money. You know that. I know that. Hence why you came to me."

Bill sighs as he has been caught out. "You can work anywhere. I was wondering if you could do your work around my daughter."

I think about it. "We have nothing in common. She has never met me. She has no idea who I am. She wouldn't even recognise me if she saw me."

Bill hesitates. "That wouldn't make any difference considering she is blind. She has been slowly getting depressed. She has no one. Her friends have tried to help but they have their own lives."

I walk over to the window. "If... I mean, if I decide to do this, I only have a few months before I head out of town. I have a book signing in about two months and I am potentially heading out of town for a television deal."

Bill smiles with hope. "So, you will do it. Look after Helen. By the time you go, she would have already had her operation to get her sight back."

I turn to him. "Does she know about the operation??

Bill looks at me in surprise. "How do you know?"

I use my instinct. "Instinct. It is what has helped me write my books. She is depressed. Anyone who is looking to get their eyesight back would be positive. I assume you have not told her as it might not work."

Bill is impressed. "That is why we have not told her."

I ask him a question. "Does she know who I am?"

Bill looks embarrassed. "No, she doesn't. She doesn't even know who her neighbours are. She has been fixated by her career and her long-term boyfriend."

I accept. "Well, I want to keep it that way. I will be over on Monday night at seven. I have a few things to sort out. I will set up an itinerary of where to take her out. Where is she living and will Bob have an issue?"

Bill finishes his drink with the remaining equivalent of a single shot. "He is out of town for a few weeks. She is living at our house in the meantime. He is only back for a few days at a time."

I have one more question. "Why was she driving at that time of night when she should have been doing a nightshift?"

He looks shocked. "How the hell do you know that?"

I finish my drink which is equivalent to three shots. "I donate money to that hospital, once in a while. I know a few people there."

Bill is ready to leave. "Thank you. I will pre-warn her. Do you observe everyone?"

I casually say. "I have a habit of reading people's body language. I have been doing it ever since I can remember. I think since I was six. I think that is the reason why people like my books. I talk about real life not fairy tales." Bill lets himself out of the house and I stay in the chill out room thinking about Helen. I remember Helen from school and from going to the same college. Like me, she stayed in Los Angeles and studied at the local university. I lost touch with her after the first year of university as I focused on my studies. I have no idea what she looks like now as it has been almost fifteen years since finishing at the age of twenty-three. I am now thirty-eight.

I eventually go up to my bed and lie in my birthday suit under the duvet. I start to think about Helen, what I remember of her. I have my right arm behind my head facing the ceiling with my other hand twirling myself while I think about her. Not in an erotic way. It is my proverbial comfort blanket.

I start to mull over what kind of things I can do with Helen from the point of view of being blind.

The next day I take my walk to the lake and sit in my favourite spot. Before I write my final chapter to the ending I decided to go with, I look up activities for the blind. The suggestions are exercise such as walking, hiking, swimming and even rock climbing. The information also mentions sensory activities such as gardening, sculpting and knitting. Reading books to her or uploading books on a computer for her to listen to are also options. I can look at buying the software to allow her to listen to books on her computer. The software has a speech synthesizer.

I did not know that there are recreational and leisure activities that a blind person can do. How would I know if I am not blind and I have never had a friend or family who is blind?

The other idea that I had in mind was taking her to a theme park and letting her enjoy the rides without her eyesight. Even if she has already been to the theme parks and went on the rides before, she will experience them in a different way. The final idea was board games. I did not realise that you can get braille and tactile versions of games such as Monopoly, Scrabble, Chess and Checkers.

The game boards have raised boundaries between the squares, braille letter tiles and braille captions indicating the word scores. Checkers can be adapted by myself, by sticking a textured surface on the centre of the red or black squares so Helen can differentiate between them. I get excited thinking about having to look after her over the coming months.

CHAPTER FIVE

Get the Car

It is now April Fool's Day, not that my family do any pranks on each other. It feels like summer already.

It is Saturday morning. I glance over at the digital clock and it says eight forty-five. Helen suddenly pops into my head, again. I could not stop thinking about her all night and I found it hard to get to sleep. I have not seen her since the second year of university. I wonder what she looks like now. Has she put on weight or stayed the same since I last saw her? I have a smile on my face, thinking that I am going to be spending time with her.

I go for a shower in my en-suite, while thinking about where to take Helen on Monday evening. I feel upbeat wishing Monday to come around quickly. I know she has a long-term boyfriend and nothing is going to come of it but this has reignited my dreams of being her boyfriend. That is enough to substitute not having a girlfriend or a wife.

My first thought is to focus on dating. I think I will have to go online dating. I thought I could avoid internet dating as it is not my preference. The thought of finding women that are focused on appearance, not the character or personality of the person, is daunting.

I plan on checking how many dating websites there are out there, and to separate the wheat from the chaff. I will do this by glancing at the people, both women and men, that use the website. I can look at the pictures and comments on the dating websites and make a good judgement from my observations. I am not interested in whether they are rich or poor. Either can be ugly, metaphorically speaking. I just want to look for a normal person who is looking for a long-term partner. Preferably someone who believes in marriage.

I am worried that I will not get any dates before I next see John. I do not want him moaning at me.

I am not really into dating. I have not brought it up in any of the sessions over the past twelve months. I only wanted help with dealing with my depression and suicidal thoughts. Finding a girl to like me was not in my thoughts.

I am comfortable with being in my own skin. I do not feel a craving for companionship, though I think about it often. I am reminded of relationships with my family under one roof. My thoughts about being in relationship contradicts my feelings of having no interest in a relationship.

I head downstairs to the kitchen for breakfast, after getting dressed after my shower.

It sounds weird for me to say, but I do not want to pay for the dating service. I do not want to spend money on a website and not end up meeting anyone or have the desperation of meeting someone, just because it has cost me so much money so far. I do not want to latch on to just anyone based on how much it has cost me. At the same time, I do not want to throw money down the drain.

Also, I do not want to meet any time-wasters or anyone that wants a bit of fun or a one-night stand. If I did meet my future partner through the process, I would want to get married. That is my strong belief.

There is no one at the table for breakfast. It looks like the maid has already tidied up, as the table is clear. It looks like the chef is preparing for dinner tonight. I decide just to have toast and a coffee. It would seem everyone else has already had breakfast and gone about their own business, whether on the grounds or out for the day.

I want to spend the morning and part of the afternoon finding the right dating website, then think of the first activity to do with Helen after that. It will be easier to do my research on a computer rather than my phone.

I decide to use my office room where I write when I work from home. I keep my laptop on top of the desk.

I go to my office soon after having my buttered toast with my half and half white coffee.

As I am waiting for the laptop to boot up, I keep looking out for anyone walking in the hallway past my office. I keep thinking that I can hear someone walking by, but it is just my mind playing tricks. I am fidgety as I do not want anyone to know what I am doing. I feel embarrassed that I am looking for a relationship. Especially on the internet.

I am independent and I do not need a relationship to fulfil my life. Admittingly, sometimes I would like a relationship to fill parts in the day, but not all the time. My brothers and sisters met their partners naturally. They did not look for them consciously. So, if I am supposed to be with someone, then I will naturally meet them. Looking for someone seems to be forcing a relationship to happen. Finally, my laptop springs to life.

After I log in, I open up the internet to search dating websites. In the search field, I type 'dating websites' and loads come up. It is a minefield. There are some I recognise from adverts on television and others that feel are new.

I know I have to go inside each website to look at the type of people on there. This is going to take ages. It has taken twenty minutes already and I have only added the different websites in my favourites, under a new folder. I have called the folder 'websites' and have saved almost twenty websites there.

I grab a notepad and pen from across the room to make notes on the clientele that is on each website.

It takes me just over an hour to weedle out the tasteless dating sites. I am left with six strong potentials. I make one more search by using 'over thirty dating' to see if there are any new names. Only a couple more came up and from gaining familiarity, I can see they were not worth perusing.

Now I have found my six potentials, I make comparisons by having six windows open, so I can flick between them. I make for and against lists, finally coming up with one suitable website.

I move away from my desk leaving the chosen website open. I carry my notepad and pen with me. I go over to the sofa to feel relaxed. I decide to start writing out my likes, dislikes, wants and education level. I then write a brief description about my personality. I want to do this properly, not go in half cocked. If it does not work, at least I can say I gave it my all. I want to attract the right people. My profile will scare off the time-wasters that want a five-minute fling.

I mull over what I want to write about myself. I will be putting up a picture and so I will have to describe myself. Ah, I know. I will talk about my height, size and weight. I will then write about what I do when I am not working or doing errands. That is pretty much nothing. I am too busy helping out family and neighbours.

I cut the grass for an elderly couple with old money. I feel sorry for them. They can barely breathe, not less leave their armchair. They think I am a student on holiday. It is my fault for giving them the impression I do not work. I also help out in a local charity that another neighbour is involved in. Then there is the odd donation I make and now looking after a blind friend. What could I possibly write that will make me sound good?

The penny drops. Why don't I just put down what I just mentioned to myself? I am not lying and there is nothing else I do. At least when I next see my shrink, I can say I did my best.

It has been two hours now and I have finished my notes. It is now time to create an account on the website. I sit at my desk in front of the laptop pondering where to find a picture of myself. It needs to be a picture with my beard. That way when I meet them, they will recognise me. I try to look for any photos stored on my laptop. I cannot see any with my beard. I check on social media to see if anyone took a picture of me and put up on their page. Nothing there. I now have to take a picture from my phone. I hold my phone up to my face at arm's length, horizontal and with the bookshelf of all my books on the top shelf. Vanity. I don't want people to think I am showing off the number of books I have written. Let's go by the window. Great, the lighting is good. Great, now I have porches, Mercedes and a Ducati in frame shot. I don't want people to think they are my cars. Let's take one against the blank wall. Ah, much better. Simple and no material belongings in the background. I can upload this photo. Let's quickly do that now before I get distracted.

Now to type up what I do in my spare time in a Word document before copying and pasting it in the field box. It also allows me to make spelling and grammar corrections. By the time I am finished, it is almost three o'clock. I am tired from the thought process. I will leave it till tomorrow, Sunday, to view potential ladies. At least I have something interesting to do and something to look forward to in the upcoming week.

I go into the kitchen, where I last left my tablet on the side, to look up restaurants on the internet. I search for restaurants close by to our road, Groverton Place.

I have no idea what restaurants are around as our chef can make any culinary dish. So, I have no reason to go out for something to eat.

I think about what type of food there may be like Indian, Mexican, Italian or even Caribbean.

My search brings up over ten restaurants. I settle for an American cuisine in Getty Centre Drive. It is easier to play it safe. I can imagine how hard it would be tasting a dish that you have never heard of before or tried, when blind. I intend to help her with eating her food.

I use my cellular to phone the number of the restaurant.

I make a reservation for half past seven on Monday night. I make it clear that I am taking a blind lady and ask if that is a problem. They are completely chilled with it. Once I book the table, I leave my tablet on the kitchen table and walk around the house for something to do.

The house is eerie with the walls a light pale green paint with brilliant white gloss skirting boards and skimmed white ceilings. This style continues throughout the hallways and stairs.

There are three stairs that lead up to the second floor as the house is very long. Each stairway is grand with dark mahogany wood. The stairs are wide with the railings curved outward. There is a minimalist feeling with the odd armchair placed as a feature in the corner or on the landing by a window. The house was built in the eighties when the land was sold by the Bel Air Country Club. It was originally owned by a stock broker who went to jail for selling non-existing investments. It was a liquidation sale. I bought it at a below value price and then redecorated the whole house.

I am bored, not knowing what to do. I finished the dating website, booked the table for tomorrow, I have no errands to do and I do not work weekends. It is times like these that I wish I had a girlfriend to fill the time. Just hang out with. No physical contact. Just a person to talk to about what we have done that day.

Even when I witness bickering between my siblings and their spouses, it does not put me off finding a relationship. I just want an easy life. No drama. I do not think I will find that. I cannot be asked to prove this to my shrink. I would rather cut to the chase, by bypassing the whole rigmarole of getting to know someone. To find that they are what you predicted. I have got by this far without a relationship.

I have exhausted walking around the house and need to get out whilst the house is empty.

I decide to go for a walk to the lake, my favourite spot. It is peaceful and quiet with the water a clean dark green colour. You can see newts and baby fishes swimming about. I sit against my favourite tree trunk that is a couple of feet from the edge. I get my cellular phone and go into my music app.

I have sombre music that is euphoric and has lyrics about being hurt and missing out on the girl you like. I use the lyrics of the music to help write my books. I use the sound of the music to help me snooze by the lake.

When I snooze, my mind wanders and my creative ideas surface for my current story and future stories. I keep a mental note and will write them down when I get home. I do not listen to the lyrics. The musical instruments and the melody helps me to drift off to sleep. Sometimes I will replay the same music over and over again while I rest my eyes in order to fall asleep. I also like to do this to make my boring days go quickly. I do not have any friends to hang out with and so I have to make do with my own company. My family have their own family lives and I do not want to feel like a gooseberry. I would rather be alone. I also like going to the cinema to watch both romantic films and action films that have a good storyline. I tend to go to the cinema at least once a week, on a school night.

As I drift in and out of consciousness, Helen suddenly pops into my head. I start to reminiscence how much I used to fancy her. I think about the amount of times I would daydream about us being in a relationship. Wondering what our lives would be like living together and enjoying being a couple. As I am reminiscing, I suddenly realise that the old feelings that I thought had died have resurfaced. I am scared as I do not want her to know that I used to fancy her at school and all the way through to university. I do not want her to know that I may have those feelings still. I will to repress them and just think about her being with her boyfriend. She will not know who I am as we never crossed paths. She did not notice me at all. I suddenly regret organising dinner as all I will do is just stare at her thinking that we are on an imaginary date. I start to think about cancelling the reservation and doing something different, like staying indoors and talking about how she has coped so far with her blindness. I do not want to allow myself to get infatuated with Helen again. Then have myself a dilemma whether to stay friends or stay away from her. At the same time, I do not want to leave her during her dark days. If it was me, I would be upset if someone left me in the lurch. I am not one of these guys that would take advantage of her situation; her boyfriend travels a lot and she is looking for moral support. Not that she would actually find me attractive. She did not notice me back then, why would she notice me now?

It is now gone five o'clock and I have been here for a good few hours. I decide to head back and see if anyone has returned from their day out. I fancy ordering in a pizza and drink a hundred-dollar bottle of red wine. Maybe two. It is not like I spend my money on clothes or fancy cars. My most expensive purchase was a fifty-dollar cardigan. Apart from the house, of course, I have not really bought anything. My clothes last me forever and I only travel between here and the office. I am not in and out of the house seeing friends or going for drinks and meals so I do not feel that it is weird to drink a hundred-dollar bottle of wine. I love my wines. The last time I drank an expensive bottle of wine was… last Friday at the family barbecue. Well that is only four times a year. I will go home, phone for a stack of pizzas for everyone and drink my bottle to myself.

When I get back to the house, it is buzzing again. Everyone is walking about the hallway, chatting and laughing about the events of the day. I walk into the family living room, separate to our parents. Everyone is sat on the sofas and armchairs getting drinks from the cabinet, of rum, bottle beer and cans of fizzy pop for the kids. When I walk in, everyone notices me and says hello.

I sit down in the only chair left empty, in amongst my family. I am passed a large glass of rum which I did not ask for. Everyone is in a laughing mood and the decision was to hear me read one of my books. Everyone wanted to end the day with listening to my voice, reading an adventure book. We wait for the various pizzas to arrive, which includes pepperoni, Hawaiian, vegetarian and meat feast. Once the pizzas arrive and everyone is settled back down in their seats, I start to read one of my adventure books that I wrote when I finished university. The story is about looking for a lost treasure in the Amazon. I ask everyone to put on the lamps darted around the living room and switch off the main lights. The room is dark now and I am ready to read.

Whenever I read a book, I tell it without any accent, but I vary my tone so I do not sound monotonous. My audience always looks gripped waiting for the next scene and conclusion of the plot. My nieces and nephews lean forward with their elbows on their laps hanging to every word that passes my lips and from the pages. My chapters always have a cliff hanger at the end.

I am reading the book that we are three quarters of the way through. We do not do this on a regular basis. The last time we sat together like this was six months ago, back in September. We are still eating and drinking during my story reading. Both the story reading and the demolishing of pizza takes about two hours. Once the book is finished, the kids go up to their rooms and chill out. The rest go out into the garden to carry on drinking. I go and finally get my bottle of red wine and drink it in the living room.

I realise that I can download the app of the dating website on my phone. Once the app logo appears on my phone, I open it up to see my profile I wrote about myself. I notice already that I have had some interest on my page. I only set it up today. While drinking my wine I have a look at their profiles. There are three interested women. As I look at one of the three women profile, I am distracted by my nephew Carlton, Chevalier and Melissa's son. He is sixteen.

Carlton stands in front of me waiting to be noticed. "What can I do for you?"

Carlton sits on the sofa next to me. "I have a problem."

I look inquisitive. "You need money. And your dad won't lend it."

Carlton pauses. "No… this is embarrassing."

I coach him. "Go on. You can talk about anything."

Carlton sheepishly blurts it out. "I met a girl!"

I am taken aback. "Shouldn't you be talking to your parents.?"

Carlton just stares at me. "You're the one who owns this house. You are filthy rich."

I have a blank face, not knowing how to react. "Okay? So, what's the problem? You didn't get her pregnant? You have an STI."

Carlton looks at me weirdly. "What is an STI?"

I ignore his question. "Don't worry about it. You would soon know if you had one. So, what is it?"

Carlton explains. "I met her at the barbecue. She lives in Inglewood. She is my first date. I don't know what to do."

I find it cute and endearing. "It is okay to feel nervous. I suggest the park and a milkshake after. Keep it simple."

Carlton looks like he has another question. "What if she wants to kiss me? I find it disgusting. My mom and dad's kisses are rough and sloppy."

I try not to smirk. "A girl does not kiss like your parents. If she goes to kiss you, then let her take the lead. After she kisses you, tell her that she tastes like chocolate and smells like strawberries. Trust me, she will be putty in your hands."

Carlton is relieved and walks off. As he is about to leave the room, he turns around. "Do you know why I asked you, Uncle Harvey?"

I have no idea. "Why's that?"

Carlton is coy. "Because of what you write in your books about women."

I smile as he smiles and runs out of the room. Little does he know that I am still a virgin. I have no idea what it is like to kiss a woman. I base it on films and other people's books. But it felt nice.

I go back to my interests on my profile. I read about a woman who calls herself Laura. She is a little younger than me and Mexican-looking. Her body type is slightly plump but she wears clothes that compliment her body. She is just shorter than me at five foot four, where I am five foot six and she is a social care worker who lives South Park.

The second woman calls herself Trudy. She is the same age as me and is Caucasian. Her body is slim with slight curves. She is slightly taller than me. She is a cashier at a bank and she lives in Lakeview Terrace.

The third woman calls herself Olivia. Again, she is the same age as me and is black. Her body type is athletic, from running. She is also slightly shorter than me. She is a dentist and lives in Brentwood.

I look at each of their profiles and see what they do in their spare time. I look for something that I find naturally interesting about each of them. I then send a message each of them, acknowledging that I noticed they saw my profile. In the same messages, I ask them about one of the things I read about them. Each of the three messages are of equal length. Each message finishes with a question of why they were interested in those things and how they go into them. I send each message one after the other. I close the app and try not to think any more of it.

It is Sunday morning around eleven o'clock. I notice that everyone is staying home today. They are by the pool relaxing in loungers and reading magazines or newspapers. I can see them from my bedroom. I decide to wear shorts and a polo top and join them.

I say morning to them all and stand around watching. I

suddenly remember to check my phone for any responses from the three women. All three have responded either late last night or this morning. I am in shock as they are actually interested in conversation. I read each message in turn.

I look at the earlier message first. This is from Trudy. She tells me that she has been horse riding ever since she was a child. She asks me when I am free for a date. She says that she is off all this week. I am getting flustered and panic what to send in response. I decide to read the other two to see if they suggest a time to meet.

I read the second message to come through, which is from Laura, the social care worker. She responded by ignoring my question and suggests meeting up to discuss face to face. She says she works nights and the only time she is free this week is tomorrow. I am taken aback by her reply. I did not expect that kind of message.

I read Olivia's message which talks about how she fell into fencing. She has been fencing since when she was at university. Her message finishes with leaving her number to call her, if I fancy going out sometime.

Each message is positive and there is no flirting before meeting up. I like that as I am not into trying to flirt with innuendos. I just want a normal get to know each other. I decide to leave it till the afternoon to decide a day, time and place with each of them. My preference out of the three is Olivia. She appears to be chilled out while the other two, I perceive as going at one hundred miles an hour. But I want to see all three before I decide to send messages to the other women on the website.

My sister, Natalya, who is feisty, asks. "Who is texting you?"

I act casual. "No one special."

Natalya pries some more. "So why were you stood there for half an hour staring at your screen. Is it some girl that you haven't told us about?"

I ignore the question. "So, you're not doing anything today then?"

Chevalier joins in the conversation. "Don't tell them you are rich. They are only interested if you have money."

Xavier sucks his teeth. "Don't worry about him. As long as she smart and kind, that is all that matters."

I wonder how they came to the conclusion that I am texting a girl. "It is not a girl. Just checking my emails."

Mercedes now joins in. "What is her name? Whoever it is, she will be fine. She won't love you for your money."

I repeat myself. "It is not a girl. I was checking my emails."

Chevalier pipes up. "It is not a girl cause it is a woman. Don't date a black girl. They give you grief. Date a white woman cause they just let you get on with it."

Montel agrees. "Exactly. Look at me, there is nothing left of me."

Natalya says. "My sister lets you get away with murder."

Melissa, Montel's wife, says. "Ignore them. Just go out for a drink. If you like her, then take it slow. Her true colours will come out."-

I have enough of this and go for a walk to the lake. Once I am sat down and resting against the tree, I read all three messages again. I respond to Laura who said her only time is Monday day.

I tell Laura that I can meet up Monday and suggest a bar for a drink. I wait for her response.

I tell Trudy that I can see her in the day time on Thursday, suggesting lunchtime. I say the same thing about a drink at a bar.

I text the cellular number Olivia gave me in her message, to suggest one evening except Monday night as I am taking out Helen. I leave it to her to choose a night.

As I am sending the last message, I notice someone walking by. I try to be discreet when I look round in the direction of the footsteps. It is Mercedes. She somehow knew I was here.

Mercedes stands there. "If you are going on a date, I suggest you find some clothes to wear."

I am curious. "How did you know?"

Mercedes sighs. "I can read you like a book. I suggest you get rid of that shitty blue Chevy. No millionaire drives a shitty car. I suggest you trim your beard. How much do you have in your wallet?"

I know I have no cash except for a bank card. "I only have my credit card."

Mercedes sighs again. "How much is left on your limit?"

I have never used it. "A mill. Here. It is in black. It was given to me by my bank. They said only people like me have one."

Mercedes takes it and looks hard at it. "It's for rich people. That will do. I suggest your budget will be a hundred thousand dollars, including the car. Grab you ID and your driving licence. I suggest the car first. Any preference?"

My mind is blank. "A Bentley?"

Mercedes looks at me with a sigh. "Keep it real. You are not a pop star or a drug dealer. I think a Mercedes will suit you better. A conservative look. Then some nice slacks and fashionable shirts. And some decent shoes."

I look at my flip flops. "I guess so."

We get to the Mercedes showroom off Santa Monica Boulevard which is only nine minutes away. Mercedes is wearing a pair of jeans with a light blue shirt and a grey blazer. I am wearing a t-shirt, blue shorts and flip flop.

One of the salesmen walks over and goes to speak to my sister. I wander off to see what cars they have. I notice the usual hard top convertible in a saloon and a two-seater. I look at the C-Class and I like how the latest model looks. In the corner of my eye is the CLS model. The design is like a half-oval shape. The interior is beige with marble wood trimming on the doors and dashboard. The car body colour is a deep navy blue. This is the car.

Mercedes is explaining. "My brother is looking for a new car. He prefers one of yours. What kind of deal can you offer?"

I walk up to them. "I found the one I want."

The salesman gives me a snooty look. "I assume you are paying for the car. Shall we check your credit score?"

Mercedes looks at him as if he was something on her shoe. "Eh err, he is paying for it."

The salesman thinks it is a joke. "So, we will do a credit score on you."

I am baffled as I have my debit card. "Can't you take cash?"

The salesman looks puzzled. "You have cash?"

I look at my sister. "About a hundred on this one. Or do you want it in notes?"

My sister smirks at me and we both stare down the salesman. He nervously smiles and gets the paperwork ready. I sit at the desk with him staring at the walls.

Mercedes says. "My name is also Mercedes. I may buy one."

I look at the salesman. "Do you do discounts? I have the money."

Mercedes puts my wrist down. "No that is alright. If I want one, I will get it myself."

I sigh. "Okay, just the one. I want the one I saw. That will do nicely. Here is my card. I can do contactless."

The salesman's jaw drops and when payment is ready, I just tap my card on the contactless card machine. Little does he know that I have an exclusive bank account because of how much money is held there. One of those privileges is having a contactless limit of one hundred and fifty thousand dollars, not the usual thirty dollars. My bank account now only has about ten grand in it. Enough for some clothes and food in a nice restaurant to say thanks to my sister.

My sister takes me to Rodeo Drive to buy a few pairs of nice trousers, jeans, loafers and smart shirts for socialising in. It took me a while to decide which clothes I preferred and purchase. Before I know it, I have a completely new wardrobe for my dates and socialising. I now need to get my beard shaved.

CHAPTER SIX

First Date

It is Monday morning and I need to get all my old clothes bagged for a charity shop. I am excited about wearing my new clothes and driving my new car. I have never owned a new car before. I have never sat inside a Mercedes until yesterday. I cannot believe I spent ninety thousand dollars on a car and two thousand dollars on new clothing to last me ten years.

I had a reply back from all three girls late last night. I am seeing Laura for definite today, at one o'clock. I am seeing Trudy on Wednesday and Olivia on Thursday night. I am more looking forward to seeing Olivia as she seems more like me, chilled out and take it or leave it. I will get around to sending messages to the other women on the website that I like the look of and particularly their written profile about themselves. I will not contact any that have no profile or no picture. If I can be bothered to put a photo up and write about myself, so can they.

Even though I am meeting these three women I am still going to look at all the women who have put their profile on the website as well. I am going to create a spreadsheet to include headings like their first and second name, age, length of time they have been on the website, date I sent them a message and outcome of response. That way I will be able to keep track of any responses and who they are without embarrassing myself. Laura, Trudy and Olivia will be the first women to put on the spreadsheet. I do not want to waste time seeing one person at a time, waiting to see if there is a second or third date. I would rather treat dating like a job search and send my profile to multiple women. I do not have any urge to want to sleep with any of them or even kiss them, including Laura, Trudy and

Olivia. I just want to speed up the process of meeting the right one. I want to meet the right person before anything physical happens. Also, if it takes a few dates to realise we are not compatible with each other then there will be no complications or miscommunication. My shrink cannot tell me that I did not give it one hundred percent.

During breakfast, the topic of conversation is my new car and the new clothes that I bought with the help of my sister, Mercedes. My family appear relieved that I disposed of what they call "the shitty blue Chevy". I miss driving that car. That saw me through work, publishing my books and meeting my agent. It also saw me through thick and thin and now I have abandoned it. I do not know what half the functions do in my new car. I am told it has cruise control, works out if you are tired to warn you and also auto brakes if I am too close to the car in front. My old car was a 1970s model, so it did not have the mod cons you can get today.

My family all say that they want to drive it, except for my parents and Simon and Alexandra, the youngest of my nephews and nieces.

I could sense that my brothers and sisters now want to change their cars now I have a new one.

It is now nine o'clock and breakfast time is finished. The house is empty again except for my parents, the chef and the maid. My parents go to the solarium to spend time attending to their plants. The house feels very empty and I feel lonely. I guess at this point I am glad that I am now dating. It does not sink in and just feels that I am meeting up with a friend. It feels surreal.

I am seeing Laura at one o'clock. I have to leave by half past eleven to allow time to drop my old clothes to a charity shop, preferably in South Park, so I am not far from the cafe. Also, it is not far from where Laura lives. We have agreed to drive there separately. If I am caught up in the shop then I will still not be late getting to the cafe.

I decide work from home today, as I will be able to unsettle. My thoughts about the date will cause me to struggle with my concentration in writing my story. I want to also change into my new clothes for the date and so I do not want to go into the office to then rush back. I will work in my study.

I plan to pay for her coffee and lunch, even though this has not been formally discussed. I have never felt right, a woman paying for a meal or a woman paying for both of us. It is a stickler and a personal issue; I do not know why. Especially when money is not an issue for me.

It would have been nice to show off my car to her but I am not like that and I want her to judge me and not my belongings. I just hope that Laura does not recognise me somehow. I do not have my photo on my website or on the back of my books, even though my agent moans at me. However, I do book signings and have had photos with my readers so Laura may recognise me from someone she may know who went to my signing and had their photo with me. I will lie about my job if Laura asks me. I will say I am an underwriter. I still remember the process and can go into great detail still, if I have to.

I am sat at my desk struggling to concentrate as I write the plot for my next book. I plan to have the manuscript ready for publishing next year. The story is about a haunted house in Kansas. I have mulled over the story in my head for about a year. I am now making notes on what topic I will write for each chapter.

I knew I would be struggling to focus on making my notes due to my first ever date. I knew this would be the case. It feels like I am in detention and I can see everyone else playing outside and having fun. I want to be on that date with Laura now. I want to be having an interesting conversation with her, rather than sat here by myself. Instead, I start to write down the feelings I am having about craving for a relationship and feeling lonely. I want to use my written down thoughts in my next romantic novel. It will make my love stories more realistic.

Once I finish writing down my feelings, I look up at my digital clock on the bookshelf that is flush against the wall. The clock is like a picture frame in chrome with red L.E.D lights against a black background. The clock is at my eye level when I am sat down at my desk. The clock is between rows of various books. I am clock-watching as I struggle to continue to write my plot down. I feel agitated as the digital minutes slowly change on the clock.

Waiting for the date feels like I am waiting for an interview for a job or an appointment with the dentist. You know you need the job or you need the toothache to go away, but you do not want to go through the motion. You want to skip the beginning and middle and just have the job or the toothache taken care of. My thoughts on the date are like that. I do not want to go through the motion of getting to know Laura, Trudy, Olivia or anyone else and just want to be in a relationship now. I want to skip the introductions and several dates to get to the boyfriend and girlfriend part.

There is nothing in the house that can distract me or take my mind off the date. Going for a swim or a walk to the lake will not stop my butterflies or thoughts. I suddenly think about how the conversation will take place when I say I am a virgin. Do I blurt it out when the woman I fall for says "Take me!" Or do I say it in front of a log fire, her back pressed against my chest and we are both naked, a single blanket covering the both of us. While we sit there gazing into the log fire, I whisper in her ear. "I want to make love to you, but I am a virgin and clueless so you have to take the lead."

Either way, it is not going to be natural. I could just pretend and say it has been a while, while I read the manual on how to find the hole. Hence why I am in no hurry to get into a physical relationship. I would be happy to just hold hands for a year. I cannot even say that I have properly kissed a girl. My romantic books are based on what I think it is like or what people have told me. All this thinking is starting to detract me from my butterfly stomach. I give up trying to write my story so I leave my office and go to the family living room.

I flick through the television channels to find a film or programme to wish the hours away. It is only ten o'clock now. I decide to have a bath to make the time go faster. When it is time to eventually leave, I look at all the apps on the screen of the car that are built into the dashboard. They are causing me to be late now, as I eventually work out how to tune the radio to my favourite station. The drive is made out of gravel so I have to drive slowly to prevent stone chips on my fresh new paint work. The car is lower than my old car and so I am extra cautious. This is making me even later. I quickly text Laura to let her know what my ETA is. The sat nav in the system is not straightforward to use. I already did an internet search on my cellular for a charity shop in South Park as well as the area code for the cafe. The arrival time for the charity shop on the sat nav is about half past twelve. Then from there it is only a five-minute drive to El Pollo Loco, where we will be eating.

The car is the smoothest I have ever driven. I cannot hear the engine running or revving.

The sat nav takes me through Century City and Rancho Park. Normally, if I was in my Chevy, I would be annoyed stuck in traffic but I am chilled out in my new car where I stop and move effortlessly. The traffic does not bother me. The sat nav eventually takes me on Highway 10. The automatic transmission of the Mercedes is smooth as it reaches ninety miles an hour in no time. The air conditioning makes the car nice and cool so I am not feeling sweaty. I wish I bought this type of car years ago. The steering is effortless. It only takes me about ten minutes to carry my clothes, in black bin bags, into the charity shop. Luckily the member of staff was not a chatty person.

Once I arrive at the cafe El Pollo Loco, on the corner of

East Vernon Avenue and South Avalon Boulevard, I park up round the back of the premises.

While I park up I start to get butterflies again. I am not nervous about the date as I am treating it like a job interview. I intend to ask Laura questions about what made her become a carer, how long has she been doing it, her hobbies and so on. The questions will not be intrusive. I have witnessed and heard all different kinds of dates so I am simply mirroring someone else's date.

I check the time to see it is five minutes past one now. I check my phone to see if Laura had replied to my earlier text about arriving late. She texted while I was travelling, to say okay with a 'x' on the end. I assume that she is already here and is sat inside the cafe. I picture her with a coffee already, half drunk, waiting for me with a casual attitude. She will recognise me and wave for my attention.

When I walk inside, she is nowhere to be seen. It is easy to see that she is not here yet, as the eating area is very small. There are only six tables with four chairs at each table. The table and chairs are only a couple of feet from the service counter, where you order your food and drink. For a second, I think she could be in the toilet so text her to say I am here now. I then think of getting a coffee or a beer. Before I decide I get a text saying she is only a couple of minutes away so I call her to ask if I should get her a drink.

When she picks up, the sound of her voice has a slight Mexican accent and is soft. She sounds very nice and friendly. She is happy to have a latte, so I get two. The cafe is half empty with about four couples with a mixture of friends, work colleagues and people in relationships. I get a table for us and sit patiently.

Laura finally arrives and to my surprise, which is not an issue, she has a young child that looks about five years of age. There was no mention of her having a child, even though the arrangement was quick. I also notice that she seemed a bit strange.

I stand up and we recognise each other instantly from

the pictures on our profile. She comes up to my nose in height. Her hair is dark brown and straight. She has a flat stomach with wide hips. She is wearing a pair of straight cut jeans with a flowery red blouse. Her face is round and slim with a slight crooked nose.

I smile nervously. "Nice to finally meet you. So, this is your daughter?"

Laura seems merry. "Her name is Sophie. She is my daughter. Really sorry, could not find a baby sitter."

I think it will be nice to sit outside. "Shall we sit outside? It is nice outside.?

She smiles. "Yeah. That sounds good."

I let Laura lead the way with her daughter. I see Laura looks tipsy by the way she is walking out of the door. I take no notice of it for now, as I want to take the benefit of the doubt.

I put our coffees down and I grab a chair from another table, for Sophie. I still stand to get something for Sophie. Smiling at Sophie, I turn to Laura. "So, you found this place okay."

Laura is apologetic. "So sorry. I actually came from a friend's house. Had a drink before coming here."

I do not pass comment. "Would Sophie like a drink? Was thinking of getting something to eat."

Laura pauses and composes herself. "Excuse me. Feel a bit woozy. I only had one drink, but it was strong."

I feel awkward. "No worries. What drink shall I get your daughter?"

Laura takes a breather. "An orange juice, please."

I smile at Laura as I go inside to order the drink for Sophie. Laura did not give me an answer about ordering food and so I get two menus while ordering the drink.

As I get back to the table and give Sophie her drink, without warning, Laura vomits on part of the table on her side and on the floor.

I do not know how to react. I casually grab paper napkins from the container on the table and mop up the watery pink colour of sick. I am too shocked to react to her vomiting.

For a split second I think about ending the date but she has only been here five minutes. I have to give her the benefit of the doubt. If it was me, I would not want her to end the date if I threw up in front of her. It is only one hiccup. I will wait to see if she does it again.

Laura looks embarrassed. "Oops, ha ha ha, it must have been something I ate."

Of course, it was. "Fine. No problem. Just cleaning the last bit. There. I'll just chuck this in the bin. Be right back."

I chuckle to myself not quite believing what I saw. I think this is down to being nervous. I sit back down pretending that that did not just happen. I make conversation to move away from her being sick.

I sip my coffee. "So how old is your daughter?"

Laura does not think about being sick. "How old are you Sophie? Are you going to tell Harvey?"

Her daughter is shy and hides her face in the palms of her hands, while pressing her face into Laura's thigh.

Laura tries to encourage Sophie by saying. "Ah, you are not shy. Tell him. She is five. She is not normally like this."

I look at Sophie when I say to Laura. "Not to worry. I was shy at that age. So, what happened to her dad?"

Laura goes to tell me when she suddenly bends down below the table. I assume for some reason she wants to talk under the table with her daughter or her daughter has done something. But no, she vomits again near the table leg. More of the same watery pink fluid poured out of her mouth. This cannot be happening to me. My first date and it cannot just be normal. Sophie looks concerned for her mom while holding her hand.

For a second, I consider ending the date this time round but it was a good ten minutes before she threw up the first time. This time she has the courtesy of not spewing on the table so at least she thought about it this time. I start to think how she and her daughter were going to get home.

She must have had a lot more than one drink. She looks more drunk now. The sun must have made it worse. I decide to give her three strikes and then end the date. I look at her daughter to look at her reaction. She is too young to understand. I pretend that it did not happen and prompt Laura to tell me about Sophie's dad.

I nervously smile. "What happened to her dad?"

Laura grabs a napkin to wipe her mouth. "He is in Mexico. He wanted to move back to live near his mom. I wanted to stay here."

I am naturally interested. "So, does he get to see his daughter often?"

She frowns as she thinks about the question. "Umm, he has not seen us since he left."

I want to know when he left. "How long ago did he move?"

Laura is quick to remember. "Three years ago. He said he was going back on holiday, for a week."

I am surprised. "When did you realise that he was not coming back?"

Laura smiles as she thinks back. "I left it three weeks and then went to his place of work. They told me he quit four weeks before. So, I worked out that he spent a week planning his leave."

I empathise. "Wow. That must have been hard. Not having a chance to save your relationship or have closure."

Laura finds my comment warming and puts her hand on mine. We look at each other before she suddenly moves her head under the table and throws up a third time.

That is, it. Date is over. I now have a dilemma. She must be drunk, so do I drive them home and risk her being sick in my car, get a taxi and she picks her car up the next day or do I drive her car and get a taxi back to the cafe. I have no idea how to flag a taxi down or have a number. I do not know how long a taxi will take to get here. It is not like New York City. I do not fancy being stuck here, nursing a drunk woman with a minor for hours. I decide to drive her car and get a taxi back. At least I know she will get home safely and I will be stranded at a house rather than a public place. Also, even though I am not short of a bob or two, I do not want to spend money on a taxi both ways.

I awkwardly say. "I think I should take you home. I think I will drive you home in your car."

Laura looks disappointed. "I can drive back. I am fine. It must be something I ate this morning."

I know she is drunk and the alcohol has had a delayed effect. "No. I will drive you both home. I will have peace of mind."

I help her up as her daughter looks at me, not understanding what is happening. Laura takes me to her car and gives me the key.

She does not live that far from the park in South Park. She has a small Chevrolet Sonic car. I get her daughter in the back seat first, on her booster seat. I talk to her as I put her in, saying that I am driving them home and mommy is a bit unwell. I then wait for Laura to get in the passenger side before I get in.

The car looks tired inside. The upholstery is worn out and there is slight dust on the dashboard. There is some crushed in food in the backseat next to the booster seat. My old car was more well-kept than hers.

The next issue is working out where she lives. I ask her for the address, but she is not really with it so I go through her handbag after letting her know.

I hope I do not find any embarrassing things like a vibrator or a packet of tampons. I finally find her driving licence, after finding her lipstick, mascara, tissue, makeup mirror and comb. I put the address in my phone app map. I can then drive her and her daughter back home.

Luckily, she was only ten minutes away from the cafe. I get them in their ground floor apartment and help Laura in the apartment first with her key. Once I am happy that she is sat in her living room, I go and get Sophie from the car. She is relaxed and happy sat in the car. Once they are both in, I ask Laura if I need to call anyone. I explain that I need to head back. Laura looks upset and I do not know if it is the date or Sophie's dad. I choose not to pry. I use my cellular to call a taxi driver, hoping they will not be long.

I feel awkward not knowing what to talk about. I sit in the armchair opposite the sofa. Sophie sits next to her mom, holding her hand.

I feel sorry for Sophie as she did not ask for this. Sophie looks sad and I wonder if she is aware of what is going on. I am aware that children see everything. They are not stupid.

I do not think that a second date is on the cards, from my side. I do not consider if she wants to go on another date herself. It feels like forever waiting for the taxi to arrive.

Laura finally plucks up the courage to speak. "I am so sorry. You drove all this way for our date. Then had to drive us home. Can I pay for your taxi?"

I do not want her money. "No. It is fine. It won't be that much. Will you be okay?" *Please say yes, please say yes,* I think as I smile with sympathy.

Laura looks mortified. "Yes, I will be fine. Do you need to be anywhere?"

I lie. "Yes. I have to go round a friend's house and help them out."

Laura remembers my profile. "I remember, you help out your neighbours gardening and offer your time up. That is what drew me towards you."

She sounds sober now. "You're the first date I have been on."

Laura is shocked. "Wow. And I do this. I suddenly feel worse."

I suddenly realise how I came across. "I'm sorry. I did not mean it like that. It's just I had no expectations or know how a date should go."

Laura smiles. "Well, this is not how a date should go… You are a great person. And I do this. You shouldn't have had to have this experience for your first date. What do you do for a living? Are you a nurse or doctor? You have a lot of patience. Ha ha ha. I don't mean patience as in patient. Any other guy would have just left money on the table and left."

I cannot lie. "I write books."

Laura has confusion on her face. "Like an authoritarian."

I smile. "Like Jane Knight but romantic and adventure novels. Touching on crime."

Laura is open-mouthed. "You must be–"

I cut her short. "Yes, I am a millionaire. You're not going to do a Norman Bates, are you? Trick me to take you home. Use a child."

Laura laughs, finding my worry amusing. I laugh with her, nervously. By the time the taxi arrives, we have, I guess, a second attempt at dating.

I am ready to leave. "I guess I better get going."

Laura looks sad. "I wish the date could have gone a lot better. I guess that car was yours, that I almost threw up on."

I remember and squint my eyes. "Ye-ah. That car."

Laura walks me to the door leaving Sophie in the living room. She is sweet when she gives me a hug. I do not know why she hugs me hard and gives me a long lingering kiss on my cheek.

On the way home, after going back to my car via taxi, I suddenly remember that I have an evening with Helen. I also think back to my date with Laura, wondering why she drove drunk and put Sophie at risk. Whether she was round a friend's house earlier. Either way, the damage has been done. I do not want to be with someone who needs a drink for Dutch courage. She was my very first date and I am still a virgin, but I did not need a drink to steady my nerves. You will not catch me having a few drinks for Dutch courage. To calm my nerves, I focused on not being late. I took a long bath to hurry the time along. She did not know about my status and so I had no confidence to build up from. It is a shame as I find her very attractive and I am hoping she was the one. She seems to tick all the boxes.

My next date is with Trudy. She is the cashier at a bank and enjoys horse riding. I am seeing her Wednesday night. I am not normally into Caucasians but she sounds interesting.

Helen pops into my head again. Grrr, I hate it when that happens. My feelings are bubbling up to the surface and are getting murky with the bullying I suffered at school. The two go hand in hand. I have never once gone to a school reunion. Why would I want to be reminded of my troubled childhood? Unfortunately, my feelings for Helen are marred with that. Also, she never noticed me when she could see. What makes me think she will notice me now, now she is blind. Right, find something else to think about. My agent wants to see me in a month's time. I have that awful book signing out of town, somewhere. I hate public appearances and refuse to wear a suit. My agent arranged it behind my back and told them I would do it. That is in three months' time. Then I have to make my mind up about the television series of one of my genre books. I wrote a series of five books about an adventurer. Finding lost treasure. They want to steal the limelight from a similar film that Spielberg did but mine is set in the current climate. The time I want a girlfriend. It is quiet and I have nothing to do, then when it is getting hectic for me, I have to go on dates. If I was doing a nine to five job, I would not cope. So, a quick recap. Agent meeting, book signing and review contract for television rights. Each a month apart. A total of three months. If I meet someone, it will be a waste of time as it is highly likely I will go off to adapt my book for television. It will mean moving to Atlantic City. Helen will no longer need me if she is getting her eyesight back in three months' time. That will be June or July. I will not have any ties to sever. I guess I will start a new life. Hopefully the shrink will completely fix me by then.

CHAPTER SEVEN

Embarrassing Moments

When I eventually get home I think about the date with Laura. I avoid my family by going straight to my bedroom, after I get my laptop from the office. I sit on the end of my bed, in the centre.

I cannot quite believe what happened on my date with her. My perception was that she was a nice girl. She just needed a drink to cope with the date. But my attitude is that if I do not need a drink before going on a date, then no one else should. I will leave it a day before I send her a text message. The message will say that I do not want to take it further as I feel that we have nothing in common. I am upset that this was not a normal date.

I just want to go on a normal date where I like her and she likes me. Where we are comfortable with each other. Thinking about it now, I am upset that it did not work out. Her approach to how she chose to cope with the date makes me see her personality as ugly. She is very attractive in my eyes, but I judge women on their personality and content of character. She can be the prettiest girl on the planet, but her character is what makes me fancy her. Appearances change over time, but character and personality do not. No matter how much you say you have changed, your actions do not. It is like the tale of the *"scorpion and the frog"*. The scorpion could not help stinging the frog, even though it made a promise not to. Even if it means your life depends on it.

Moving on, I am focusing on the next two dates. I decide to also peruse all the girls on the dating website. I list all the girls I like. I find a total of twenty girls from the website and I put their details on my spreadsheet, which takes me ages. Once I finish, I update my spreadsheet about Laura to remind me why I am choosing not to go on a second date. Not that I need reminding why. I thought she would be sick once and put it down to something she ate. But three times. I felt sorrier for her child as she had no choice but to come along.

I keep forgetting that I am seeing Helen tonight. I just hope that she does not throw up as well. Especially where she is not able see where to be sick. At least this is not a date and so I cannot be let down. Admittedly, I am not in the mood to take her out now. I am in the dumps about my disastrous date. It has put me in a foul mood. I am not in the right frame of mind to try and entertain a woman who is depressed and I have to try and cheer her up. I wish I could rewind my offer of taking care of her. I still do not get why her boyfriend cannot look after her. Just because I do not have an office job, it does not mean I have lots of free time on my hands. She is probably big and fat, with a massive scar down one side of her cheek from the car accident. No longer attractive anymore. I am guessing she has a really ugly personality and that explains why her boyfriend will not look after her. I reckon she is a cow who thinks she's it, because she had all the guys after her in school.

I suddenly think about the time, guessing it is six o'clock and check my clock to see that it is almost seven instead. Damn it, I have to go. I still have my clothes on that I wore for the date. It does not matter as she is blind, so she won't notice and it is not a date. So why make an effort, even though I am wearing nice expensive clothes now. I quickly rush down the stairs and out of the door. I am glad I have my new car now. I love the smoothness of the drive. I feel like I want to cruise the streets all night.

I am stood at Helen parents' door. I do not know why I am nervous. I put it down to having to take out a blind person. I have not seen Helen since university. Our cul-de-sac is not a practical estate to be able to naturally bump into your neighbours. Each house has its own long drive, far from the main road. You need a taxi to get to the houses from Groverton Place Road.

After I ring the door bell, I wait patiently for her dad or mom to answer. After a minute, I start to wonder if her parents and Helen have forgotten that I am coming over and that the three of them went out for the night. I ring the doorbell a second time. Ah, I did not hear the doorbell ring the first time. The sound of the bell is louder than ours. You could hear it from space. It must be loud, so you can hear it in every room.

Their house is a different design to ours. Each house in the road is different. Their house has five steps leading up to a plush porch. The steps and porch are a light grey stone; Greek looking finish. They have twin double doors, in black, with thin black bars horizontal from top to bottom. As the door opens, I can see the floor is marble, creamy white with slight orange swirls. It is very plush. Our house has solid oak flooring. Maybe I should get marble flooring. Their butler opened the door. Wow, maybe I should get a butler. But saying that, I have a maid and chef. That is enough.

As I walk inside, the butler closes the door behind me. We both wait there, as I expect the butler to call for someone. The main entrance is big with a stairway in the centre of the entrance hall. The stairs look like they are from a Cinderella scene, where the railings are made out of stone. The stone railings flow down the stairs, wide and straight, then at the bottom of the stairs the railings bend outward with the steps widening at the bottom. The stairs are flush against the back wall, so you cannot walk behind them. I notice that there is a chandelier directly above me that is in the centre of the hallway. The chandelier looks like it is made out of real crystal, as it leaves star-like sparkles on the floor. Looking at it directly makes your eyes dazzle.

On the right side of the hallway is an open door to another room or a narrow hallway leading somewhere.

Bill comes running down the stairs at a trot. "Harvey,

come, come, into the reception room. I really appreciate this. Helen is still getting ready. Her mom is helping her. Can I get you a drink?"

I look around the hallway, slowly spinning around. "Uh, yeah, but something soft. I am driving. You have a nice house… Mr Simms."

Bill chuckles. "I said before, Bill. So, I notice you changed your car. And your fashion sense. Midlife crisis. Windfall on the National Lottery, again ha ha."

I am still distracted by the interior of the house. "did not want the neighbours to know who I was. I am a private man. Apart from the quarterly barbecues, which my family organise. For the car, it will do. I had my other car since I finished uni. Thought I would go for a change. I needed to get new clothes as my old clothes were bought in 1999. You have a nice house Mr… Bill."

Bill waves his hand as to say 'shucks'. "Your house is grander than ours. You have an extra hundred square footage, solarium and swimming pool."

I correct him. "And a tennis court. But it is used as a basketball court or a playground. It was what I could afford at the time."

Bill looks at me with a disapproving look. "You are the richest kid on our road."

I am not impressed with his comment. "Not everyone has a large family to house. It is a necessity, rather than a want. I thank God every Sunday. So how was your day?"

Bill gives me my drink of ice-cold orange juice. "No one went to jail this time."

I look at him with a worried look. Wondering if he has an axe to grind.

Bill notices and laughs. "Your face, I am kidding. I am a corporate lawyer with offices in Chicago, New York as well here, downtown."

I am intrigued what that actually entails. "So, you deal with mergers, acquisitions and intellectual property?"

Bill smiles. "Exactly. My last deal was between Larzen and Anderson."

I have no idea. "Who?"

Bill puts his drink down. "They are in the music business. Country and Western. Not hip hop."

I give a slight acknowledgement. "Never heard of them. I don't exactly listen to a lot of music. Only certain types. How much did you make?"

Bill ignores my question. "Ah, Helen, Martha. I will leave you two to it."

I turn around to look at both Helen and Martha. I greet them with a smile, not knowing what happens next.

Helen's blindness makes her eyes look as if she is seeing past me in the distance as she speaks up. "So, you are Harvey. I believe you are stuck with me for a while."

Helen has not changed one bit since I last saw her in the first year of university. She still looks cute. I look at Martha to take Helen's arm from her. I then help Helen to an armchair in the reception room. I sit in the chair next to her. Martha leaves us to it.

I struggle to know what to say when Helen speaks first. "You don't say much, Harvey." She says it with a straight face, looking like she is staring into the distance passed me.

I look away from her. I am not sure what to talk about. "I hear you are surgeon."

Helen abruptly says. "Was."

I correct her. "Still are. Just because you are not practising it, does not mean you are not. Hence why the word 'qualification' is used."

Helen almost smiles. "I stand corrected. Retired surgeon."

I correct her again. "If you are retired, you would have received a pink slip."

Helen starts to smile. "Okay you got me. What do you know about me?"

I do not tell her that I have known her since elementary school. "You already know that I know you are a doctor. You were in a car accident. You have a boyfriend. And... he is away a lot and so you live here with your parents, for company."

Helen scoffs while smiling. "He is a sales executive. He travels a lot for his job."

My opinion is he does not want to deal with his girlfriend's disability. He would rather work late at home. I choose not to accept her reason for him not looking after her.

I realise it is twenty past seven. We should be going. The restaurant I booked is called West Restaurant and Lounge. It is about a four-minute drive luckily, along Sunset Boulevard, crossing over Route 405. The venue is on the seventeenth floor of the Hotel Angeleno. I have never been there. I chose it because it overlooks the city of Los Angeles with panoramic views. Even though Helen will not experience the view, she will sense the venue is tranquil and spacious. I almost picked an Italian restaurant with similar views but it overlooks the sea at the end of Wiltshire Boulevard, at The Huntley Hotel. I wanted home-grown American food.

I help Helen to her feet and steady her as she stands up. "Let's go to dinner. I hope you enjoy the ambiance and the smell of home-grown food. If you are lucky, I will feed you grapes."

Helen grins, trying not to laugh. "If you are lucky, I won't stare you out."

I quickly respond. "How will you know if I blink first."

Helen laughs and we head to my car. I help her to the passenger side of the car and open the door for her. I hold her arm as I rest my other hand on her head, to prevent her from hitting the door trim or the roof of the car. I am glad I bought this car as there is ample space in the foot well. Helen would have struggled in my previous car.

We do not say much in the car on the way to the restaurant. Helen is happy to be with her thoughts in silence. I adjust the climate control panel of the car, so we are nice and warm. Helen makes a comment about the car smelling new. At first, I smile and nod my head.

I suddenly realise that I should not use facial expressions or hand gestures, because she cannot see. In a delayed reaction, I say thank you. I notice the street lights, cars, people and the weather and feel I should let her know what I see to make the journey less boring for her. I guess all she can see is black space.

I speak up. "This must feel weird, not being able to see the road, the street lights and the people."

Helen looks like she is in deep thought. "I am still not used to it. I have been a hermit for the past six months. I do not go out in the car that often."

I ask her how it feels to be blind. "What is it like travelling as a passenger, blind. Does it feel like being in an elevator? You know where you are, but you do not know what is happening behind the scenes."

Helen seems to perk up. "That is a perfect analogy. I know I am in the car. I know where it is taking me, but I cannot see what the journey is like."

I decide to describe what I see. "We are driving along Sunset Boulevard. I see a couple in their early twenties, on our right, window shopping for clothes, a woman walking her Shih Tzu. The road is fairly quiet for a Monday. It looks like there is a band playing at the local club; people queueing round the side of the venue. It looks like a young band as the people look like teenagers. The weather is slightly hazy clouds with the sun struggling to come through. My car says the temperature outside is mid-twenties. Anything else you would like to know?"

Helen thinks about my question. "Is your wife worried about where you are?"

I chuckle. "No, I am not married. The closest I am to getting married is the Pope becoming gay."

Helen laughs which I was not expecting. "We are here now. We'll get inside and continue talking. I am just parking up. Here we go. Perfect. Wait for me to get you out. We have to take a lift."

Helen nods her head to acknowledge what I said. I quickly get to the passenger side and hold her right arm and rest my other hand on her back between her shoulders. Helen eloquently gets out of the car.

She came out wearing a pair of bootcut jeans with red high heel shoes. She has a dark blue shirt with a creamy brown leather looking jacket. We both look similarly dressed.

Once we get to the restaurant on the seventeenth floor, we stand at the waiting area by the lectern. There is indistinct chatter inside the restaurant. I describe to Helen what the other customers are like and what the waiters are doing. I describe the atheistic of the restaurant. Helen wants me to take the lead and is happy to go along with whatever I do.

The maître d' finally arrives to check our booking, made under my name. He then shows us to our table. I walk in front of Helen while she keeps hold of my left arm for guidance. The table and chairs are quite close together, so I move the chairs in or aside so Helen does not stumble.

Helen lets me help her sit in the chair. The waiter hands us a menu each, to read. It makes me realise that people with no disability are not always observant. It is not for me to suddenly be all high and mighty as I am just as bad. Just because I am with a blind person, it does not make me knowledgeable all of a sudden. I know I will have a steep learning curve.

I take the lead. "I am thinking of reading out what is on the menu, so you can decide what you will like."

Helen smiles. "Yes. Unless you can magically get my eyes back."

This is the first time ever that I am having a conversation with her. "Right, so what type of food are you thinking of? That way I do not waste time reading out food that you will not want."

Helen takes her time. "Um, huh, fish. What fish do they do?"

I scour the menu for fish dishes. "They do a Scottish salmon with asparagus risotto, roasted cherry tomatoes and preserved lemon beurre blanc. The next one is fisherman's stew. That has clams, mussels, shrimp, swordfish, linguica, chard, saffron lobster broth with grilled ciabatta. And… that's it."

Helen ponders. "I will go with the fish pie. What are you going to have?"

I fancy the lamb shank. "I am going for the Persian lamb shank. Do you want a starter?"

Helen still looks like she is staring into space. "No. I will have desert."

I suddenly realise that we do not have drinks ordered. "I almost forgot, what drink would you like?"

It does not take Helen long to decide. "Red wine. Any."

I wait for a waiter to walk by to grab their attention. Once I give him our order and drinks, I start a conversation about her boyfriend. Helen is happy to talk about him with joy in her face.

I ask about how they met. "Where did you meet him?"

I can see Helen is thinking back with nostalgic, fond memories. "It was when we were at university. We met in the student bar. Through mutual friends. Is there anyone you are interested in?"

I think about when I used to fancy her. She has not changed physically and for the first time, I am getting to know her. "Sorry, no."

Helen picks up that I appear distant. "You don't want to talk about it."

I decide to ask for advice. "I decided to try out internet dating. I haven't dated since forever. I have two more dates before I start looking for someone I like. I bet you never had any awkward dates."

Helen has a quizzical look. "How do you mean?"

I decide to tell her how my date went today. "My first date was earlier today. It was embarrassing, thinking about it now."

Helen is now intrigued. "In what way?"

I reluctantly tell her. "I met her at a cafe near where she lives. Just as we get to know each other, she throws up."

Helen bursts into laughter. "Ha ha ha ha ha. You're joking. Was she eager to blurt out how much she liked you? Ha ha ha."

I wished I hadn't told her. "Not only did she throw up, she did it three times. Just in case I missed the first time. I had to use napkins to mop it up."

Helen is in a fit of hysteric. "Three times. At what point did you think that was going wrong?"

I feel embarrassed. "I'm glad I amuse you. I thought I would give her three strikes."

Helen continues. "You have made my day. Ha ha ha, aaah. That was funny. I thought my day was bad. So how did you leave it?"

I feel stupid. "I ended up having to drive her home. I decided to text her tomorrow that it is not going to happen."

Helen is smiling and trying not laugh. "Well, that doesn't beat my one of my dates."

I am now intrigued. "What did he do? Bore you to death?"

Helen tries not to laugh while she attempts to tell me her previous date. "He was a few years older than me. A friend set me up with him. Ha ha ha. He had a glass eye which she neglected to tell me."

I am open eyed. "Wow. So, what happened?"

Helen grins as she is telling the story. "As we were talking over dinner at this fancy restaurant, he decided to take his glass eye out of his and casually roll it along the table, side to side, between his hands. He does this while we are still talking. I decide to pretend that what he is doing is not really happening. Then he decides to squeeze his glass eye between his fingers and thumb, when suddenly it slips out of his hand, across the next table into someone's soup. The splash makes the soup go all over the front of this dainty old lady next to us. Ha ha ha."

I burst into laughter. "You are kidding me. You got to be joking. What happened after that?"

After Helen finishes having her fit of laugher and

composes herself, she continues. "The guy was profusely apologetic once he realised what he had done. He quickly asked for the bill and we go. Then he forgets that he did not get his glass eye so he has to embarrassingly walk back to the old lady and politely ask if it would be okay to fish out his glass eye from her soup. She is too shocked to respond. He ends up putting both his hands in the soup bowl to dig out the glass eye. I just stand there worried that we will be arrested or something. Ha ha ha ha."

We are both in stitches as I am imagining what that must have looked like. It made my date look normal. I had no idea that Helen was like this. My stomach is in knots as I am trying to control my laughter.

After what seems like five minutes, I finally control my own fits of laughter. "Aaaah, that was funny. I can beat that. I can beat that. One time, I was in the college library with some other student friends and we were sat around a table doing our course work. A girl came up to us asking if we knew how to use the photocopier. None of my friends wanted to go with her, so I obliged. When I get to the photocopier machine, I cannot believe how gorgeous she was. She had a skirt on and her legs were very sexy. I did not realise when I was showing her how to use it that I had a huge erection. What made it worse, is that I used to wear trousers. She was more focused on my erection than me showing her how to use the photocopier machine."

Helen face is open-mouthed. "You are kidding."

I say. "No."

Helen suddenly burst into laughter again. "Ha ha ha ha. Aaaah. That was funny. I can do better than that. One time I was in a rush to get to a wedding. I thought I would be smart and go without any underwear as I was running late. No one would know as I had a normal knee-length dress. Well… to get to the wedding, you had to walk up some flights of stairs. It was in a private ground. I slipped up the stairs and as I slide down the stairs–"

I can imagine. "Nooo. Nooo."

Helen laughs. "Yep. Yep. My skirt rides up past my

waist and there you have it, my birthday suit. The men did not know where to look. Lucky it was just my bum."

We laugh till our eyes are watery. Our mains arrive shortly after, so we stop discussing our embarrassing moments.

Helen starts to get flustered with how she is going to eat her food. I guess she has not eaten out in public before. She has her hands on the table, either side of her plate. She forms her hands into fists and then opens her hands up. She does this intermittently. I wait for a while to see if she asks me for help. I assume she learnt how to feed herself in the dark over the last few months. But I guess her mom or dad have been helping her to feed. After I see her hands shaking slightly through nerves or embarrassment, I have a sudden urge to hold her wrist and rub it to calm her down. I then take her knife and fork and cut up her food like I am going to feed a toddler. I then collect a tiny bit of the salmon with a tiny bit of asparagus and cherry tomato on the fork, before putting it in her hand. I then wait to see if she motions me to help her. I leave it a few seconds, when she eats off the fork for herself.

Helen closes her eyes and gives a look of *When Harry Met Sally*. "Hmmm. Hmmm I miss this. God this is great."

I smile. "Going out or the meal?"

She continues to groan. "The food. This is great."

I look at her body. "Don't your parents feed you. There is nothing of you."

Helen hurries her food and speaks between chewing. "Sorry. I did not realise how much I missed this."

I roll my eyes. "I know. I can see in your face."

Helen swallows her food. "This. I cannot think the last time I did this."

I am surprised. "How long are you talking?"

Helen takes a long think. "About three years ago."

I almost spit out my wine. "You're winding me up. Didn't you go out with friends?"

Helen is not kidding. "I miss this."

I think of what plans I have over the next two months between now, April, and end of May. "Well, just as well I have made plans."

Helen smiles as I tell her. In a soft voice, she says. "Yeah."

I smile at her. "Yeah. I am going to see you three times in the week and on Saturday. The other days, you can see your friends or tell your parents what we got up to."

I continue to collect food on her fork, so she can feed herself. I still have my meal in between helping her eat her food. I notice there are some couples looking over at us and I feel awkward. I realise that they are staring because I am helping Helen eat her food. They are empathising rather than showing sympathy. One old lady is resting her hands on her chest and praising me for my effort.

Somehow Helen senses something is strange going on. "What is it, Harvey?"

I am honest. "People are staring at me helping you eat. I think they think we are a couple. I hope they are not expecting a rendition of *Nine and a half Weeks*. I don't have any honey."

Helen laughs, almost spitting out her food. "I hope you are not going to throw up on this date. One date is enough."

Helen cannot stop laughing. We decide to have pudding and coffee after our main. I cannot stop staring at her with fondness. I am glad she is blind as she cannot see me admiring her beauty.

Our conversation moves on to why she chose to become a doctor.

Helen gently feels for her coffee cup. "I saw a car crash, of all things. My father was driving by at the time. I saw a woman fighting for a child's life. Giving resuscitation. The child didn't make it. But I decided there and then, that I wanted to be a doctor."

I ask about the car accident. "What do you remember about your accident?"

Helen's face looks blank. "I think about that all the

time. I have no idea why I was there. I do not remember the impact, being in hospital… except waking up in hospital. The only thing I remember is going to work that night. I have no idea why I was driving, when I should have been at work."

I listen intensely. "So, have you asked anyone or checked your phone, in case it was an emergency?"

Helen twists her lips as she thinks. "My phone was lost in the car crash. Also, I have lost my memory, so I cannot remember whether I spoke to anyone."

I suddenly remember her memory. "Of course, and they never found your cellular on the road or in the car."

Helen shrugs her shoulders. "That goes round and round in my head. Once I find out why, I will understand what I was doing in the car."

The conversation dries up, but we are comfortable with the silence. I start to imagine what it would be like to kiss her. It is weird looking at her as if I was a pervert, Helen not having any idea that I was doing this. She is so cute and I still fancy her as if it was yesterday we were back in elementary school and high school. She has the cutest nose and dark brown eyes. She reminds me of Halle Berry with long hair, flowing down to her shoulder. It is not a surprise to me that she is now engaged to get married. The ring on her wedding finger is a big giveaway. It sparkles quite brightly when she moves her hands and it catches in the light. I noticed it when I was at her parents' house, but I chose to not to mention it.

I decide to ask about her engagement. "When did Rob propose to you?"

Helen's face lights up after I ask her. "When I got home from the hospital. He felt he should be making an honest woman of me. Also, he wanted to reassure me that he will be with me always."

I question Robert's motive. "Well, you have been together twelve years. Better late than never. Yet he is suddenly busy with travelling. Don't you find it strange?"

Helen feels put out of joint. "He can't help it if work is

busy now."

I am curious what he does for a living. "So, what does he sell?"

Helen feels interrogated. "He sells… medical drugs."

I think seasonal. "What type of drugs?"

Helen looks embarrassed. "Antihistamine."

I am close to making it obvious that the drug is most likely seasonal for hay fever. "I was just curious. It makes sense now."

Helen gets defensive. "What are you trying to say? He is avoiding me?"

I change the subject to asking what she wishes she had done before going blind. "Is there anything you regret now you are blind?"

Helen thinks about my question. "I always wanted to go travelling. Through South America. Visit Guyana, where my parents are originally from."

I surprised. "Wow, my parents are also from Guyana. We could be related."

The change in conversation has helped to make Helen feel more uncomfortable. I am suspicious now of Robert, as he is suddenly busy selling a drug that is seasonal in the summer. I know it is April now, maybe pre orders for the summer. But her accident was in October last year.

I think about what she said earlier about the last time she went out with Robert on a date. Helen said three years ago. They were together for nine years then. I wonder what would have changed. Both of their careers would have been established so there would be no need for a change in them spending time together.

Helen is quietly sipping her coffee. I cannot help wondering if her relationship with Robert is okay. I decide not to try and pry anymore into her personal relationship. We sit in silence the rest of dessert and coffee.

When both finish our dessert and coffee, I ask for the bill straight away.

There is no awkwardness when we leave to go back to

the car and drive home. We do not say anything to each other on the way back but the silence was not uncomfortable as if we had a cross word. I put the radio on to break the silence.

When I get back to her parents' home, I help her out of the car and walk her to the door. I ring the doorbell for her and wait with her until she is inside. The butler answers the door and acknowledges us.

I am about to leave when Helen says something with her back to me. "I had a wonderful time. I look forward to seeing you again."

I am taken aback as I thought she may not want to see me again after questioning her relationship. "I will see you on Wednesday. I will be round about ten o'clock in the morning."

CHAPTER EIGHT

Reflections

Helen is already awake and does not know how long she has been lying in bed awake, as she has no sense of time. She is lying in bed under her duvet, in her childhood bedroom.

She sits up, feeling for her two pillows to push upright and vertical. She wants to rest her back against her h board before she gets up to go into the shower.

She showers by herself and gets herself changed. Helen has a carer but she prefers to use her assistant to get downstairs and help her eat her breakfast, lunch and dinner.

She naturally does not know what time it is, as she sits up on her bed. Helen cannot tell if it is day or night via shades of light and dark. Helen can only know what time it is by using her voice speaking clock that her father bought for her.

She just has to feel for the button on top of the clock to allow the time to be electronically spoken to her. She has the time spoken to her in the twenty-four-hour clock format. This is so she can know straight away whether it is morning, afternoon or night time.

Helen already checked the time when she initially woke up, so she already knows it is morning. She presses the clock button again to find out what time it is now. Helen hears the clock say that it is now nine twenty-eight. She has been awake now for an hour, listening to the local radio, not keeping track of interval times provided by the presenter.

Her clock is on top of her bedside three tier drawer, on her right. There is nothing else on it, so she does not have to worry about knocking over a lamp or an accessory. Her bedroom is minimalist as she does not live there permanently anymore and all her belongings are back at the flat she still shares with her fiancé.

Her parents decided to hire a full-time carer to look after their daughter as they both still work full-time. Helen's carer lives at the family home and sleeps in the bedroom next to her. Her carer is in her early forties and reminds her parents of the black comedienne named Wanda Sykes. She has similar mannerisms and moans about everything but she is great at her job and does not take any rubbish from Helen. Her name is Florence.

Florence's routine is naturally waking up at eight o'clock in the morning and then getting herself ready before she checks in on Helen. Florence knows that Helen needs help if she can hear the bell ring. Helen keeps the bell inside her bed while sleeping, so she does not have to search for it. Helen only rings the bell if she has no way of getting herself out of any predicament. She also has a bell in her en suite, so she does not forget to leave the bell in her bed.

Helen decides to take a shower and slides herself to the side of the bed that her clock is on. Her en suite is on the same side as well.

Once she is sat on the edge of the bed, she uses the bedside drawer to gauge where she is and stands up resting her right hand on the small three tier drawer. She then sticks her left arm out to touch the wall to her en suite, as she stands upright. She then shuffles her body, with tiny footsteps, along the wall while using her right arm to slide along it. The palm of her hand can feel the wall's surface imperfections; the raises and dents along the surface of the wall. Helen can remember where the imperfections are as she has done the same routine over a hundred times now. She finds the journey to the en suite and walk-in shower second nature now.

Helen has been living at her parents' house now for four months since the middle of December. Both Helen and her parents wanted her home for Christmas.

Helen uses the door frame of the en suite's entrance to know when she is there. She has counted how many steps she is away from the door entrance from her bed. Every time, she counts twenty-one steps. She thinks that one day it will change, somehow. She can feel for the triple grooves in the joinery of the door frame. When she gets inside, she pictures in her head where the towel rack is from memory and grabs the towel. She feels the shower glass on her left, that is from tile floor to ceiling. She uses the glass to find the edge which tells her the entrance of her walk-in wet room shower. She places her towel on the Persian style floor tile next to the shower glass before the entrance to avoid getting wet by the water splashes.

She then stands underneath her shower head which is plumbed into the ceiling, centre of the shower unit. Her shower tap is already set to her thirty-five Celsius temperature. She is lucky as the water falls out instantly at the right temperature so she does not feel the initial cold before it warms up to the right temperature.

She keeps her shower gel, shampoo and face scrub on the floor, under her shower tap. She is able to tell the difference by having the shower gel with an elastic band. The face scrub is small so if she does not remember which way round she left them, she does not use the wrong one to shower with. She keeps her flannel to wash her body on top of the shower tap.

She learnt all this, thanks to her parents searching the internet for tips on being blind.

Now she is blind, her other four senses are more heightened. Her sense of smell is stronger and this makes it harder to accept unpleasant smells which make her feel sick. If she smells sick or a bad toilet odour, she is almost sick herself. She carries a scent spray to counteract any such odour. Under the circumstances, her sense of smell would not ordinarily notice her personal hygiene. Now her sense of smell is heightened, she can easily tell if her personal hygiene is offensive. She now feels that she has to shower twice a day; sometimes three times. She gets paranoid that other people can smell what she can. She realises that her genitals give off a dull musk that seems inviting after she has showered.

Sex for her is now heightened when she makes love to Robert. She gets lubricated more quickly and she can smell Robert's genitals more clearly now. She can feel his orgasm shoot through her body as he climaxes inside her. It has made her sexual appetite increase, which at times tires Robert out.

One time Helen demanded sex from eight in the morning till gone mid-day with brunch in between. Robert was surprised he was still able to relieve himself, in between brunch. Helen felt guilty as he was a bit sore in that department after their five-hour session. He could not sleep on his front for two days. He also had to have a steaming hot bath to relieve the spasms in his back. He had to tell his clients that his mattress springs were digging in his back, as he had a hunch back.

Helen's new-found sexual appetite has caused her to get a vibrator to fight the urges. It was awkward for her when one day she was using it in her en suite. She forgot that she did not shut the door, not much lock it. As she was buzzing away and overcome with the moment, she could suddenly smell a coffee aroma in the room. She heard her mom clear her throat and say. "Once you are done, take a coffee break." Helen was totally mortified and reminded of the downside of being blind. Her mom could have just quietly pretended not to have noticed and left the drink in the bedroom. Helen thought about this while showering and started to giggle to herself. She also was glad she did not remember that when talking about embarrassing moments with Harvey.

While she is showering still, Helen questions herself: why she was not at work and where was she going in her car on the day of the accident? She hates herself for getting in that car and being involved in the accident which resulted in her going blind. The first couple of months she cried herself to sleep every night.

Her mom struggled at first, not knowing how to make her daughter feel better. Martha is disappointed in her daughter's fiancé Robert, not making himself available to look after Helen. Martha found it weird that Robert chose to propose while Helen was still in hospital. But is not here to support her now. Martha's husband offered to support them both financially until Helen gained her sight back.

A lot of people have the misconception that blind people see pitch black, whether born blind or who go blind later in life.

A person born blind cannot say if they see black as they have never seen colour before. A person born blind sees shades of light and dark so they can see light, whether it is soft or hard. There are no shapes or shadows for people who are born blind. A person born blind has eyes either grey, white or a mixture of blue and white in colour. A person born with sight but later in life becomes blind, does not see blackness or darkness. Their eyes are the same colour they were born with.

Helen sees mixtures of colours that change within minutes. She tends to see a dark black background, like space. In front of the dark black background are blotches of green, purple, yellow, blue and white. The blotches then have various shades of gold blotches. The blotches are like seeing through a camera lens at various clear view lightbulbs in different colours. The lens is out of focus and so the lightbulbs are blurry. That is how Helen has described it in her own words.

When she showers herself, she has to mentally think in what order to clean herself so she does not miss any part of her body. She has to feel the texture of the shower gel, so she knows she has enough to create a lather. She starts on her boobs first, making sure she gets underneath them. She then soaks her areola's in soapy lather to ensure they are properly clean. She then cleans her vagina, making sure she has cleaned it thoroughly. After that, she then cleans her bottom thoroughly. After she has scrubbed her boobs, genital and bum, she then cleans her back, tummy, legs and feet.

Once she is happy that she has cleaned herself all over, she will let the waterfall rinse off the excess soap suds. She knows when it is all washed away, by rubbing parts of her body to see if it her fingers judder along her skin. She rubs the face scrub on her face with the palm of her hands and then looks up under the shower head to rinse off. She then turns off the shower and crouches down to feel for her towel she left on the other side of the shower glass by the entrance. Once dried, she puts the towel back on the rail. She prefers to walk back into the bedroom naked so she does not have to go back, repeating the whole exercise again.

Once she is finished, she repeats the same method to get back to the side of the bed, feeling the air cascading over her naked body. Again, she is in autopilot counting the twenty-one steps back to the bed.

Back in her bedroom, she sits next to her bedside drawer to pull out her underwear for the day, and a bra. She does not care about getting her underwear colours mixed up as no one can see. At the same time, her taste in colours are not garish or loud but neutral so you would not really know if she mixed the colours up. She keeps her tights, underwear and bras separately in the three drawers so she knows where to get them from.

Her whole routine of showering and getting changed takes her about fifty minutes, because of her disability. She was able to get ready inside twenty minutes before she lost her sight.

Helen's staple clothes, now she does not go to work, are jeans and polo shirts so she does not have to struggle to work out what clothes she is putting on.

Helen thinks back to when she first woke up out of her coma.

The first few days for Helen were tough. Each time she

woke up, she expected to have her eyesight back, only to be reminded that she still cannot see. When she awoke, her vision saw the various colours and shapes, as described before. At first, she thought it was her eyes fighting to gain sight back.

She had a few work colleagues visit her during her stay at hospital. Only a handful of friends out of work visited her at least once. Her fiancé did not come to visit that frequently, blaming it on his heavy work schedule. Her parents visited every day during her two months in hospital. When Helen had no visitors, she would just sit up in bed looking at the patterns and colours her brain was producing. The doctors and nurses checked her obs every few hours on her eyes and her injuries sustained in the crash.

The nurse would feed her breakfast, lunch and dinner.

Helen was scared about not getting her eye sight back. She would suffer panic attacks, needing a nurse to calm her down and soothe her. The panic attacks would be in the evenings after visiting hours.

When she left hospital in December, she had counselling to deal with the life change. Her counsellor saw her up to end of February, a month ago. Helen's father drove her there each week and waited outside in reception.

Helen used to have her ornaments and various pieces of furniture dotted around her room. After a period of walking into her furniture and knocking her ornaments over, her dad had them moved out of her room. Helen would have bruises on her thighs and knees.

When Helen was discharged from hospital, her mother said straight away that she was going to stay with her and her dad. Martha did not like the idea of her daughter being home alone most of the time. Robert did not give any signs of taking time off work. Martha always questioned why Helen was with Robert.

While Helen is still thinking of the past, she is interrupted by Florence. She came into the room without knocking, knowing that it did not make a difference to Helen.

Florence checks in on Helen every morning at ten thirty on the dot. Whether Helen is butt naked, half-dressed or still asleep, she will walk in to check she is alright. Helen is used to it and it does not embarrass her, quite the opposite. It is a comfort for her as she has a constant in her life.

Florence looks at Helen in just her underwear. "You're not dressed yet. You are lucky I am not a lesbian; I would have jumped your bones by now."

Helen smiles. "I have got going to the shower and back, down to a tee."

Florence responds. "I expect you to do cartwheels next. If you want, I can put a roller skate on the floor. See how you get on then."

Helen bursts into laughter. "Maybe that will get my time down from fifty minutes to twenty."

Florence waves her hand. "Shucks, it takes as long as it takes. It's not like you have to be anywhere."

Helen sighs in agreement. 2Can you pass my clothes over, please?"

Florence looks on her bed for her clothes and passes them over, then taps on her shoulder to indicate next to her.

Florence asks. "Do you want me to give you a hand?"

Helen wants to try on her own. "I want to give it ago. About time I tried. How hard can it be putting on jeans and top?"

Florence is stunned to see her underwear. "For a start you have put your thong on wrong. Are you trying to go for the Mankini look? Or accentuate your lady part. Either way, it is not a good look."

Helen feels deflated at not being able to put on a simple piece of underwear. "Ah, can you help me?"

Florence jokes. "Does this constitute sexual assault? It is only me in this room with no witness."

Helen burst into laughter again. "Depends if I make a pass at you. Works both ways."

Florence helps her out of the underwear to correct it. Then lets Helen dress herself. She manages to get her clothes on properly.

Florence wants to know more about why Robert is never around during the week. She has noticed he only comes over during the day on a Saturday and is gone early evening.

Florence wonders how to broach the subject. "When are you next seeing Rob?"

Helen is happy to talk about him. "He is around this Saturday as per usual."

Florence asks about phone calls. "I notice he never calls to see if you are alright."

Helen makes excuses for him. "He knows I have you. I am in safe hands."

Florence, without a sound, screws her face in disagreement. "If I had a boyfriend or if my late husband was around, I would call him every day and text. In your situation, have the text read out."

Helen again makes excuses. "He is not into text messaging. Besides, you would get fed up reading out the obscene conversations we would have. You would go red in the face."

Florence asks. "What does he do for work again?"

Helen can tell what Florence getting at "He is very busy travelling across America, selling medical drugs. It is not easy for him to come and see me often."

Florence is not convinced. "Why does he not go to his boss to get time off work? Doesn't his boss know about you?

Helen feels ruffled. "His boss is hard on him. He is on his back all the time, pushing sales."

Florence is still not convinced. Robert comes around to her parents' house to see her only on Saturdays. Helen would have nobody if Florence was not there to keep her company, much less care for her. Helen sees her parents every night when they are home from work. Her dad works normal office hours while he waits for her operation that has been scheduled for June. Thankfully, an anonymous person funded the medical unit for the operation. No one in the hospital found out. The operation is to try to get her eyesight back. There is a fifty-fifty chance of it working. The doctors thought Helen's eyesight would return once the swelling of the brain had subsided.

Now that Helen is ready, Florence helps her to walk down the stairs to eat the breakfast that their butler prepared and left in the oven to stay warm.

Today is scrambled eggs and salmon, with buttered toasted brown bread. While Florence helps Helen to eat her breakfast, Helen starts to think about Harvey. Until last night she had not left the house since the accident. She is worried that she has scared him off, after having a heated discussion about Robert's absent and their relationship. But at the same time, Harvey did say he was coming over tomorrow morning. There has been no contact to say that he has changed his mind. Her dad has not said anything to the contrary.

Helen did not realise how much she missed going out until last night. She found Harvey funny and very different to Robert. Helen had not remembered to touch his face to get an idea of what he may look like. She decides that she will do that tomorrow before leaving the house. Helen has not made any plans for the day and wishes that Harvey was coming today, as well as tomorrow.

For the first time in four months, she has not thought about her fiancé. Her mind is preoccupied now, knowing she has plans made for her. She is intrigued what plans Harvey has for tomorrow. She remembers that he is coming round for ten o'clock in the morning. While Helen is still thinking about tomorrow, Florence thinks out loud. Florence is looking at the newspaper Helen's dad has delivered. It is one of those respectable newspapers, unlike gossip papers. "Say what!"

Helen almost jumps as she was not expecting it. She is snapped out of her thoughts. "What is it?"

Florence is emotionally charged. "That idiot Trump is saying that Putin was not involved in rigging the election. I haven't heard so much crock in my life. With hair like that, no one should be in charge of a country. If you can't sort your bald patch out, what chance have you got sorting out the shit hole of America?"

Helen smirks and shakes her head with bewilderment. Helen finds Florence's moans refreshing and funny. She thinks what her life would have been like if she had a different carer. Like her parents, Florence reminds Helen of the comedienne Wanda Sykes but Helen does not know what Florence looks. She has not touched her face and felt her what skin feels like. She does not know if she is old and wrinkly or fresh-faced. She has not found the right time to ask but she can imagine her looking like the comedienne with her character and the sound of her mannerisms. She suddenly realises that she can use Harvey to describe her when he comes round.

I have gone into the office today, now I have no social commitments. I have made headway with my new story. Once I finish one book and organise for it to be published, I cannot hang around for the royalties to come in before starting on my next one. Also, I cannot just sit around taking a break before moving on to my next book. While I am writing, I cannot stop thinking about Helen. She has not changed since school and university. She is even cuter now she relies on someone to help her around as a blind woman. I am surprised with myself that I am not prejudiced towards blind people. I have never been put in a situation before to determine if I was prejudice. It is something you would not know unless you were put in that situation. It has not put me off fancying Helen. I am glad that I am already in the throes of trying to meet my future wife. I said it. I am ready to meet my future wife. There, I said it again. I am trying to meet my future wife. It still sounds strange as I repeat it in my head. It is not just going on dates to try to get laid. It is about finding my companion. I do not know what I would have done if I was not looking for my own partner. My feelings would spiral out of control with Helen and maybe I would have made a pass at her with Robert hitting me in the face.

My office is across the hallway from my two brothers' offices, that are next to each other, both facing my office. My desk does not face the hallway but faces the window. I like having an office away from home as Mom and Dad are a distraction. My parents do not get what I do for a living. They think I come up with ideas for my brothers' business. When I bought the house, they thought I had won the lottery. I have told them on numerous occasions that I write for a living. I have not used the term 'author' as I feel uncomfortable saying the word. I guess I have never come to terms that I am an author. I see authors as having knowledge on their field. I have no idea if I have knowledge in my field. I just write what I think I would feel or what people have told me. I have not experienced sadness, loss of a loved one or being a hero but I have an ability to help my readers escape their day-to-day life for a few hours. My craft has allowed me to buy things and live my life. It is what has allowed me to live next door to Helen.

Around lunchtime, Chevalier and Xavier sometimes come into my office to take a break and catch up. They like the idea that I do not get phone calls from customers or have deadlines to meet but they do not realise how lonely it can be. You are guaranteed not to bump into anyone if you choose not you. I do not regret choosing to become an author, as I love discussing topics like affairs, illnesses and disabilities. I enjoy explaining to my audience what it is like using my characters and stories that I make up. I do not use family or friends directly. I base my characters on my family and friends and then embellish them. I try to have humour to lighten the story. I have, on numerous occasions, incorporated my experiences of embarrassments and unsuccessful adventures, as I have plenty of those.

My new story is about a man who is trying to settle down and keeps meeting the wrong kind of woman. It is a story about the pitfalls of dating and getting wires crossed. It is weird that I happen to be starting dating while writing this book.

During my clicking of the keyboard on my laptop, my brothers come into my office and sit down on the two seats in front of my desk. They bring a Chinese takeaway that they had delivered to the office. I saw a Chinese man walk in a few minutes ago and drop off a white bag at reception. My brothers assume that I would have the same dish I usually have and order it for me. They were right: egg fried rice and chicken curry. Chevalier plonks the white bag on my desk next to my laptop and unpacks it. Xavier goes to my cabinet behind me to my right to get out paper plates and some plastic knives and forks that I keep in there. I stop what I am writing when I get to a natural stop of a sentence. I look up to see where they are with putting the food on plates.

When they have finished filling the plates up, we sit together eating our own dishes. Xavier starts the conversation first. "Christine keeps moaning at me, not spending enough time at home to help out with the kids."

Chevalier responds with a negative attitude. "Christine is asking too much. This is a business where we cannot just stop everything. If she is struggling, then get a nanny. It is not like we are on the breadline."

I roll my eyes. "She is not saying she is struggling; she wants adult conversation and to feel like a family."

Xavier jumps in. "Exactly. But we have this new contract and it is early days. I cannot relax until it is at a workable stage."

Chevalier is not convinced. "She wanted a second baby, now she is struggling. Now what is happening with you and this girl, Laura? I hear she almost blew it. Ha ha ha. Get it?"

Xavier laughs as well. "I heard she spilled her feelings over you."

Chevalier raises his hand at Xavier and they do a high five together. "Boy, you sure pick them."

I feel embarrassed. "Who told you?"

Chevalier says. "Mercedes, of course. She also told us what happened on the date."

Xavier is interested to know when my next date is. "So, when is the next date?"

I am hesitant. "Um–"

Chevalier interrupts. 'He doesn't want to tell us."

Xavier is curious about his decision to date Laura again. "So, are you going to see Laura again?"

I misunderstand Xavier's question. "Of course, I am. I made an agreement to look after her until she gets her eyesight back."

Xavier looks surprised. "I wasn't talking about her. I was talking about Laura."

I feel caught out. "Huh um, I assumed you were talking about her."

Chevalier wants to know as well. "Well, so do you still have feelings for Helen. Considering you assume we were talking about her."

I lie. "No! She is… ugly now. She has got really big."

Xavier looks at me. "The same girl I saw the other day. I suggested to her father that you look after her. That girl. The last I looked, she looked fine. Apart from the blindness. But that is great, right? That means she will go out with you, now that she doesn't have to see your ugly head. She can picture a black Brad Pitt. A Denzel Washington when she is making love to you. Apart from the paunch you carry."

I exaggeratedly laugh. "Very funny."

Chevalier joins in. "Yeah. She can think up anyone if she has a good imagination. May have to do that to get a climax. Maybe read one of your books, if you fail to bring her off."

Xavier suddenly has a thought. "Does she know you

are a self-made millionaire? That you are an author?"

I think back. "No. She doesn't. I prefer it that way. I won't be around come June, July anyway."

Chevalier is curious. "Why's that? You've never left home once. Since when are going to fly the coup?"

Xavier changes the subject to dating again. "So, when is your next date? Have you told Laura that you are not going to date her again?"

Chevalier backs up Xavier. "Yeah. I thought you told Mercedes that you are going to call it off."

Just as I am about to say that I am going to call it off, I get a text from Laura which I was not expecting. I presumed that she would know that I would not be interested in getting to know her further. I read the text saying. "Hi, thought I would see if you fancy going for another drink. This time I will not drink. I can pick you up this time." It would have been easier had Laura not sent the text. It would have just been a formal confirmation of not taking it further.   My brothers are looking at me with the expectation that I will read out the text or summarise it.

I look at them begrudgingly. "She wants to meet up again. I told her I am a millionaire. She is only asking because she now knows."

Chevalier gives his helpful advice. "Sleep with her, then ditch her. She will only drain you dry."

Xavier reminds me of the obvious. "She did throw up. Not once, not twice, three times. Three strikes and you're out."

Chevalier bursts into laughter. "Ha ha ha. So, what are you going to do?"

I look at the text, pondering. "I have to text her to say it is over. But I will wait. I will text her to say that I need to look at my diary and see what that week is like."

We finish eating our food after I text Laura saying. "Only if you promise me that you will not throw up on our date again. There is spilling the beans, but that takes it to a whole new level."

CHAPTER NINE

Second Date

It is Wednesday morning and I am already dressed and ready to go over to Helen's.

Last night I found a great place to take Helen. I did not need to book. We just need to get there for eleven o'clock.

As well as finding this place, I finally sent twenty individual messages via the dating website. It took me three hours and some numb fingers. If I don't find someone after this, then I don't know what. The twenty women I like the look of, as well as the look of their profile, vary from curvaceous to slim and hail from Mexico to Budapest. I have no qualms what race the women are. My only concern is that they are kind, can communicate and they want to be with me for who I am. I have not had any response yet. I feel good as I will get my shrink off my back. Deep down, I don't think I want to meet anyone. I am self-contained. I have lived almost half my life without a companion, so I can do another thirty odd years. The only person I want to be with is Helen. I sort of lied to my shrink that I want to meet someone.

I am in my office at home making additional notes to my story so I do not forget to include them in my latest novel. As per usual, everyone has left to go to work. My parents are sat in their living room watching rubbish television. I am clock-watching so I am not late getting to Helen's. From door to door, it is only two minutes by car.

I sense in myself that my feelings for Helen are still there. They never left. I am glad I am arranging the other dates, so I can be distracted. I will try to use Helen's blindness to deter my feelings for her. I wish I was not looking after her.

I must not forget the gift voucher I bought online and printed. I will be giving it to her carer as a token of appreciation. No one knows and I want it as a surprise. Helen's dad, Bill and I thought it would be a good idea. I know that her carer, Florence will love it. I spared no expense and so I hope she still goes to the "*Beverly Wiltshire Hotel*", despite the extravagance. I think Florence will like it. I think I am more excited than she will be. Bill warned me that she knows who I am and is a fan of my books. She does not know that I am coming over though.

When I arrive to pick Helen up, I am hesitant to ring the doorbell. I have no way of knowing if Florence will put two and two together from my name. I do not have my picture on the back of my books or on my website but my name is unusual. I am worried she will let on to Helen. I don't want Helen to know as I do not want her to like me just because of my job. I want her to notice me for who I am, not what I do. Bill was not clear on the phone what he had told Florence. I wonder if Bill told Florence that I am an author and if she knows of my work. Also, that it is me coming round. I had not asked Bill if Helen was within earshot, when he spoke to Florence.

I do not want Helen to know about my background because she never noticed me at school or uni. I do not want Helen to, all of a sudden, show an interest and forget who I am. I just hope the butler answers the door again. Thinking about it, where was Florence when I came on Monday?

This time round, the door is opened within seconds of ringing the doorbell. Obviously, they now know that it is me coming over. Shock horror, the carer opens the door. Florence is open mouthed as she looks at me in surprise, at her favourite author. Helen looks bewildered as she does not know why there is silence. "Who is it. Isn't it Harvey at the door."

I smile awkwardly at Florence and remember to put my index finger to my lips and whisper to Florence. "Sssh. She does not know. I want to keep it that way." Florence turns to Helen trying to think of something to explain her behaviour. "Huh, Nothing. I was expecting…the mail man. Come in Harvey."

Helen is standing a few feet away from us, patiently waiting for us.
Helen picks up on the whispering. "What? Not say it is you?"

I quickly defuse the confusion. "Ah, I think your carer has mistaken me for someone. She thinks I am on a wanted poster. Everyone thinks I look like someone."

Florence goes along with me. "Aaah. That's it. I thought he was…that opera singer. Maybe we could go on a date."

Helen is anxious at not being involved in the conversation and does not understand what we are talking about. "What is that?"

Florence reassures her. "Nothing, Helen. This is between me and this hunk of a man. You didn't say he was handsome."

Helen tries to be funny. "So, it isn't Harvey, then." And then smiles.

I find Helen annoying. "You're not funny, Helen. Shall I just leave you here and take Florence out instead?"

Helen thinks I am serious. "No, no. I take it back. I need to get out. Not that Florence is not great company."

Florence smiles. "Are you sure? He has a cute butt," she says as she bends round me to take a look.
After the conversation naturally comes to a close, I get out the voucher I printed. I look at Florence and pass it to her.
Florence squints at the paper wondering what it is. "Is this for the bin? I ain't no butler."

She makes me smile. "Look at it. But don't shout. I am already deaf in one ear."

Florence's eyes open up wide. "Holy shit. Are you for real? I know you can afford this, but you are shitting me?"

Helen is nosey now. "What is it?"

I jump in and lie. "It is a tax bill."

Helen screws her face up in annoyance. "If you dent want to tell me, then that is fine."

I smile as I have wound her up. I whisper to Florence. "Take a friend. Put the tab under my name."

Florence goes to get ready to go to the Beverley Wiltshire Hotel Spa, leaving me and Helen alone. I help Helen walk to the reception room as we have over half an hour before we have to leave. After we are sat down, Helen hesitantly reaches her hands out towards me to touch my face. She looks nervous as she goes to feel my cheeks. I let her continue, moving my face to make it easier for her to feel. I keep my eyes open as she feels my cheeks, eyebrows, forehead and my ears. She looks at me with full concentration. I can smell her perfume and I could just kiss her. God, she is beautiful.

Helen smiles at me. "I see you have a beard. I mean, I feel your beard. I am picturing in my head what you look like. Your nose is wide and round, which tells me you are black. Your lips are full which also suggests you are black. Your ears are small which is cute. Your cheekbones are slightly protruding which means you are slightly slim. Learning from Ray Charles, your wrist is slim which suggests you are not fat."

I am not impressed as it takes a lot to fascinate me. I expected her to be able to map my face. Helen did not ask what I did for a living. I was half expecting her to ask me but she did not. It was now time to leave for our day out. I am taking her to an eating course for the blind so she can gain more confidence.

We get there just before eleven o'clock. There are about fourteen other blind people with their friends or partners. It is a good turnout. We are standing around waiting for the teacher to start the course. There is indistinct chatter among the other people. I explain to Helen what the turnout is like and the type of people here. Helen is appreciative of me telling her.

The place has tables and chairs, like a restaurant. There is a kitchen at the back. The course is about learning how to realise the texture of different meat, fish and salad.

The person who is taking the course finally shows up. The lady is flighty. "Thanks for coming. My name is Rosie. As in the rose. I am going to read out the register. To make sure that everyone has arrived. Just say yes. For those accompanying the blind, thank you. They couldn't have got here without you."

After Rosie does the roll call, we have to find a table to sit at and start the course. The food is already cooked and Rosie brings the food out with a couple of assistants.

Rosie explains what is going to happen. "We are going to use our knife and fork to feel the texture of the food. We are going to do a competition. You will have to guess what food is on your plate by only using your knife and fork. There are five different food types. No help from your partners. The winner gets a voucher for a restaurant of your choice. My assistants Enrico and Melissa are putting the food in front of you."

I look at Helen, who seems to be getting into this. "They are putting your food down now. Right. Time to test your skills."

Helen starts to feel for her knife and fork. "I reckon from the smell, it is pork, some kind of fish and pasta. The vibration through the knife and how easy it tears, suggests that it is pork. I can cut through this too easily, so this has to be pasta. I am not sure what this is. Assume it is fish, but not sure."

I do not give her any hints. "So, you think it is pork, pasta and some kind of fish. I am not sure if you have to be specific. Your final answers?"

Helen is confident. "Yes."

Rosie goes to tell the participants what food is on their plates. "Has everyone decided what is on their plates?"

All of us say in unison. "Yes."

Rosie continues. "Right. On your plate is lamb shank,

which you could have mistaken for pork. The next food is squid which you may have thought was pasta. And finally, the third dish is tofu that you may have thought as fish. Did anyone get all three correct?"

No one correctly guessed the food. It is an eye opener and I am surprised. Helen is completely shocked that she did not get any of the food right.

Helen makes me smile when she says. "I am surprised how easy it is to get confused with what food is on the plate."

Rosie finds it funny and explains. "This is why this course is a great one to come along to. We will teach you how to work out where your food is on the plate and how to use the clock to know where your food is on the plate. The way to allocate your food is to have your meat at twelve o'clock on your plate, then your sides at nine o'clock and three o'clock. The aim of today's session is to teach you how to avoid seasoning your food wrongly and avoid spilling your drinks on the table."

Helen turns to me and thanks me for taking her to this place. I knew that this would be more practical than just going out for the sake of it. I find it interesting myself. The teacher shows us to put the salt and pepper in your hand, so you know which, is which. Then sprinkle from the hand. Take note of where you hear the drink being placed on the table, then place the glass to your eleven o'clock or two o'clock so as not to spill it. Helen is taught how to use the knife to taste the food before eating and how the texture of different meat feels. Rosie made us laugh throughout the course.

The final part of the course is to put into practice what was taught so we had a three-course meal after one o'clock. I am impressed with how much Helen has taken in from Rosie's lecture. It is like it is second nature to her. We start to talk about the course.

Helen is testing out her side dish. "I am so grateful for you taking me here. You are so practical."

I am halfway through chewing my food. "No problemo."

Helen smiles at me. "Problemo?"

I just look at her. "Yeah, so what are your plans tonight?"

Helen sighs. "The usual. Dinner, listening to the TV, then bed. How about you?"

I think about the date that I have with Olivia. She finally texted me late evening on Tuesday suggesting tonight. I naturally said yes. I want to ask Helen for advice. I decide to ask her when we are close to finishing our lunch. I am not shy telling her. "I have a date tonight."

Helen looks up at me. "So, what is her name?"

I lean forward on the table. "Her name is Olivia. Can you give any advice? Considering my last date."

Helen smiles. "Ask lots of questions about her. She is a lucky girl."

I am taken aback. "Why do you say that?"

Helen smiles again. "You are thoughtful. You put the other person first."

I feel humble. "This is just second nature. If I can think of this, anyone can. This is not a hard thing to think of."

Helen has concentration on her face. "Any girl should be lucky to have you."

I start to feel embarrassed. "That means a lot."

I think to myself that I could just kiss her. She has the cutest eyes and nose. I wish she was my fiancée. I don't care she is blind.

I can see that she has become more relaxed with feeding herself, now she has been given the tools.

Helen has something else to say. "Since I became blind, each day has been depressing. From today, you have given me a light at the end of the tunnel. For that, thank you."

I am touched. "That means a lot. We have a whole three months of this."

Helen smiles. "Yes, we do."

After we finish, the group of us that attended slowly

disperse their own ways. Helen and I did not socialise with the other attendants. We were only interested in the course and having our own private conversations.

When going back to the car, I noticed a couple of people whispering among themselves, as they noticed me helping Helen in my car. After I closed her door, one of them crept up behind me. I was taken aback as if I was being stalked. The woman looks like she is in her eighties and with a sweet smile asks for my signature. I smile with a nod to acknowledge her wish. I ask her what she wants me to write. I write her name, Fran, in the book. I also write. "To a sweet old lady who recognised me at a blind person course. Of the places to spot someone. Love H." She is open-mouthed with my comment and skips back to her friends.

When I get inside the car, Helen asks what we were talking about. I lie and tell her that she was asking for directions. Helen contradicts me by saying that she sounded like she knew me. I pretend to have a blank look and tell her that I do not know her from Adam.

During our drive home, Helen asks me more about what I know about Olivia. I tell her that all I know about her is that she enjoys fencing. Not the garden type. That is pretty much all that I can tell Helen.

Helen mentions the smell of the car and notices that it is brand new. She says that she can tell from the feel of the seat and the smoothness of the ride. I tell her that she is very observant. She says that she noticed on our first date but was too nervous to mention it. I correct her by saying that this is a friendship outing. I ask her what she wants to do on Friday. She asks me to surprise her.

I ask Helen where I should take Olivia on our date.

"I have to text Olivia where to meet up. Where would you suggest?"

Helen pauses. "Um, I would suggest a nice quiet bar. So, if it goes nowhere, you can leave quickly."

I think of Laura and decide to do a U-turn. "I need your advice. I mistakenly agreed to go on another date with

Laura. But have changed my mind."

Helen looks like her mind is elsewhere. "Me. What do I know?"

I continue. "I don't know how to tell Laura that I am not interested in her."

I can see Helen thinking about her answer. "I would text her to say, 'I have had a change of heart. I do not want to take this any further. It was nice meeting you.' Leave at that."

I am happy with her answer. "Thanks."

Helen changes the conversation to Florence and asks me about why Florence was acting strangely. "What were you and Florence talking about behind my back? You two were very quiet."

I play it down. "It was not behind your back. It was in front of you."

Helen pushes me for an answer. "So, what were you talking about?"

I naturally lie. "Your father told me that she was a fan of some writer. He knew that I could get a signed book so I managed to get her one. Then your father thought he would treat her to a spa as a token of his appreciation."

Helen still does not seem convinced. "So why were you two whispering?"

I make a joke of it. "She thought I was some dodgy salesman. I had to quiet her as I did not want you frightened. Florence was worried for your safety."

Helen smirks.

We finally arrive back at her parents' house. Her butler answers the door and Florence is not back yet. I feel that I should wait till either her parents get home or Florence. I do not feel confident with her butler looking after Helen by himself.

Helen suggests that we go in the living room. This will be the first time that I have been in there. For me, it will give me an insight into her parents' lifestyle. Helen tells me that their living room is the door on the left at the back of the wall. The door is beyond the stairs. I walk holding Helen's arm to guide her. Her butler goes back to the kitchen to finish preparing dinner.

Their living room is dark and cosy. The wall is painted an off-colour brown, almost beige. The skirting boards are a brilliant white. There are two three-seater sofas facing each other and an armchair creating a u-shape. The sofas and chair face the television. There are coffee tables with flowery lamps dotted around. The curtains are cream. This gives me the impression that her parents are humble and do not need lavish items. It also tells me that Helen was brought up not to be money-orientated.

I help Helen to sit down on one of the sofas and we make idle chat.

I ask her about her Robert again. "So how often do you and Robert talk on the phone?"

Helen is defensive. "He is busy so it is not easy to call me."

I get the feeling he will be around when she gets her eyesight back. "Does he text you?"

Helen finds my comment funny as she stares into space. "A bit pointless considering I am blind."

I am sarcastic. "You can store them up for when you get your eyesight back."

Helen finds me funny. "There is no point."

I suggest a way round it. "Buy a voice application to read out your text messages. Get Florence to read out your messages."

Helen does not react from my comment. We hear the front door open and I guess it is Florence. It is too early for one of her parents to be home now. I let Helen know that I am taking a look and walk out into the main entrance. I tell Helen to wait there.

When I go and check, it is Florence. She looks revived and on cloud nine. Her face is glowing. I walk back into the living room to let Helen know. I tell Helen that I will see her on Friday and I will bring Florence in. Helen acknowledges me and says she is looking forward to testing out her new skills. She also thanks me before I leave.

I am on my way to see Olivia, after going home and having a shower with a change of clothes. I texted Olivia while helping Helen into her house. I decided to meet Olivia at the same restaurant I took Helen. "West Restaurant & Lounge." I found the restaurant was nice and quiet. I listened to Helen advice and went with going to a quiet bar. I arranged to meet Olivia outside of the building so we can go up together. Out of the three women I have initially made contact with from the dating website, Olivia is my preferred choice. I am to still meet up with Trudy. I arranged to meet up with her tomorrow, Thursday. That was organised on Sunday.

I am already in the car thinking about my night with Helen at the restaurant. I remember us talking about our embarrassing moments. I still find it funny thinking about her story of the one-eyed man. As I approach the building, finding a car space, I think I notice Olivia standing by the entrance.

I am not bothered if she sees what I drive. I am not in the mood to pretend something that I am not. Once I park up, I walk up to Olivia and we both recognise each other. We smile at one another as we acknowledge each other from our photos on the dating website.

When we get to the restaurant, we both choose to sit at the bar. We can overlook the city, with the panoramic view. The sky is a hazy grey and the sun is setting.

Olivia is wearing a nice simple knee-length black dress. She is not wearing tights and her legs have a nice sheen to them. Her hair is relaxed and falls to her shoulder. She has the cutest nose. She has full lips that are welcoming. She is helping me to take my mind off Helen. Olivia is well-spoken and is quite funny. After I pay for our drinks, I ask straightaway about her like for fencing.

She has made me feel relaxed. "I have been burning to ask about how you got into fencing."

Olivia smiles at me trying not to laugh. "I saw it on a notice board and thought they meant a garden fence. So, I went thinking how cool it would be to make a fence."

Olivia makes me laugh. "What gave it away, there being no white picket fence?"

Olivia laughs with me. "Come on. That was an easy mistake."

I ask. "Do you still fence?"

Olivia is coy. "Yes. And?"

I picture her in the outfit and find her sexy. "I think you look cute in in a fencing kit. What do you call it?"

Olivia explains to me the gear. "The trousers are called 'breeches with braces. You have what they call a 'plastron' which is like a bulletproof vest, but like a t-shirt. It is protection. Then you have what you call the 'jacket'. The thing that is like a leotard. You have what is called a 'lame' which is further protection. It is like a jumper but is foil or cotton-like. Then you have the mask."

I am curious about the cost. "How much does that all cost?"

Olivia thinks about it. "It cost me about... seven hundred dollars. Less than a grand."

Olivia wants to ask me questions. "So how do you find the time to date if you are busy cutting neighbours' lawns and helping local charities?"

I find myself laughing. "Well I was given the night off. What made you want to become a dentist?"

Olivia smiles while drumming up an answer. "I fell into it. When at school, we had to choose a work experience. It was the only one going." She makes me laugh again. "That is one way of choosing a job. Can I get free work?"

Olivia is sweet. "You won't need free dentist work. Your teeth are fine."

Olivia asks me the question that I have been bracing myself for. "So, what do you do for a living?"

I nervously tell her. "I am a writer."

Olivia eyes light up. "Wow, for what? A newspaper or magazine?"

She is a breath of fresh air. "No one has ever made an assumption like that. I am an author... But I used to underwrite insurance."

Olivia is intrigued by the change. "So, how did you go from being an underwriter to becoming a writer?"

I notice the irony. "I wrote a few stories while growing up and edited them. Then one day, I was unhappy. I thought about what I really would want to do and being an author was it so I published a few books until it was enough to change career."

Olivia is not interested in my books. "Tell some. I might have read one."

I don't think she has. "What kind of stories are you into?"

Olivia thinks. "Have no preference but I have a preferred author. His name is similar to yours, which is why you stuck out. What's his name? Can't think."

I change subject. "So, what is your family like?"

Olivia goes to answer. "Shit. The penny's dropped. I know why you stuck out. I am so sorry. You are going to think that I set this up."

I am worried now. "What have you done?"

Olivia is apologetic.

"I am embarrassed. I don't want you to get the wrong impression of me. I didn't do this on purpose."

I try to reassure her. "Whatever you think you have done, trust me I don't think any less of you. Please tell me what you think you have done wrong."

Olivia pauses before she hesitantly tells me. "I know who you are. I now know why I wanted to go on a date with you. I just didn't realise what I was doing."

I try to encourage her to just get it out. "Are you a stalker?"

Olivia finally tells me. "My favourite author is Harvey Spade. I thought it would be funny to date a person with the same name. I didn't think I would actually date the actual man. I found it funny that you used that name. I thought you would be fun to go out with. Not that you are not fun to go out with. I just didn't expect someone like you to go on a dating website. This is coming out wrong. Of course, you would. You are normal, like any other person."

I hold her hand to slow her thoughts down. "It's okay. It is too late. You already made me laugh."

Olivia stops and looks at me. "Well you got me at 'How did you get into fencing?'" She smiles afterwards.

I decide to make this into a dinner date rather than drinks. "Do you want to leave here and go somewhere for something to eat?"

Olivia smiles. "I would love to."

I try and think of where to go for food. "Here? Or somewhere else. Do you have a preference?"

Olivia already knows where. "I like Caribbean food. There is a place down town. It might not be your scene."

I am not bothered. "If the car gets trashed, I can buy another one."

Olivia laughs. "We can go in my car. If you are not embarrassed to go in an electric car."

I smile. "That depends if you are a stalker. Or you plan on kidnapping."

Olivia smiles. "I keep my other favourite authors in my basement."

We go to her favourite restaurant in her car and we do not stop talking. Olivia is a fresh of breath air, talking about our families and her asking me what my hobbies are and wanting to come along to one of my charity events. During dinner, she expresses herself with her hand movements and arms flailing as she describes her conversation. We both laugh in the right places. Then we come to a natural lull in the conversation. Olivia broaches the subject of Helen as I said on my profile that I am now looking after a blind woman. I do not mention about my infatuation about her, but who she is and how I know her parents. Olivia is really taken aback by what I do and how I put other people first.

By the time we finish eating, we are the only people left in the restaurant and they are waiting for us to leave. We are so engrossed in our conversation and at staring at each other, neither of us noticed that it was already closing time. I pay the bill and we walk back to her car. She drives me back to my car and we do not say anything to each other. We are comfortable sitting in silence. Helen is no longer my distraction as I look at Olivia while she is driving and think she is gorgeous, funny and cute.

We finally get back to my car and I think I have already made my mind up to give this a go. She parks right next to my car and turns the engine off. Neither of us is in a hurry to say goodbye.

I start first. "I had a really nice time."

Olivia reciprocates. "So, did I. I have not had this much fun in ages. You make me feel like myself. No airs or graces."

I feel the same way. "I know what you mean. Can I say something?"

Olivia is apprehensive. "Of course. I can understand if you don't want to see me again."

I smile and it is quite the opposite. "I have another date with a girl called Trudy tomorrow–"

Olivia gets the wrong idea. "It's okay. She will be lucky to date you." I quickly reassure her. "I also sent twenty messages to other girls on the website. But there is no other person I would rather date."

Olivia is happy to hear me say that. "So, what are you trying to say?"

I go shy. "Would you like to meet up again?"

Olivia gives me the cutest smile as her nose wrinkles. "I would love to." I suggest our next date. "Would Saturday be okay?"

Olivia looks into my eyes. "Can I kiss you?"

I smile at her and have no idea how to kiss her. I let her take the lead and react to how she kisses me. As a result, there is no awkwardness and I can smell her perfume. She smells sweet and her lips are delicate, like a cushion. She slips her tongue into my mouth slightly before she pulls away. I get out of her car and wait for her to drive off before I get in my car and go home. I did not expect my date with Olivia to lead onto a second date.

She texts me to say she had a wonderful time and that she will definitely call me tomorrow from work. I text back saying that I am glad she made it home okay and that I wish the night would never end. She put a lot is x's on the end of her text which I found sweet and personal. I repeated the same after my message. I felt on cloud nine and Helen was no longer the affection of my heart.

CHAPTER TEN

The Shrink

I am at my fifteenth session with my psychotherapist.

I see my shrink once a month and I have been looking after Helen and dating Olivia for three weeks before my next appointment. I feel a lot has happened since I last saw him. My shrink is in his mid-fifties, with a beard. His hair is short, dark grey and frizzy. He wears trousers and a single cufflink shirt. His shoes are brown suede. He is not your usual type of shrink. He is always chirpy and interacts with you rather than just sitting there and listening to you. He seems to remember everything I have said to him, even reminding me of things I forgot I told him. He charges me a hundred dollars for a forty-five-minute session. He is not strict with the time and the first few minutes is a general catch up, with what I have done in between each session. He then becomes abrupt and starts the session.

He thinks I have a long way since he first saw me fifteen months ago. I do not feel that I have changed myself and no one has said anything either. The only area I feel I have changed in is that I feel I can be more open about my feelings and if something does not agree with me, I will say. However, I will not be rude and offensive when being openly honest. But my shrink thinks that I have changed more than that. The conversations we have are two way and we talk about anything I want to talk about with him, explaining the reason for it.

I always have one of his coffees as it is made really creamy. He uses some kind of coffee maker where you have to put in both a coffee capsule and milk capsule. It has a rich creamy flavour and he offers me a cup every time. He makes it while catching up with my life.

The shrink asks how I have been since I last saw him.

"It has been okay. Finally finished my book. I have been offered to have one of my book series turned into a television show."

The shrink looks happy. "So, are you going to take it?"

I think about the offer. "I don't know. The meeting is not until June so I have three months to worry about it."

The shrink asks me why. "What is holding you back?"

I reply with. "Money does not motivate me. I am worried about the show and not making my books to their true form."

The shrink questions what if. "So, what if the show is nothing like your book. Does it really matter? Your readers know work. You have earned it."

I am still on the fence. "My series talks about how I see the world. If the show does not portray that exactly, then it will distort my thoughts."

The shrink asks me why again. "What does it matter if they get that wrong. The show will encourage people to read your book. Then people will see what the show tried to do."

I am still not convinced. "I still don't know. It is not like I need the money."

We move the conversation onto the task he gave me about dating lots of women.

The shrink mentions about the challenge he gave me. 'So, did you do what I asked you to do?"

I joke with him. "I had my first taste of caviar. It was nice."

The shrink knows that I am skirting the question and gives me a stern look. "So, how many women did you date?"

I tell him direct. "I spent like two hours writing about myself. Kept deleting and restarting. I had to think about what my hobbies and interests were. I realised that I don't do anything. I just cut the elderly couple's lawn and attend a few charities, donating money. Then I had to put down what I did for a living. I left it blank."

The shrink asks me to move on. "So how many women did you get a chance to meet?"

I start with Laura. "Well, my first date was interesting."

I wait for the shrink's response. "What happened? Did you have sex on the first date?"

I disappoint him. "No. She decided to throw up."

The shrink is open-mouthed. "You are kidding."

I continue. "Not only did she throw up, she did it with a kid."

The shrink bursts into laughter. "That is so funny. Ha ha ha he he he ha ha. Ah, that was funny."

I feel embarrassed. "I am so glad to amuse you. Just laugh at my misfortune." I try not to smirk or laugh.

The shrink finally controls his laughter. "Ah, sorry. Very unprofessional. Maybe that was her way of putting everything on the table. Ha ha ha, see how I did that?"

I am not amused. "I am here all week."

The shrink moves on. "So, did you have any other dates apart from her? Or did that put you off?"

I tell him about the rest of my dates. "I had three women respond initially to my profile before I sent any messages. I arranged to date all three. After Laura, it was Olivia. We hit it off. Which lead to me cancelling my date with Trudy. I also told the seven women who responded out of the twenty messages I sent. I feel that I should have dated all ten before making my mind up with Olivia."

The shrink reassures me. "And if you did, do you think you would have chosen someone else? Once you meet the right one for you, that is all that matters. If it only takes one date, then you are in the small minority. Think yourself lucky. The average number of sexual partners you have before meeting the right one is twenty."

I am shocked. "Wow. I did it without sex."

The shrink explains about dating. "The only reason people have serial dates, is because they think they know what they are looking for and do not see what is in front of them. You, however did. You continued until you thought you met the right one. It does not matter if she was your first, second, twentieth. All that matters are that you met the one you want to be with."

I question his explanation. "But what if there were three potential women? I prevented myself from meeting them."

The shrink has another counterargument. "If there were three, you would have met them. The profiles would have stood out. If Olivia's profile did not stick out, you would never have given it a second thought to contact her. What stuck out for you?"

I tell him about her hobby. "She is into fencing."

The shrink is quick to explain. "You were looking for a girl that was different. Someone who did not follow the norm. If she did not do fencing, then you would not have chosen her. If everyone did Fencing, you would have looked for something else in her. You want to be with someone who is unusual. That is what you want from a relationship. You want to meet someone like you, different. And you found each other. Let me tell you a little secret: you are not different."

I disagree. "I don't do what other people do. I don't play sports, go out."

The shrink says. "You are not the only person who doesn't do anything. Look at your parents. Do they go out or play a sport? You are one of thousands that are like that. Just because you cannot see them, it doesn't mean that they do not exist."

The conversation changes again to what else I have done.
I think of Helen. "I am looking after a blind woman now."

I can see the shrink is interested Helen. "So, should Olivia be worried?"

I play it down. "A neighbour asked me to look after their daughter."

The shrink asks me further questions. "So, what does 'looking after' involve?"

I tell him what we have done so far. "I have been

getting her out of the house so I have taken her out to dinner, helped her to be able to feed herself. Took her to fun fair and a number of other things."

The shrink asks if Olivia is okay with it. "Does Olivia know that you are spending time with a blind woman?"

I feel awkward about him questioning my ethics. "I told her that I look after a blind woman. I don't think it is relevant for her to know what we… I do with her."

The shrink suspects something. "Why do I feel that there is more to it?"

I feel like a deer caught in the headlights. "Shouldn't you have been a detective?"

The shrink wants to know everything. "So, you can start from the beginning."

I unwillingly tell him. "I know her from school. But she never noticed me, even though I noticed her. Her father looked me up in a school book thinking she had old friends. I was the only one who was around."

The shrink has put two and two together. "I am guessing you used to fancy her. I am also guessing that you took the offer so you can be near her again. Please don't tell me you like her as well as Olivia."

I have to think about whether I still like Helen. "She already has a long-term boyfriend. They are engaged. I thought I liked her until I met Olivia."

The shrink gives me a disapproving look. "So, are you going to tell her about feelings towards Helen?"

I feel like I am being put under the spotlight. "I don't think there is anything to discuss. I have not done anything. It is purely platonic."

The shrink says. "So, tell her about Helen. I guarantee you that if you don't tell her now, it will be harder when it all comes crashing around you."

The session goes on for twenty-five minutes more. The conversation finished with the shrink being disappointed in me and strongly advising me to tell Olivia. We then moved on to have a lecture on how a relationship works and ensuring that I do not mess up with Olivia. I arranged to see the shrink in another four weeks, in May.

Now I am going to see Helen to take her to the theatre. I booked it a couple of weeks ago and did not mention it to Helen when I saw her last week. Helen told me that she was going to go with her mother to find a dress for a special occasion. She thinks that her father paid for the private plane to fly to New York for the play.

I get to Helen's for five o'clock to pick her up and drive us to the local airport to catch a private plane. I kind of wish it was me and Olivia going as I think she would have liked it as well. I picture what it would have been like taking Olivia to the theatre.

I arranged to have us sit in one of the balconies, close to the theatre stage. The theatre caters for blind and deaf people. They provide headphones with the audio in various languages, including English. This allows Helen to hear a description of what is happening in the play, as the story unfolds. The story is verbally explained as the play is performed. It took me ages to find a theatre that accommodated the blind as I knew that Helen would be interested in going. I looked at different States that we could fly to using a private jet.

The butler walks me to the living room and tells Helen that I have arrived. I see Helen is already dressed for tonight and is sitting on the sofa. Helen smiles when her butler says my name. Helen's parents are also home and are sat on the sofa opposite her. Her parents give me a welcoming smile as I sit down next to Helen. I find it strange that they are sat with us, as they are never been home before six o'clock. They seem to want to stay and make conversation with us. I feel strange as I have never had any real conversation with them since I started keeping Helen company. I do not know what to say and just look around the room.

I feel that we are going on a first date, and her parents want to check me out to see if I am good enough for their daughter. Her dad has a glass tumbler of iced rum in his hand and her mom has a tall glass of some clear alcohol. Maybe vodka. I feel that this is ominous and Helen is not in a hurry to start a conversation.

Bill asks me how work is going. "When do you go away for work?"

I keep work vague. "I have a meeting in June which is to be confirmed."

Martha asks what I do for a living. "So, what line of work are you in, Harvey?"

Bill is the only one who knows what I do for a living. "I push paper around and write reports."

Martha looks confused, not knowing if she had an answer. "So, where are you two going tonight?"

I look at Bill and Helen. "We are going to the theatre. An Italian play with audio. The programme is even in braille But I know that you cannot read braille."

Martha is chirpily looking at us. "What time do you need to be there?"

Helen pipes up. "I think it is eight o'clock. We're flying at… six o'clock?"

I agree with her. "Yes. It is an hour's flight."

Bill has found out that I am seeing someone by saying. "Helen tells me you are seeing a girl now."

I nod my head. "Yes. Her name is Olivia. We have been dating three weeks now. She is really nice."

Bill is trying to tease me. "So, does she know you are taking a lovely lady to the theatre?"

I have been open with Olivia to a certain degree. "She knows that I am taking Helen. She is not interested in theatre. Her thing is cinema."

Martha asks Helen about Rob. "Is Rob coming over for dinner on Saturday? Need to make sure we have enough for dinner."

Helen is thinking about the question. "I will ask him when he calls tomorrow. Before you say it, he has a demanding job."

The three of us – Bill, Martha and myself – say at the same time. "Yeah."

Helen smiles with no idea that we think he is an idiot.

We finally leave to go to the airport. I drive us there while we are both in comfortable silence. I have Olivia on my mind, visualising her naked and us making love in my bedroom. While I am imagining us making love, I feel myself getting a hard on. Luckily, where Helen is blind she cannot see my crotch. I have not slept with Olivia yet and we have only got to first base with heavy petting.

Olivia has not made any effort to get to second base. A couple of times, she has brushed my crotch or accidentally leaned the palm of her hand on my crotch unintentionally, when lying on her bed. One time we went to the beach, with her reading a book and myself writing my current novel. I was in the middle of writing an erotic plot and Olivia was ready to get a drink from the beach bar. She wanted me to go with her and I had a massive erection from writing my erotic paragraph. I could tell that Olivia noticed and she just played it cool, to save my embarrassment. I sense she consciously walked in front of me to prevent my modesty from being seen by other people on the beach. When we were at the bar, she put her hand in my pocket, brushing her finger against my cock. I knew she was teasing me but she pretended not to notice. She also bent over at the bar and motioned me to stand behind her while we wait for the drinks to be poured. I was trying not to sustain my erection by staring at the sea or looking for overweight women or women in their eighties but Olivia still acted, oblivious.

While I am having these thoughts, I almost veer off the road, not realising that I was daydreaming. Luckily, Helen did not sense that I was not focusing in the road and I used the excuse of a cat running in front of us. Helen is chilled out and does not think anything of it. I decide not to think about Olivia anymore as I am worried I will wrap my new car round a lamp post.

I am happy that my feelings for Helen are being replaced by Olivia and that I have stronger feelings for

Olivia, than I ever did for Helen. After twenty years of fancying Helen, I finally meet someone who I can see myself with long term.

Helen is starting to feel for Harvey and she wants to naturally put her hand on his. But she keeps being reminded that she is engaged to get married to her long-term partner. She likes the way Harvey smells and wonders what he would be like to kiss. Helen would never make a pass at another man or jeopardise her relationship with Rob but she cannot control her feelings, which are starting to grow for him. She feels that they are already married and he is driving them to a dinner party. A couple of times, she thinks her hand has maybe brushed against his body.

Helen wishes that Rob would take her out to things like the theatre as what Harvey is doing. She wishes that Rob was with her instead of Harvey. She senses that her feelings are starting to form for Harvey. She has created an image of what she thinks Harvey may look like, based on what she felt when she touched his face with her fingertips on their second outing. She imagines Harvey to look like a lot younger version of Sydney Poitier.

Helen starts to make comparison between Rob and Harvey, with regards to how Harvey is attentive and puts her temporary disability first. Rob has not asked how she has been since the accident. He is letting work get in between them. Helen sees Harvey as prioritising her over work life.

When we get on the private jet, I sit opposite her. Helen looks anxious and I assume it is the take off. I decide to move over to her side, to sit next to her. Once I am comfortable I feel an urge to hold her hand to give her comfort.

Helen blurts out. "I hate flying."

I feel guilty now. "I never knew that."

Helen looks curious. "How would you know?"

I suddenly remember that she does not know how much time I have spent learning about her. "Of course not."

Helen looks slightly more relaxed. "I did not want you stopping me from going to the opera. I didn't want to spoil your plan."

I am liking this moment. "I have been enjoying organising these little things."

Helen thinks about the time flying by. "It is May now. I only have a month left with you."

I think about the meeting that my agent has arranged. "I can't believe that I only have a month to go for my meeting."

Helen still does not know about my life after her. "What meeting do you have to go to?"

I lie again for the umpteenth time. "I have to travel for work."

Helen does not want this moment to go. "You have made me realise that being blind is bearable. I don't want this to end. This moment. I don't know what I would have done if you were not around. Rob is only around on a Saturday, if I am lucky. The highlight of my week is you coming over and whisking me away."

I feel flattered. "I have enjoyed it. It will feel weird when you get to go back to your life."

Helen looks sad. "I don't want our friendship to end."

I am realistic. "You are getting married. Rob will be freed up with work and your life will be busy with work and planning your wedding."

Helen is delusional. "No, I won't. We will have a year of planning the wedding. Rob will still be busy with work. So, we will still be able to meet up four nights a week."

I see it as it is. "You work shifts so you will not be home by six each night. Practically, you will not be around every night."

We eventually land in New York and a hire car waits for us. Olivia calls me while driving to the theatre. Olivia wants to arrange for us to be at my place for dinner. She will bring food and cook for us. She is in a chirpy mood by the way she sounds on the phone.

I look at Helen while still talking to my girlfriend. Helen looks a bit sad while listening to our conversation. I think she is realising that this is how a relationship should be.

Olivia checks what food I do not like. I tell her that my family will be in the way and that our chef will be put out. Olivia has plans to use the pool house and get away from my family. We finish the phone call with arranging a time for six o'clock, to eat for eight.

Helen says that she is jealous. After I ask her why, she admits that she and Rob do not behave like this. They are robotic and unspontaneous. I shrug it off to suggest that there is nothing wrong with different types of relationships.

When we finally arrive at the theatre, I get us drinks and describe the architecture of the building. I also talk about the type of people that are here. Helen finds me funny as I describe everything. There is loud indistinct chatter at the bar area and lobby.

I finally tell Helen that we are going to see *Tosca*. Helen is speechless as it is a play that she has always wanted to see. She cannot believe I organised tickets for the play. Personally, I will fall asleep. She will not notice.

It is time to go to our balcony. I have Helen use my arm for support as we walk up the stairs.

When we get to our balcony, I give Helen her headphone that is provided by the theatre. I was told that the audio will be in English.

The play begins with the curtains opening as the performers start to act before the curtain fully opens. I wonder if I should have had headphones myself. At the same time, I plan on falling asleep. The music is moving and I can see Helen getting into it. Seeing her being engrossed in the story makes me happy.

I text Olivia through the play. I give her a blow by blow account of the enactments. Olivia tells me off for texting her while I am meant to be with Helen. It is one of the things I like about her.

I order more drinks and ice cream during the interval and Helen gives me the lowdown of the story so far. She keeps thanking me for taking her, holding my hand.

Helen starts to compare Harvey to Rob, with Harvey on top. She feels that Rob would never think of doing something like this, blind or not. Helen is worried that her feelings for Harvey could be starting to grow, even though Harvey has not tried to influence Helen emotions towards him.

She feels guilty as she loves Rob and she can see herself being married to him. She cannot see herself being with Harvey or marrying him. But she feels like he can be a long-term boyfriend.

After the play finishes, Helen wants me to take her for a walk. The streets are buzzing with noise and the traffic of people going about their busy lives, dressed to impress. I make sure Helen is tightly close to me as we walk against the flow of people traffic. I feel more and more like her boyfriend and wondering what the strangers of people are thinking.

Helen feels like Harvey is her fiancé and likes the feeling of being proud to be with Harvey.

Helen cannot remember a time when Robert made her feel special, like how Harvey does.

Helen starts to notice how strong Harvey arm is and how solid he feels.

Olivia texts me to say she is jealous and that she misses me. I text back to say that I will do whatever she wants. It is a nice feeling to have a girlfriend that wants to be with me. She likes me for who and what I am. She found out who I was of her own accord. She is adorable. We have not done the deed yet. At the same time, I have not been with anyone so I am no hurry embarrass myself. Olivia is a nice girl and so she is in no hurry to sleep with me.

Helen has been quiet while I have had my mind elsewhere. She seems to be in deep thought herself. We are both comfortable in our own deep thoughts.

I notice an all-night diner and I suggest we go in to have a bite to eat before getting back to the plane. We both make idle chit chat about the play and what each other is doing at the weekend. I tell Helen that Olivia wants to spend the whole weekend with me at my place. I explain that I want our privacy and so I want to spend the weekend in the pool house. The pool house is self-sufficient, with an integrated kitchen and a separate all-in-one bathroom with shower room. Finally, a bedroom with only a double bed. Helen assumes that Olivia and I will be sleeping together all weekend. I make it clear to Helen that only Olivia is sleeping inside the pool house. I will be in my own bedroom. I explain that Olivia has not hinted that she is ready to sleep with me yet, as she is a slow burner. Helen says that Olivia wants to spend the whole weekend with me for that chance of making love with me. I brush Helen comment aside and come up with reasonable arguments to suggest otherwise, arguments that Helen squints her face at and despite being good arguments, she bugs me with the love making angle. To change the subject, I ask her when the last time was her and Robert were intimate. She sighs as she thinks about it and comes up with two years ago. I almost choke on my steaming hot coffee, almost burning my throat. Helen does not feel embarrassed when she tells me. Her face is glazed over as I watch her pain through her eyes. I change the conversation to say that we should be going to catch the plane.

During our flight back, Helen speaks up. "I am jealous of you, Harvey."

I look at her in bewilderment. "Where did that come from?"

Helen smiles. "You have been seen Olivia almost every other day. Olivia likes you more than you think."

I question her statement. "How would you know?"

Helen raises her eyebrows. "I may be blind, but I know when two people are in love."

I laugh off her comment. "I don't think so. It has only been a month. Statistics say it takes anywhere between one month and three months to fall in love. Three months being the average time it takes. I do not fall in love on first sight. It is lust in the beginning."

We eventually land and it is raining in Los Angeles. I help Helen off the plane and we run to the car, while she is in my arm and her head buried in my shoulder. I get her in the car before I get in the car myself. I am glad I have this car now as it de-mists the windows quickly. Also, the car sticks to the road, like it is on rails as I drive through the puddled road. Helen puts herself in a foetal position, facing me, falling asleep. She looks cute as I hear her breathing through her cute nose. I put the car seat heater on to make her feel cosy. I rest my head back on the headrest, as l let the car drive itself while barely holding on to the steering wheel.

It does not take long to get back to her parents' house. I gently rouse her from her sleep and whisper to her that we are back. Helen looks disappointed that the evening is over. I help her out of the car and wait with her at the door, until someone lets her in. I decide not to go in, as I would rather give Olivia a call on my way home. Helen thanks me again for another great evening. I think nothing of it by saying to Helen that it is no bother.

When I get back in the car, I give Olivia a call, wondering if she is going to answer.
Olivia picks up with enthusiasm in her voice. "Hi babe. How was your night then?"

I smile as I hear her cute little voice. "It was okay." Playing it down.

Olivia talks about this weekend. "I am looking forward to coming over for the weekend. I want to cook for you. I will be bringing food over to cook."

She makes me feel warm inside. "That sounds good. I will briefly introduce you to family, then I will take you to the pool house. There is an oven and stove there. Also, a barbecue if it is sunny. I think it is going to rain over the weekend."

Olivia is not bothered by the weather. "I plan to stay in all weekend. I have some ideas of what we can do."

I joke with her. "Twister, chess, Scrabble."

Olivia laughs. "That is right. There is something that I want to tell you."

I am curious. "What is that?"

Olivia is vague. "Nothing to worry about. Just want to have a chat."

My heart starts to sink as I think the worst. "Is it serious?"

Olivia's voice does not give anything away. "Seriously. Nothing to worry about. I would rather say in person as it will be kind of embarrassing."

We talk for another minute with Olivia saying that she was jealous about me taking Helen out to the theatre tonight. Olivia knows that I paid for everything and I sense she wishes it was her instead of Helen. One of the things I like about Olivia, is that she does not sulk and we both get excited when we see each other. Olivia is very affectionate when we are not in public and finds any moment to have a kiss and cuddle.

CHAPTER ELEVEN

No Worries

It is now May and the weather is starting to become more like summer.

I go round to Olivia's place to chill out for a change. We decide to stay in and watch a DVD. Olivia has already chosen the film which is a Romance about a couple, one being surgeon and the other a celestial. It reminds me of Helen and the man is me. Olivia still made an effort to dress nicely, even though we had plans to stay in tonight. Her apartment is smaller than my pool house with only a bedroom, small living room and poky kitchen. It does not bother me feeling cramped in her apartment but it is in an affluent area and land must be expensive.

I think Olivia is comfortable to let me come over or else she would not have suggested it. I am not shy to bring it up in conversation. I guess the shrink has helped me to come out of my shell.

When we are ready to watch the DVD, I quickly ask if she is embarrassed of her place. "Just a quick question. Are you okay me being here?"

Olivia look puzzled with my question. "How do you mean? I thought you were happy to come here."

I make myself clearer. "You don't think I am judging where you live. I feel that you think I could be comparing your apartment to my house."

Olivia makes light of it. "Like your bedroom being the size of my apartment. Is that what you mean?"

I smile at her humour. "Something like that. We have been spending a lot of time at my place. I want to make it clear to you that I am happy to spend more time here. Please don't think that I prefer to be at my place."

By the time the film finishes, we are cuddled up on her sofa with Olivia almost falling asleep. We talk about the film saying that I have a copy of the DVD as well. Olivia looks like she is pondering as if she wants to tell me something.

Olivia hesitantly says. "Will you do something for me?"

I look worried. "What is that?"

Olivia plucks up the courage. "Prostate cancer is more prevalent in Black people. Can you have yours checked?"

I look at her as if she has two heads. "You are being serious?"

I have never seen Olivia so serious. "I care about you too much. Will you?"

I decide to do it for her. "Okay. So how do I arrange a pro…"

Olivia smiles. "Prostate cancer. You just call your doctor and they will give you an appointment."

I ask her why. "What has brought this on?"

Olivia looks down. "My uncle died of cancer a few months ago. Now I am with someone I care about. It sounds silly–"

I tell her straight away. "It is not. I understand exactly what you are talking about. It is fine. I will book an appointment tomorrow."

The next day I phone my doctor about doing a prostate check and my appointment is for the following Thursday, at four o'clock. I get to my doctor's appointment in good time. Like a lot of surgeries, you have to log yourself in on a touch screen, rather than speak to a person on reception. I have to press the option tab for acknowledging I am here. I have to touch a number, and abbreviated month, followed by typing year.

The screen then confirms my name and appointment time as well as attending.

Once I check myself in, I go to wait in the reception

area. I feel nervous as I have no idea what the doctor will do to check my prostate. I have not tried to search on the internet as I do not want to give myself a scare.

There are only two other people here at this time of day. I look on the television screen that shows which patient is next and with what doctor. When the television is not showing the next patient, it advertises medical issues. At the moment it is advertising how bad smoking is. I read the screen about how smoking causes ailments. This helps to while the time away as I wait for my appointment.

Eventually, my name comes up and I have to go to room four to see Doctor Truman. I think it is appropriate to tell Dr Truman my real reason, why I am here, and that is my girlfriend is worried about my prostate.

I do not think I will be comfortable having a man check me out but it is important. Olivia told me it is prevalent in black people.

I cannot think of the last time I saw a doctor. When I reach the room, I knock first in case he is not ready for me. I hear a faint murmur, so I push the door open.

Doctor Truman is a woman. "You are Mr Spade?"

I confirm. "Yeah."

Doctor Truman reads her screen on her computer. "So, you are worried about you prostate. Any pain or blood in your urine?"

I tell her. "No. I have a girlfriend and she suggested I come for a check-up."

Doctor Truman smiles. "You have a good girlfriend. If you could go behind the curtain and pull your jeans down."

I nervously do as she says, feeling strange. I wouldn't have felt comfortable a man checking it and I feel no more comfortable having a woman do it. I am having doubts about agreeing to do this. It is becoming real now. What if she finds my prostate to be cancerous? I have only just met someone who I genuinely care about. If I had not met

Olivia, I would not have entertained the idea.

I hear Doctor Truman put medical gloves on from the sound of rubber snapping against her skin. I then hear her come behind the curtain.

Doctor Truman puts surgical gel on her forefinger and index finger. She whistles quietly to herself as she limbers up to shove her finger up my bum. She asks me to relax to make it easier for her to insert her forefinger and index finger into my rectum. Her fingers are entering inside my bum hole, making a squelching sound as the gel allows the rubber glove to slide in easily.

Doctor Truman talks me through it. "I have inserted two fingers inside your rectum. I am now going to proceed to find your 'donut'. A technical term for prostate."

I am not instilled with reassurance. "Now I know what it is like to be gay."

Doctor Truman does not give me any warning. "Here go…"

I feel a scrape. 'What the fu…. Did you put any gel on that finger?"

Doctor Truman licks her lips as she searches. "It is two fingers. Almost there. So, what are your plans for tonight?"

I think this is the highlight of her day. "At this rate, I am going to sit in a bucket of ice. When do you know you found it?"

Doctor Truman looks puzzled. "Normally by now, I would have found the donut. Yours must be small… ah, there it is. Gotcha. Now, how are them apples, pardon the pun."

I am not amused. "So, is it bad or not? I assume it is fine, if it took you a week to find it."

Doctor Truman finishes palpating my prostate. "I am just stroking your prostate. It feels good. Best one I have caressed to date. Yep. All done. You have nothing to worry about. See you showered. You are one of the few."

I try to be humorous. "A gay man would have loved

me."

I could sense that Doctor Truman did not know what to make of my comment.

I feel her pulling out and I am worried I will follow through after her. It feels like I am going for a number two as she pulls out her fingers.

I hear her pulling the gloves off. I have a sudden vision of a lump of poo on the end of her finger. My inners must be clean as a whistle now. This brings a new meaning to the term 'colonic irrigation'.

Doctor Truman says that her examination is finished and that I can pull up my jeans. I hear her feet walking back towards her desk. I assume she is typing up her thoughts on my examination.

As I pull up my jeans, it is uncomfortable, so I carefully pull my jeans over my bum. I am going to walk like John Wayne, all bent over. I just had another thought. There is a high-end gay bar around the corner. When I leave the hospital, people will think that I am struggling to walk, because I went there for a close encounter. I will need crutches to avoid people thinking that.

When I am ready, I walk over to her desk to see if there is anything else she needs from me. I walk gingerly, with small steps. She motions me to sit, but I am happy to stand. She smirks at me, as I stand like a ninety-year-old.

I screw up my face to indicate that I am not amused. She uses her eyes to point down. I look at her and say that I know how ridiculous I look standing here. She smirks nodding her head to say no and points at me. I look at her puzzled and think my flies are undone. When I look down, oh my. I only have an erection the size of the Empire States Building. I am mortified. I quickly turn around and try to get rid of it. I think of non-arousing thoughts, like smelly socks and a prostate examination.

My sore bum completely distracted me from noticing I had an erection. The soreness outweighed the feel of an erection. She only now mentions that she may have brushed past my perineum, that I now learn is inside my rectum and can be aroused. Hence why homosexual men enjoy things inside their bums.

I ask how long the sensation lasts and explain that it feels like I have had a spicy curry. She says that it will calm down after a few hours. I ask if she can supply pain killers, as I have to drive home. I don't fancy taking my chances trying to keep the car in a straight line. She goes inside her desk drawer and passes me a packet. I could really do with ice wrapped in a towel and shoved down my pants. I definitely won't have trouble going for a number two later.

The doctor suggests that I have my sperm checked out for any anomalies. She gives me a sample pot to put my sperm in. She says she will make an appointment for me to drop it off. I have to allow for a two-hour window before my substance goes off. She says I will get a letter through the post with an appointment.

What turned out to going for a prostate check, is now having to jerk myself off. I leave her room and go back to reception.

I end up calling Olivia to come and pick me up, as it is all her fault that I am in pain in the first place. Olivia cannot stop laughing on the phone as I explain my discomfort. She is finding it hard to compose herself on the phone. I tell her about the erection under my breath as there are a couple of people waiting in reception. I can imagine her visualising how I described the examination and the doctor pointing out my erection.

I have asked Olivia to leave her car at work so she can drive us to my place in my car.

When she comes, she looks at me, trying not to laugh at my posture. I am resting against the wall with my bum not touching. The pain killer is not working.

Olivia gives me a hug and holds me by the waist as we walk to my car. We go at my pace. She is cute slowly putting me in the car, frequently asking me if I am okay.

During the drive home, we just have random conversations range from how I am feeling to how her work is going. She tells me that she had a call out of the blue from an old college friend.

Olivia is surprised as they lost contact about ten years ago. She is just telling me to get the information out in the opens. She did not want me to react or form an opinion. I am finding it hard to focus on the subject because of the pain. Olivia is aware of my discomfort and keeps glancing over at me to see if I am okay.

As we approach my house, I can see Olivia still gets bewildered by the size of the house and grounds. The more she comes to terms of me being a millionaire, the more she becomes overwhelmed by it all. She does say to me that she does not see me as wealthy. My mannerisms and behaviour throw her every time. Apart from the car, she cannot put my success and me together.

I ask Olivia what she wants to do: stay for a bit or go straight home. Olivia admits that she feels guilty and wants to look after me for the night, before she goes home. I suggest going to the pool house for alone time. Olivia welcomes it and so we go straight there.

After a few minutes in the pool house, I suddenly need to go to the toilet. I am crapping myself because of the thought of the pain or it just falling out. I am on tenterhooks and Olivia looks at me with worry. She asks me what the matter is as I pace around anxiously.
Olivia looks at me concerned. "Are you okay. Is there something I can do?"

I nod my head no. "I need the toilet. Number two."

Olivia realises and gives me a pitiful look. "Oh, poor you. Do you want me to help in some way?"

I go quiet. "I just want to get this over with. I will have a shower straight away."

Olivia gives me a passionate kiss. "I feel really guilty. I will make it up when you come out of the shower."

I take deep breaths as I sit on the loo. Olivia is sweet asking on the other side of the locked door if I am okay. I am too nervous to reply as I get ready to release my bowels. I cannot stop thinking about the fingers up my bum as I brace myself to go to the toilet. Phew, thank you, God. THANK YOU, GOD. It was not how I imagined.

Olivia shouts through the door. "Are you okay? What is going on in there?"

I reassure her. "I am fine!" Under my breath. 'It is all good."

I decide to go for a shower to make myself feel human again. I am cautious when it comes to cleaning myself down there, as I am still reminded of the examination. It was felt really weird having a woman putting not one, but two fingers up there when I am not sexually inclined that way. I have heard of men who like the sexual acts of having their rectum licked or a finger inside their anus, stimulating their perineum. I am too prudish for that and I would freak out of Olivia turned around and said she was into that.

While I am showering, I wonder how I will handle the moment if the time comes to making love. I start thinking about being a virgin still and try to imagine how it will come up before having sex. We have been open and both of us do not want to have sex until we both love each other. My shrink told me that on average it can take about three months to fall I love. It can happen instantly but can be confused with lust and that love can last as little as three minutes.

After I get out of the shower I feel a little more like myself. I put on slumber clothes for the rest of the evening and go back into the main room.

I notice that Olivia is sitting on the couch watching television and is startled when I walk over. Olivia nervously smiles at me as I walk over and sit next to her. I lean on my thigh as a precaution. Olivia switches the television off and turns her body to face me and puts her legs up onto the couch.

Olivia touches my leg. "So, are you feeling a lot better?"

I do feel a lot better. "Yes. I needed that shower. The pain has gone now, but I am still jumpy thinking that it is going to hurt if I sit on it." I change the subject. "Thanks for picking me up. No one has ever done that for me. I didn't know what to expect. I just wanted you to be there, not family"

Olivia looks flattered. "Of course. You mean a lot to me. I wouldn't do it for anyone."

I give her a meaningful look. "I want to show my appreciation. You can have anything in the world."

Olivia gives me a meaningful look in return. "All I want is you."

Our eyes interlock and we both gravitate towards each other as we go to kiss passionately. There is nowhere else I want to be right now. For the first time, I have allowed a woman into my life and know about the most intrusive, embarrassing and sensitive experience of my life. I am starting to fall in love with her and it has only been two months. My heart is longing after her and I want to be inside her, under her skin. Making love will not get me closer to her. Olivia reciprocates and is trying to push herself even closer to me. I start to move myself, so I am lying on the couch and she lies on top of me.

Olivia starts to breathe deeply as we passionately kiss. "I don't want to go. I just want to stay here with you."

I do not say anything but press my lips against her even harder in response. I feel her body getting warmer and her heart feels like it is trying to break out of her chest. I push her body away so I can see her face, brushing her loose hair away from her face. I smile at her and she responds almost smirking, before I pull my head up to continue our passionate kiss. She is so gorgeous with her cute nose and dark brown eyes.

Who thought that my day would go from having a

doctor's finger up my rectum to having this sexy, intelligent and beautiful woman in my pool house making out with me. Despite her knowing what happened to me and still finding me attractive, I feel blessed to have been able have met her. I think I am ready to make love to her now, but at the same time I do not feel it is right and too soon after my bum recovering. Olivia does not show any signs of wanting to make love herself as she does not motion for us to take our clothes off or move to the bedroom. She looks happy to just make out on the couch.

Without warning, we both fall off the couch and I hit my head against the coffee table. "Well, that was not how I was hoping for this to go."

Olivia bursts into laughter. "Is your head alright? Come here, sweet pea."

We continue where we left off, on the floor now. I feel myself getting aroused and as she adjusts her position on top of me, she looks down towards my crotch and notices my erection through my jogging bottoms. She does not make a thing of it and looks up at me and rests her crotch on top of my erection. We then continue kissing passionately. She grinds her body against my erection as we fight to get close to each other as much as possible. We are almost trying to outdo each other, with who can get the closest. I cannot hug her any tighter and she cannot press her lips against mine any harder.

After making out on the couch and floor, it is almost nine in the evening. We did not get to second base, but I enjoyed our intimacy just as much. Olivia tidies her hair as I managed to scrunch it up as I get us a drink and ask for my chef to make up a snack. Olivia finds it strange that I can just get a home cooked meal made up just like that, as if we are in a hotel. She looks like she feels special having me in her life now.

Olivia walks up to the kitchen worktop and I am standing behind it. "I feel like we are in a hotel. You ordering food on the phone? Won't it be late? You told me he goes home at seven."

I open one of my secret stash of Latour wine. "Yes, he does. He travels about six feet to his home. He lives on the ground. He makes a note of additional hours and bills me."

Olivia is open-mouthed. "I didn't realise. You actually have a chef living in your house, as well as your family?"

I smile. "Yes. I hope you like this. It is my favourite wine. It is not cheap, so if don't like it, I will drink it."

Olivia jokes. "How much? Twenty dollars? Thirty?"

As I finish pouring my glass, I casually say. "A thousand."

Olivia is shocked. "A thous–"

I interrupt her. "Yes. I love my wine. I do not buy many things. All I have is this… pool house, a car I only purchased last month. I have everything I need so I treat myself to a case of Latour. I order it online and normally only drink it at the quarterly barbecues we have each year. But now, I have someone to share it with."

Olivia takes a sip and then frowns as she tastes it. "Not bad. That is the best wine I have ever tasted."

I casually say. "I hope so. Twenty bottles per shipment. Three times a year, roughly."

Olivia almost chokes wine she sipped just now, still her mouth. "You spend…" She counts in her head. "Sixty thousand dollars on wine alone."

I smirk at her. "Now you put it that way. Realistically, that is interest from my money in the bank. So, in theory, the bank pays for it. With a little change from the interest."

Olivia laughs briefly and takes another sip before moving forward to kiss me on the lips. "I am falling for you, Harvey. It scares me as I have never met a man like you who is so caring. I am scared of losing you."

I reassure her. "I am not going anywhere. I do not even own a plane."

When the chef brings in our snack, I thank him before he leaves us to it and we eat at the table next to the kitchen area and drink our wine. The chef made us eggs Benedict with salmon. I can see Olivia is impressed and enjoys the first bite, making a groaning sound of her approval. I smile at her while holding my glass of wine close to my mouth, before taking a sip. We sit in silence enjoying our snack together. I wonder if Olivia wants to stay over, with her in the pool house and me in the main house in my bedroom. We do not stop glancing at one other, gazing into each other's eyes. Not in a vomiting way but showing affection for one another.

Half way through eating I ask Olivia. "Do you want to stay?"

Olivia almost says yes but she looks like she has remembered something. "I get up early in the morning. I would be more relaxed waking up at home, so I can get up and leave the house for seven. I will have to get up earlier and find a taxi."

I totally agree. "I didn't think. Of course. I would be the same."

Olivia laughs. "What are talking about? You don't have to go to a nine to five job. You can just get up when you feel like." Olivia thinks about Harvey's work. "How do you come up with your stories?"

I am quick to answer. "I just have ideas pop in my head. I think how they would work in a story, then just write. A lot of the time I get my inspiration from films and real life. I would criticise certain films and think to myself I could do a better job than that. Or I think, why has no one thought of a story like that? Then I just write. I draw a timeline which helps me to focus on the story's plot and where I want it to go."

Olivia's eyes show interest in what I am saying. "That is a gift. I couldn't come up a story and write a hundred thousand words."

I explain how I do it. "I give myself a goal of about five thousand words per chapter. I will then have two or three plots inside that one chapter. By the time you have described the plot and proofread it, it doesn't take long to suddenly write a hundred thousand words. Also, it is completely made up. You are not writing a theory or dissertation and it is not as hard as you think. Anyone can tell a story. It is more to do with. "*can you be asked.*"

Olivia laughs at my last comment. "If I had an idea, would you write it for me?"

I think about it. "Yeah. It is a term called 'ghost writing', where I would write the story on your behalf and then have a pseudonym or my name on the book. You get a cut of the royalties and in theory, I do. You come up with the idea and I put it into words."

Olivia looks starry-eyed as I explain about writing and becoming an author. She is surprised how easy it is nowadays to get a book published, regardless of genre. I tell her about how I first published my book and did not waste time getting as many of my stories written as I could. Olivia cannot believe that I was eventually headhunted by my now agent who romanced me for a few weeks, at the time I was about to make my first million. After a few minutes talking about me, I let Olivia know about my sperm check that the doctor suggested and that I am waiting for an appointment to come in the post.

Olivia looks pleased and asks when the appointment will be. I tell her that I did not ask and that I would just wait until the post arrives. I explain to her that I am not looking forward to having to drive my sperm to the hospital. Olivia thought she would be helpful by saying that she could help me to get my sperm. I wonder how she will help. Does she mean she will do it for me? Olivia suddenly realises what she said and feels embarrassed, but erotically says that she would still help me if I have a problem in that department. I smile at her and say that if I need help, I would rather get a nurse to do it. Olivia jokes by saying that with my luck, it will be an obese woman with hairy armpits. I try to tease her by saying that it will be a blonde woman with legs up to her armpits and will have the technique to an art form. Olivia looks jealous now and I walk around the table to give her a cuddle to reassure her that I will be totally professional. Olivia jokingly pushes me away and hits me in the arm for saying that. On a serious note, Olivia tells me how proud she is of me for taking her and the health check seriously. I tell her that I am glad she mentioned it and that I see it as important as well. I also tell her that I am glad I met her or else I would never have considered it.

We finish eating our snack and then together we wash up the plates and knives and forks. I wash and she dries. We continue with banter while washing and drying about my day at the doctors, my erection and how she wishes she could have been there. I tease that the doctor really sexy and wearing suspenders. Again, Olivia hits me in the arm with all her strength and I just laugh it off, comparing her to a three-year-old.

After we finish washing up and drying, I tell Olivia that I will drive her home now that I can sit down without pain. Olivia welcomes the offer with a smile and she gets her things together. She cannot believe how nice my car is and how I paid for it using contactless. I explain about my exclusive bank account. Her mind is still blown away with that story, that I can just wake up one day and choose to buy something without any hesitation or any thought about it. I remind her that I did drive an original Blue Chevy shown in the *BEVERLY HILLS COP* until only a few weeks ago, before I met her. I wanted to make it clear that it was not an irrational decision.

I sense that Olivia is still blown away with my ability to just buy things without financial struggle. I do not explain myself further and change the subject to when I will be able to see her again. She asks me when I am next seeing Helen. I tell her it is not until Sunday and so we can make a weekend of it. Olivia says that she is up for that and suggests that we spend it at her place. She is feeling guilty about spending too much time at mine, taking for granted that there is lots of space to spend time alone. I am very chilled out and make it clear that it does not bother me at all. I also make it clear that it is nothing to do with how small her apartment is.

When we get to her place, we are both too tired for me to come up for a night cap. I have an early start tomorrow morning with finishing my current book and the two glasses of red wine I had with our snack has made me tired. We kiss each other briefly before she gets out of my car. I watch her walk up the steps to the entrance of the apartment before I drive away. She unlocks the entrance to the lobby of her apartment and partially opens the door, before turning around to wave me goodbye. I can just make out the silhouette of her body as she finishes waving and turns to go inside.

Tonight, was great and has left me feeling good inside. Our relationship seems to be getting stronger by the day as we spend more time going out. It still feels weird being in a relationship as I did not imagine ever, that it would happen. I just entertained my shrink with the idea that it could ever happen.

CHAPTER TWELVE

The L Word

It is the middle of May and I think I may be falling in love with Olivia. It has only been a month and a half since we first met. I am worried if I am weird for falling for someone so quickly.

It is the day I go to the hospital hand over a specimen of my sperm. The letter that came in the post a few days later, after my doctor requested an appointment on my behalf, stated that I was to go in on a Wednesday at two o'clock in the afternoon. This is a couple of weeks after my prostate examination.

Since then, I met Olivia, time has flown by. I have been juggling between seeing Olivia and Helen on alternate days and nights, so my time with both of them did not clash.

After showering and having breakfast, I decide to go to the pool house to get my specimen. I do not feel comfortable relieving myself in the main house, knowing there are other people in there, such as my parents, chef and maid. Not that they would barge into my bedroom as I am watching a porn film, sat on my bed with my willy hanging out.

I have already prepared how I am going to achieve my sample late last night with the help of Olivia. When everyone was in the house getting ready for bed, I pretended to walk Olivia out of the house to her car. We then went to the pool house to drop off some bits that will help me along the way. While we were leaving the pool house, Olivia was mocking me by rubbing my crotch with the palm of her hands and kissing me at the same time.

She told me that she could not stop thinking about me playing with myself while looking at some dodgy porn website. Olivia wishes that she could be there to watch.

When I know my siblings and their kids are not around, I go to the pool house. I feel like I am sneaking about with guilt, as if I am going to do something seedy. Not that I think having to make myself cum is not seedy.

Once I have my laptop and connected to the Wi-Fi in the house, I search the website that Olivia's friend suggested. I did not ask how her girlfriend knew of the website as she came across as a prude. The website pops up and has pages of individual porn videos with a description such as the title of video, sometimes the name of a porn star, production and time length of video. I wonder if Trump's fling, *Stormy Daniel,* is on this website, not that I know what she looks like. I have no idea what video will make me aroused. I notice that there is a vertical list on the left hand side of the webpage, listing various genres of sex videos. I can see themes like threesomes, choices of sex positions to watch and themes like dominatrix, superheroes and doctors and nurses.

I have no idea which type will help me to get turned on. I do not look at porn as a part of my itinerary for the day so this feels strange to me. I just randomly click on one of the videos from the list in the centre of web page. The video I pick is a video of a black man with a huge penis having sex with a white woman who looks barely out of their teens. I had no idea how big a cock can be. I thought I was big enough, but this porn star makes my cock look like a pea. This is having an adverse effect on getting me turned on. I quickly close the video before I get a complex and choose some other mediocre video.

The video that I next pick looks interesting. The gist of the role play is a woman looking at a car engine with smoke coming out. She has a lowcut t-shirt and fake boobs. She is also wearing a pair of shorts that looks like a belt and is pretending to know what the problem is.

Then the shot changes to some random guy pulling over to help the stranded blonde bimbo. So here we go. I think this will do it for me. I fast forward the video to get to the sex scene. The guy is giving her one from behind with the steam from the engine making her top see-through. Oh yes, this is turning me on. I forget I have to take my trousers down to actually jerk myself off. I quickly pull my jeans down, struggling like I am taking off a wet suit. I fall over with my jeans stuck round my ankle, knocking over the coffee table, almost breaking it. This is not what I envisaged when trying to make myself cum. Once I get my jeans off properly, chucking them aside in frustration, I pull myself up to look at the porn website. Oh great, the video has finished. I have to put it back on again and skip back to the scene of the doggy-style sex over a hot engine. As I am trying get myself sexually aroused, I cannot stop thinking logically of the practicality of having sex over a hot engine. Realistically, you would be at risk of burning your hands on the radiator or getting scalded by the steam. All these thoughts are not getting me to the end results.

I close the video and try and find one that is more realistic and not going to make me give a critique of the realism of the video. Perfect, this one will do it. It is on a picnic blanket in an open space green. Nothing to see that I can give a critique on. Perfect. The girl looks more attractive. I do not feel inferior by the man's cock. All perfect. Now let's get these foot soldiers out in the open. Oh yeah, I am getting into this. It is not long before I get to the climax and I have built up quite a sweat now. I am almost there, almost there, yeah baby. That is what I am talking about. Damn it, where is the pot? Where did I put it? No no no, I cannot lose the rhythm. Oh crap. I lost the climax. Right, have to find where I put that pot. I eventually find the pot behind the kitchen worktop on the floor. Must have knocked it over when I put the laptop on the work surface. Right, now I have the pot ready. Let's play the video back and get myself in the moment again.

As the scene switches from the old cliché of chat ups,

the man is behind the woman who is on all fours, giving her one up the anus. I only just realised it is going up the anus. Nope, not doing it for me. Nah nah nah. Let's go for third time lucky. No big cock, no girl who looks barely out of their nappy and no anus. Ah, found one. This is it. A really fit brunette with a fake suntan and looks like she is in her mid-thirties. Natural boobs this time and again, the man has a normal size dick, so I do not feel inferior. This is definitely going to get me those little white soldiers. Three minutes into the video and the man and woman are in a sauna. Ignore the safety aspect of the coal nearly singeing her ass, just focus on the sex. Forget about the fact that realistically, they would hyperventilate from the heat, just go with the sex scene. This time it is in her correct hole doggy-style again. That is what I am talking about. Yeah, this is turning me on. I start to build up a rhythm again with my stroke actions and I feel myself getting a climax again. Oh yeah, I am definitely going to cum this time. Ah! Yes! Come on… and finally I have lift off. I quickly grab the top, biting the lid off and quickly pour the specimen into the pot as I hover the pot under my willy. I cannot believe how much I have filled it up. The pot is almost half full. Oh yeah, I am the man. Olivia would be proud of me.

As I put the lid on and look up, I sense that someone is looking into the pool house. I slowly turn around to notice the gardener peering into the glass wall cheering me on. If it wasn't for the glass being thick, I would have heard him wolf whistling as well. The gardener looks like a porn star himself with a thick moustache. All he needs is a gold medallion hanging on his hairy chest. I cannot believe it; the gardener was watching me jerk off in front of my laptop with my bottom half of my body naked. And he can see my erection still there. Perfect. Can this day get any worse? Now, how do I fire him without having to disclose the reason for firing him? Also, does this constitute sexual harassment? The gardener realises that I am not amused and embarrassingly waves and scurries along. This is another embarrassing story to tell Helen, as well as Olivia. I could write a book about this. Change my name, of course.

The next step is to pull my jeans up and get to the hospital as quick as I can before the sperm becomes obsolete. I have a two-hour window to get there. I check the time to see how soon my appointment is. The time is... noooo. It is gone quarter past one. I started jerking myself off from midday. How can it take me over an hour to get a sample? It felt like twenty minutes. I only have forty-five minutes to get to the fertility clinic. Luckily it is only a ten-minute drive to get to the Ronald Reagan UCLA Medical Center. That will leave me forty minutes to find what floor it is on.

When I get in my car, I have a sudden thought that the lid to the pot may have flipped open. The movement of sitting in the car may have caused the lid of the pot to rub against my thigh, inside my front jean pocket. I imagine there being a wet patch where it looks like I have either wet myself or cum in my pants. I quickly look down and phew, no wet stain. I then put my hands carefully inside my jean pocket to take the pot out and put it in the centre compartment by the gear stick for safe keeping. For some reason the compartment has climate control. I am able to keep the sperm at a constant temperature.

While on my way to the hospital, I imagine "what if" scenarios. I can imagine my sperm spilling on my upholstery and the odour lingering in the car for days. Worrying that passengers will query the smell and then having to explain it.

My thoughts move on to whether the results will say I cannot father a child. I wonder if that would bother me or if it would not be a surprise. Would Olivia be disappointed? These thoughts temporarily put me off dropping my sample off but then I remember it is about my health and I need to do this for that reason.

Before I know it, I am already at the hospital and going

into the car park.

Only have to park up now. I am anxious that it will take me ages to find a space. Driving to the top floor will be quicker to find a space. As I head up near towards the top of the car park, I think about what would have happened if Helen was at work. It would have been embarrassing having to explain why I was here.

Once I park up, I check the time in the car and have half an hour to get to the clinic.

Once I am in the hospital, I rely on the signs hanging from the ceiling and on the walls at eye level. The fertility clinic sign is in yellow, so I just focus on the colour yellow, rather than the wording. The yellow signs lead me to the lift and to the fourth floor. I am conscious of the pot being inside my jean pocket. I almost squashed it again on a car door mirror, while squeezing in between the parked cars to take the shortest route.

Finally, I arrive at the fertility clinic. There is a reception desk so I go there to enquire where I drop off my specimen.

The lady behind reception is speaking to someone else, so I wait. After a few seconds, I introduce myself.

I feel awkward thinking of how to say. "Um, I have a sample. Do I leave it with you?"

The lady is professional. "Yep. How long ago did you produce it?"

I have to think. "About half an hour ago. My appointment is two so I thought I would check in now."

The lady is chilled out. "No worries. I have recorded you in. Just take a seat."

I am seen five minutes early by a man who calls out my name. I acknowledge myself to him and walk over. He asks for my pot and I give it to him. I wait for him to say it is okay go.

He seems hesitant. "This is the wrong pot."

I am confused. "Pardon?"

He repeats himself. "This the wrong pot. I will give you the correct pot. Are you in a hurry?"

My mind is doing somersaults. "But the doctor gave me this. Don't you two keep the same pot?"

He is not interested. "Can you fill this pot up?"

I am getting flustered. "What, do it again?"

He has a stern face. "Yes. It could deplete the sample if you swap it into the correct pot."

My heart sinks as I struggled to produce the first one. "Have you got a room that I can go in?"

He looks disappointed. "There is no spare room. Can you do it in the toilet? Just outside here on the left."

I get flustered. 'I don't think I can do it. It was a struggle getting this one."

He is encouraging. "Give it ago. Or you have to make another appointment. Now you are here, it doesn't matter how long you are."

I think about my current sample. "So, what do I do with this?"

He is not bothered. "Throw it away."

I walk away with a disheartened expression on my face to the toilet.

When I get inside the toilets I notice there are two cubicles and three urinals. I can see both doors are open on the cubicles, so at least I am by myself.

I lock myself in one of the cubicles and stand there agitated. I think about taking my jeans down again. As I pull my jeans and underwear down and try to arouse myself I hear someone come in and hear the sound of the other cubicle door locking. Great, I have to try to rub one out with a man next door to me. As I try to blank him, I struggle to give myself a hard on. While I struggle, I hear the man passing wind rather loudly as he is trying to go to the toilet. I still try to blank his bowel movements. I am struggling to jerk off as he continues to pass wind and then hear him heaving to push out his last night's dinner.

That's it, I cannot do it so I decide to risk swapping my original sperm into the new pot. I make sure I am careful as I do not want to lose a drop. I rest the pot, with my sperm inside, on top of the toilet cistern, hoping it does not slide off onto the floor. I then open the lid on the new pot. I am being quiet so the guy does not hear me. As I watch my sperm pouring into the new pot, I am trying not to be sick, looking at my semen close up. As I am gagging, almost wanting to be sick, I can hear the man is making heaving noises as he is trying do a number two. In between gagging and hearing him trying to get his children to go for a swim, I am thinking again, 'only me'. After I have transferred my semen from the old pot to the new there seems less in the new pot so I shake the remaining semen from the old pot to try to get the last dregs. The last drips of my semen look gloopy as it clings on to the side of the old pot. I decide to shake the pot some more and suddenly a speck of my semen goes into my left eye. I almost drop my pot with the transferred semen on to the floor. I quickly close the lid before I lose it, I then unlock the cubicle door to get to the sink. I run the faucet to splash my left eye with my free hand. I am quick to avoid the man coming out and seeing me holding my sperm and cleaning my eye full of semen. I am scared I will go blind. How do I explain that to friends and family? After I have finished clearing my eye, I notice my jeans are under and around my ankle. The man is about to unlock his door. I quickly hobble, trying not to fall over to get back into the cubicle, so as not be seen. Phew, I made it. I rest the new pot on the toilet cistern and put the old pot in my jean pocket.

Once I am back upstairs, I go back to reception to explain what the nurse asked me to do. The person gets the original nurse out to collect it. I just hope he does not notice that it is the original semen. When he comes out, I just smile sheepishly, praying that he has not noticed.

Mission accomplished. After asking how long the test will take, I leave quickly. I am told I will get a letter of the results in a couple of weeks.

A few days have passed since my sperm incident and I am going out with Helen for dinner. She has come on in leaps and bounds with feeding herself. You wouldn't think she was blind.

I tell the story of what happened a few days ago with having a prostate cancer check and having to supply my sperm for further health check. Helen is in a fit of hysterics as I am telling her. I ask if she is okay as I don't think it is that funny. She takes deep breaths in between her fits of laughter. I was hoping for some sympathy.

We change the subject to how soon her operation will be. We are in May now, with only a few weeks left before it is June. Helen looks anxious when the topic comes up. She is honest with me that she is scared the operation will fail. She is happier not knowing than going ahead and finding out it did not work. Up to this point, I never saw Helen as being blind. I just saw it as a temporary thing. The thought of the operation failing, makes it real that she is blind and it could be permanent.

Up until now, she has seen it as a temporary issue. She has had seven months to cope with it. I cautiously tell her that if the operation fails, I will be there for life to take care of her, despite her boyfriend, Robert. Helen is touched, half believing my words.

Helen asks me how it is going with Olivia. I tell her that I think I am in love with her, even though we have only been together for two months. Helen asks if I have told Olivia that I love her. I say to Helen no as I have only realised I am in love in the last couple of days. Also, I have not seen Olivia while coming to terms with it. Helen blurts out that she is jealous. The expression on my face is of bewilderment. I ask her in surprise and the look on her face is of wanting what I have, Robert to say that he loves Helen. She says that she cannot remember the last time

Robert said he loves her.   She quickly says that she does love him, but it has been a long time since they mentioned their love for one another. I guess she can interpret the sound of my voice as joy.

I play it down by saying that it is not the be all and end all. That working together and accepting each other faults makes a relation fun, not love. I tell her that one of Olivia's habits that annoys me is that she always sees the good in people and that she leaves her cups everywhere. Helen finds my moaning amusing.

It is weird that two months ago I could not stop thinking about Helen and how cute she is. Imagining us being a couple. And now all I can think about is Olivia and how much I would rather be with her now and not Helen.

When we finish dinner, I drive Helen straight home and do not stay for a night cap.

A couple of days later, I make arrangements to take Olivia to a hotel. I play it down, saying that it is a motel. I mention that it has a communal pool outside. She is overjoyed and hopes it is better than my pool house. Now I know why I love her. She does not care where we go, so long as we go together. She is oblivious that I am joking.

Friday comes along and I pick Olivia up and check her packing for the hotel. I tell her the motel is in Beverly Hills. She looks at me, puzzled. I know she is thinking that there are no motels in Beverley Hills but she just shrugs it off as she watches me checking her suitcase. I tut and sigh to myself as I look at her poor packing. She defends herself saying that no one has taken her to a motel before. I ask her if they have taken her to a hotel. She sarcastically laughs at my humour. I question her comment and she talks till she is blue in the face. I ask if she has ever visited relatives. She is defensive again, saying her family all live in here in Los Angeles.

I finish checking the suitcase, taking out a towel and

cleaning products. I then walk up to her, seeing her with a lost puppy look after criticising her packing. It makes me love her even more. When our noses almost touch, she asks me if there is something wrong. She looks worried. I blurt out that I love her. She breathes a huge sigh of relief. She then smiles and says she feels the same and wanted to tell me over the weekend. We both kiss each other passionately then talk over each other, asking when each other knew. Then we become competitive about who was first.

We are in the car, not far from the hotel. Olivia notices immediately that there are no motels. She sarcastically looks at the Beverley Wiltshire Hotel and asks if that is the motel. She then moans saying that we are nowhere near a motel.

I have been planning today as a surprise for Olivia. She does not know that we are staying at this particular hotel. I pretend to be annoyed and tell her that I will stop outside the next hotel. Will get directions from them to get to the motel. After I pull over outside the hotel, I turn around to her to say that I will not be long. I go reception to collect the key cards, before going back to Olivia. When I get back to the car I tell Olivia that our room is ready. I booked their cheapest penthouse. I tell her it was a steal at three thousand dollars. Four if I had chosen a room with a balcony.

Olivia's jaw drops. She thinks I am pulling her leg. She sits there and waits for me to start the car and go to the motel in another part of town. The concierge comes up to our car and offers to park it. A bell boy opens the trunk to take our luggage out. Olivia thinks that there is a big mistake and tries to explain that we are not staying here. The concierge asks her if we are not Mr Spade and Ms Johnson. The penny has dropped. Olivia is almost tearful. I get out of the car to let a valet get in the car. Olivia gets out of the car watching our things being carted off into the hotel lobby.

We walk up to the reception desk to get a set of two plastic gold keys. We then take the lift to the most expensive penthouse, as it was the only one left. I have already paid everything upfront as I hate surprise bills.

We conduct ourselves as friends in front of the bell boy, who escorts us to the lift and up to our room. I give him a hundred-dollar tip which he welcomes with a shock. I give the same bill for the concierge and valet, giving him a stern look. He understands and leaves straight away. Olivia is looking around at the size of the room.

Olivia is open-mouthed. "This bigger than your house and my apartment put together."

Nothing impresses me. "I hope not. The house cost me a cool two mill."

Olivia looks at me. "If I forget to say, I had a really nice time."

I look at her with a frown. "*PRETTY WOMAN*. That was the cheap room."

Olivia smiles runs up to me and kisses me passionately. This it feels different, more intimate.

Olivia says quietly. "I am ready."

I half get her. "Food."

Olivia smiles. "I am ready," She says, nodding her head.

She takes me to the bed and pushes me backwards onto it. She then falls on top of me and we continue to kiss. After a while, I pluck up the courage to tell her that I have never done it before. Olivia does not know what I mean and thinks I mean in a hotel room. I stop her kissing me and say with a concerned look that I have never had sex. She looks at me and then says. "I know." As she goes to kiss me, I stop her and question if she is serious. She replies saying it was obvious.

I look worried that she will want to leave me if I am rubbish, as the sex is bad. She suggests getting naked and so we undress in front of each on the bed. As I see her stomach and her underwear, my heart starts to palpitate as I find her a turn on. She looks like a pro as she casually undresses herself seductively, without trying. She takes control by pulling the duvet off the bed and motions me to lie down. She talks me through it like an instructor and reassures me that we will go at my pace. She straddles me and starts to rub my cock with the palm of her hand. She strokes it with the length of her hand. It is not long until I get an erection. Once I am hard, she uses her fingers and thumb to pull it up vertically, before she lowers herself on it. As I feel the tip of my cock resting against the wall of her vagina, my heart starts racing. It feels like I am struggling to stay afloat in water. My breathing elevates as I see my cock going inside her vagina.

She looks at me whispers if I am okay. I nod my head as my breathing still quickens. I take slow breaths to control my breathing. I cannot believe that at thirty-three, I am finally having sex. I still have my head raised to watch Olivia move her hips slowly, up and down. I feel friction inside her vagina like sand paper but not painful. After a few moments, it starts to feel like hot oil has slightly poured inside her vagina to lubricate friction.

I can see the concentration on Olivia's face, that I have never seen before. It is as like she is trying to remember the past. As her vagina has virtually no friction, she moves up and down more smoothly. My cock feels like it is growing more inside her. Eventually Olivia slows down and gently shudders as I watch a thin layer of white fluid clinging along the length of my shaft. Her vagina looks small around my cock as I see it going up and down, swallowing my cock whole. Eventually Olivia's body goes into spasm as if she has been tasered by a gun. I have not managed to come.

This is too overwhelming as I thought we would both cum. I do not cum and Olivia is has fallen on me still having post-orgasm shudders.

I am surprised when she says that is the first time a guy made her cum. I didn't do anything. I just lay there. It is not like I did a shimmy shake or a rain dance. She would have had the same effect with a dildo. I am too shy to say it wasn't me.

We lie facing each other. It feels surreal that we are finally in bed together. We are both in love with each other. We peck each other on the lip infrequently.

I start the conversation. "I cannot believe that I am no longer a virgin."

Olivia smiles. "So, was it what you thought it would be?"

I think about the question. "I had no perception. I thought I would need to do something to make you cum. You did all by yourself."

Olivia laughs. "Trust me, you did that."

I am open with her. "Once I reached a certain age, I did not think I would find anyone. I only joined the website, to get… someone off my back. I didn't think it would actually work. I just didn't want him on my back."

Olivia is curious who the person was. "So, who is your friend? I have to thank him."

At first, I think about lying, but decide not to. "My shrink, actually."

Olivia is thrown. "Wow."

I cannot read her expression. "Are you scared?"

Olivia is chilled. "For a multimillionaire, I did not see you needing to see a shrink. Do you mind if I ask you why?"

I am relaxed around her already. "I was suicidal. But not the kind who cried wolf. I knew I would do it within a year if I did not go to one."

Olivia is now intrigued and has an open mind. "I am so sorry. You are the most handsome, considerate and generous man I have ever met. Intelligent. Extremely intelligent."

I think about what she said but struggle to believe it. "The horrible stuff is easier to believe."

Olivia is close to tears. "Now I know why you write your books the way you do. You have a gift. Don't let anyone tell you differently."

I wipe her tear away. "I have never told anyone."

Olivia smiles through her tears. "Thank you for telling me. I feel privileged"

I fight my tears now. "You're welcome."

We embrace each other, wrapping our arms round each other, kissing emotionally. We end up making love again and our emotionally-charged minds makes our sex more electrifying. This time I get on top in a missionary position, slowly entering her. Olivia responds by gently biting on my shoulder as her body shudders under me. I suck on her ear lobe – I read somewhere. She moans softly and after a while shudders again from her orgasm.

I can smell our sweet aroma and for a second, savour this moment. This is what making love feels like. This moment.

Olivia's pert breasts, that I have seen for the first time, glisten with beads of sweat. I cannot help but suck on her nipples interchangeably. They are hard and fleshy. Olivia welcomes it and holds my head to guide me to how she likes them touched. I gently bite on them between my teeth and suck on them alternately Again, I read about this somewhere and wrote it in a book. I start to think about the descriptive stories I wrote in my books about intermate foreplays. This is it. Astonishment that I am here, with a beautiful girl, getting up close and personal. Butterflies in my stomach, my heart racing and the thought of "*I do not want this moment to end. Be caught in a time loop that will never end.*"

Olivia stops me and indicates that she wants to do the same to me, below. I lie on the bed and part my legs to make it easier. I feel I have gone from nought to sixty. Rather than first base one day, second base another day and then third base, all three have merged into one. It feels weird to me experiencing a mouth on my private parts. It feels like my hand has been caught in a water pump and the pressure is sucking on my hand. It does not feel uncomfortable. I rest my head back to feel her tongue whirling around and flicking the end. I realise how sensitive the tip of my end is when suddenly a bolt of nerve endings causes fireworks. I feel like I want to cum. I start to wriggle as I cannot handle my nerve endings reacting to Olivia's tongue flicking it. I groan deep in my throat and sit up, resting my elbows to see how she is turning me on. The sight of her concentration and focus on my cock is a turn on for me. Watching her gently bob her head up and down causes me to come close to climax. I widen my legs to try and get her closer to my cock. Eventually I cannot contain the sensation anymore and my climax explodes. The feeling of my cum flowing out of my cock is like the feeling you get when you are dying for the toilet. My body cannot contain the climax as I start to wilt from the explosion. I brush my hand over her head as if patting an animal. It is a way for me to acknowledge my appreciation. She still bobs her head up and down to finish me off. She then lets my cock fall out of her mouth and lie back next to me. She has a satisfied look on her face as I still recover from my ejaculation.

After we have both exhausted ourselves, we get into the shower together. I find myself getting aroused, watching the water splash on her boobs and cascade down them. She notices me and smirks, knowing that I find her boobs fascinating. She starts to rub my cock with a big soapy sponge, enjoying the reaction of my cock. She knows that soaking my cock in soap suds is arousing me, as she starts to laugh.

I get childish and start to rub her vagina with the palm of my hand, slipping my finger inside slightly. I can see from her face that she is enjoying it. I realise that I cannot get enough of this feeling she has shown me. I do not want this feeling and moment to end. I want to stay here forever.

Once we have finished showering, we decide to go downstairs to the sauna.

It is quiet and we are the only ones in the steam room. We are sat next to each other on the first of a two-tier cedar wood bench.

Olivia brought with her a two-piece bikini in banana yellow. Her mahogany skin accentuates against the colour of her bikini. I did not realise how pert her boobs are in just a bikini top. All she wears is polo jumpers and polo shirts so her boobs are not out for show. Not that I would like her to wear low tops. Her bikini bottom covers the whole of her front and back, not leaving any sexual thoughts to the imagination. I am wearing board shorts that surfers wear. They are reddish pink with a psychedelic faded white and blue dot pattern.

We make idle chit chat about what we think of the hotel facilities. Olivia likes the staff and I mention the shower in our room. I have a thing about how powerful I like my shower. I compare it to my en suite shower.

We both struggle to make conversation as our new-found sexual appetite is intruding into our mundane conversation. We find ourselves moving along the bench, leaving no gap between us. We are drawn by our lips as we kiss passionately. Olivia reaches down to my cock, causing an instant erection. I part my legs slightly to allow easy access. I sit back as she grabs my cock with her hand through my shorts while we still kiss passionately. She gently slides her hand up and down in a smooth action. I slip my hand inside her bra and use my forefinger and index finger, with my thumb, to tweak her nipple. I feel myself starting to get rock hard just before you feel yourself cuming. She smiles, almost laughing, as she feels how big my cock grows.

As we are getting into each other, a pair of couples in their fifties open the door and we stop immediately. Luckily, we are sitting side by side to each other, before they have a chance to see what we are up to. The shock has taken away our sensual intimacy. We look at each other, smirking like two little kids.

The two old couples smile at us as we decide to leave.

The two women smile at me, like I am their grandchild. I just smile back at them politely in return. The two men look around, ignoring us. I do not smile at them. When we are outside the steam room with the door shut behind us Olivia stands in front of me covering her mouth bending over in fits of laughter. You would think I had my eyebrows shaved. I look at her with an expression of 'what'?

Olivia points at my crotch and I look down to see if I have a stain on my shorts. Only me, only me. I had an erection all that time when we left the steam room. That's why the women were smiling at me and why the men did not know where to look. I curse Olivia for not doing something before walking out. Olivia cannot speak as she is taking deep wheezing breaths to control her laughter. She is useless for sympathy. She eventually hugs me and kisses me to apologise which arouses me again as my cock is pressed hard against her vagina. I end up grabbing a towel to rest against my crotch as we go into the jacuzzi. Luckily, there is no one else in there. Olivia is trying to be intimate and I push her away as a way of punishment and avoiding a second embarrassment. Olivia finds it amusing.

We spend the late afternoon through to early evening eating food ordered to our bedroom, including a bottle of chilled champagne in an ice bucket, with strawberries. We order a seafood platter that comes with prawns, mussels, calamari, squid and a lobster cut open with lemon and parsley drizzled over it. The other seafoods have no dressing apart from chilli dip and mayonnaise with lemon and a touch of finely chopped parsley dip. We are in our thick, soft, brilliant white robes with the hotel emblem on them. She still looks sexy and cute. We laugh about the steam room incident with us struggling not to spit our food from our mouths. We then laugh about my prostate check and sperm delivery to fertility clinic, as well as the gardener.

I could not enjoy this day any more with anyone else. We made love again, daring ourselves to make love on the balcony with her bent over the stone mason balcony, where we could get spotted from the street below.

CHAPTER THIRTEEN

Insight

It now the first week of June and Helen is to have her surgery the following Friday.

The next seven days are going to be hectic. I have to pick up Helen on Thursday to let her sleep over before taking her to the hospital the following morning. The Monday after, I finally have my meeting with the producers in Atlantic City to turn one of my series of books into a television series. Then on the Wednesday I have to do a book signing at a local book shop where the whole of LA will descend. I chose that shop as it has free parking and the people who read my books are ordinary people. My followers are not the rich kind or well to do. My readers are people who want to escape their existing life, whether because of hardship, childhood scars or what they could be going through at the moment.

Olivia and I are going really well. She is currently in Miami and has been there for almost a week. She has gone away for two weeks. She wanted me to come but I have Helen to take care of for one more day, the business deal and the book signing. Finally, we have our barbecue a week on Friday. So, too many things to be taking two weeks off.

The doorbell goes and I know it is my agent. Once I let him in I briefly introduce him to Helen as a friend coming over to pick some work up. I also mention that he is a work colleague and we work in the same department. My agent awkwardly agrees with me and says hello to Helen. I ask the maid to walk Helen to the kitchen and that we will only be about fifteen minutes.

My agent reminds me of the late John Candy. He is big,

with a big character to go with it. He has such a presence that everyone knows he is in the house. My family tolerates him as he helps himself to our dinner and expects second portions. He helps himself to the table as if he is family but he is not rude or annoying. As I said earlier, he saw how well my sales were going and how I wrote my books. He guaranteed me money and knew how to get my books further out there. He has good spin doctor skills. All he asks for is two percent of my sales and he does the rest. He has copies of all my first edition books, he keeps at his house.

My agent knows all about Helen and Olivia and has been like a real friend. I catch up with my agent every couple of months and so the last time I saw him was just before spring barbecue in March. It was then that he first mentioned about this prospect of signing a potential million-dollar contract that takes place soon after Helen operation. My agent has planned for the meeting to take place around the middle of June. If it is successful, I potentially have to move to Atlantic City by the end of June or start of July.

No one knows about the deal except for me and my agent. I have not even told my family as nothing has been signed and I do not see myself moving to Atlantic City for a million dollars.

We move from the lobby area by the front door to the living room that the rest of the family use. I see my manuscript on the sofa where I left it this morning before bringing Helen over. The manuscript is like a film script, thick with paper. My agent always likes to skim through my work from the front and middle pages to the end to get a flavour of the book. As a creature of habit, he also likes to be the first to read my manuscripts. I pick the script up and pass it over to my agent. He has glee in his eyes as he takes it off me and rests it by the drinks trolley that has various spirits like whiskey, vodka, liquor and rum. Their favourite drink is a fifteen-year-old El Dorado rum from

Guyana. I import a case of twenty once a year and when it is gone, it is gone. My siblings drink it like it is water, once you mix it with ginger ale. This takes the kick away and you can drink it like orange juice. My agent loves it and always takes a couple of tumbler glass shots. He helps himself as if he lives here. Once he hurriedly pours himself a neat glass of the rum, he relaxes and starts reading my latest script. He murmurs to himself with the odd um and huh.

In a quiet voice he says. "Wow. This is great. This is beautiful. I like the girl and I like the usual touchy-feely stuff. The middle is good. Wait, wait. What happened to the end?"

I have not decided yet. "I don't know which end to use."

My agent looks slightly frustrated. "You know I like having the original proof before going into production. You're the only client whose work I enjoy being the first to read."

I correct him. "I am your only client."

My agent raises his eyebrows. "True. But you are filthy rich so I don't need anyone else. Thanks for your accountant, by the way. He sorted out my backdated tax."

I nod my head. "You're welcome."

The agent asks me about the girls. "So, who is that one in your house now?"

I sigh. "That is Helen. She is over here because she has an operation tomorrow. She wants me to drive her in."

The agent then asks about Olivia. "So, where is Olivia? Does she know you fancy her?"

I look at him with an expression of annoyance. "No, And I don't fancy her anymore. Not since Olivia. She's the past. Besides she will get her eyesight back and then she will go back to her old life."

The agent tells me how it will go if the operation fails. "If she does not get her eyesight back? Her fiancé will do a runner. She will cling on to you. Where will Olivia stand?"

It is too much for me to comprehend. "I would have to end the current set up with Helen. See her when I am not seeing Olivia. Or we have no plans."

My agent is not convinced. "Good luck with that one. She will cling on you like rice on a stick. She will use you for an emotional crutch."

The agent changes to the deal. "So, D-day is next week Monday. We have to be in Atlantic City. Have you found a lawyer?"

I am not interested. "I don't need one. I just want three percent of sales. Nothing else."

The agent is disgruntled. "What about my fee?"

I stand up and walk about. "I will be twice as rich and you will be accustomed to whatever you do."

The agent asks about Helen's operation. "Does Helen know you funded her operation?"

I am annoyed. "No! And you are not going to tell her."

The agent is annoyed now. "Just like you funded her mother's hospital unit. How about some charity my way?"

I am standoffish. "What I do with my money is my business."

My agent disapproves. "So, how would you feel if Olivia didn't tell you that she paid for her ex's penis enlargement."

I am lost. "What are you talking about? I am doing good. I am not giving her an advantage?"

My agent gives up. "The moment you chose to look after Helen, you already started a relationship. You are sharing her experience of being blind is an affair. You cannot get any more intimate than sharing a fear and vulnerability. You do not need to have sex to have an affair. I don't know who is more blind. Does Olivia know what kind of conversations you have had?"

Whether I am naive or not, we agree to disagree. I have not given him an ending to the book. My agent leaves after necking his remaining rum. The meeting ends with him arranging the travel and the time where.

He has wound me up, trying to tell me that Helen and I

have been having an affair. I scoff at the idea, even at the mere thought of it.

I go into the kitchen to look after Helen. We make idle conversation. Helen asks if I have a book to read. She wants me to read to her. I guess she wants a distraction from the operation tomorrow.

I take her to my study room and sit her in the sofa. I try to decide which book of mine is appropriate.

I find one of my earlier books which I wrote when I was at college. The book is about a woman who has only a few months to live. She wins the National Lottery by coincidence, at the same time she gets her diagnosis. I think this will put Helen's life in perspective.

I have already read a few adventure stories with some sauciness in them. I did not know if she would take offence at first, but she enjoyed them. This book will be my fifth read to Helen.

Helen likes to lie her head on my lap as I read to her in a soft-spoken voice. She just keeps her eyes open with her face staring away from my stomach and listens to the story. I think about what my agent said as I read to her. It is eating away at me. We have only talked about what we like, don't like, what we have been up to during our time apart. I do not see what my agent sees.

I read the book till I get to the middle. It has now gone nine o'clock in the evening. We have been sat in my study for six hours. Helen is still awake lightly rubbing my arm with her finger tips, which is resting across her stomach. I tell her that I will finish reading it tomorrow in hospital.

I take Helen to her bedroom the maid prepared for her. She asks me to stay until she falls asleep. After she changes for bed, I lie next to her, as she snuggles into my chest. She looks at peace as she slips into a deep sleep.

I carefully move her head on the pillow and gently slide off the bed. I go to my bedroom and take my clothes off and sleep naked in my bed.

It is D-day. We are already at hospital and Helen is prepped for surgery. She has her own room and I am the only person here. I am continuing the book, reading in a soft-spoken voice again. She is holding my free hand as I read to her.

Her parents are on their way back from holiday, knowing that Helen's operation is today. Sweet Olivia texts me to ask how Helen is. I jokingly text back, asking what about me. She texts back a face of a tongue sticking out.

Olivia went away a couple of days before to catch up with her friend in Miami. I remember Olivia mentioning her when she picked me up from my prostate check. She said that her friend was desperate to catch up. She is back in a week's time after the family barbecue, next Friday.

My meeting in Atlantic City is on Monday. Perfect timing. Helen will not need me anymore. Miraculously, her boyfriend will be back on the scene, planning their wedding. Olivia is not around, so I will have a whole week to myself to sort work out.

It will feel weird not having to go around to see Helen. I will be at a loose end after business is taken care of.

The surgeon comes into the room, recognises me and explains to Helen what will happen in surgery. He is confident that she will regain her eyesight. He has looked at her x-ray and it is a simple procedure. Helen has been holding my hand the whole time.

Once the surgeon finishes talking to Helen, the porters come in to wheel her into surgery. Helen asks for reassurance that I will still be here after the operation. I kiss her on the forehead.

During Helen's operation I phone my agent to finalise transportation and to find out what I should expect. My agent asks how Helen's operation is going. I tell him that she is just going in and I will not know anything for a couple of hours.

Helen comes out of surgery and is still under the local

anaesthetic with her eyes bandaged. The surgeon is about to tell me how the operation went. Suddenly, her parents come walking up the corridor with what seems like her relatives, huddled together. Before the surgeon gives me a chance to tell me, her relatives bombard him with their questions. Helen fiancé is also with them. The surgeon looks overwhelmed with Helen's relatives ambushing the surgeon asking simultaneous questions. I feel like they are fans trying to get his autograph and I was the first one here, getting pushed aside. The surgeon looks at me as if he wants to help from me. I guess my work is over. I stand there looking at her large family showing an interest in Helen. I decide to slope off quietly. I take one more look before I leave the corridor. I all I want to do is call Olivia and be with her.

Helen finally wakes up from her anaesthetic with her bandage still covering her eyes. Her mom notices her stirring and quickly gets a nurse outside of the room in the corridor. The nurse nods at Martha and says she will get the surgeon. When the surgeon arrives, he carefully takes off her bandage and asks Helen to keep her eyes closed. The surgeon turns the light off so Helen's eyes do not hurt or have an effect on her eyesight. When Helen opens her eyes, she says she cannot see and panics. But her eyes are adjusting to the room and she has not seen for eight months. Her eyesight gains focus and she can see everyone in the room. The doctor uses an otoscope to see behind her eyes. He can see that everything is okay.

Helen is overwhelmed with her parents and relatives, while Rob pushes through to see her. The only thing she wants to see is Harvey. She looks around to see a face she does not recognise and every face she looks at does not resemble a stranger. She sits up and moves her head around to look beyond her relatives. She is disappointed and gives an uncomfortable smile as she has been ignoring them while trying to find Harvey. Helen is sad that Harvey is gone. She asks her dad where Harvey went and he has not realised that he left already.

I sit in my car in the multi storey car park and phone Olivia. She picks up straightaway. It is a nice feeling hearing your girlfriend's voice. She is bubbly on the phone, not allowing me to get an edgeways. She tells me how great Miami is and that her friend has shown her around the place. She wishes that I was with her and hints about me coming over before she heads back. But I have too many commitments here to be able to go over there. She finally asks how Helen's operation went. I say that it went well and that she can see now, even though I was not there. I just know. After we have caught up with everything, Olivia has to go as her friend wants to take her to the beach. I am sad to hear that she has to go.

Realising that I will not see Helen again suddenly hits me. It is like a piece of me is missing. It was a big build up to the operation to preoccupy her and take her mind off being blind. Then out of the blue, the pressure lifts off and I am left with an emptiness, where I do not have to go around to see her. I am so used to seeing her every two or three days for the last three months. I do not know what I am going to do with those days now. My book is finished. I have no plans to write for a while.

It is Monday and I am at the airport waiting for my agent to arrive. I have already checked in and am sitting at the departure lounge for our flight to Atlantic City. He finally arrives out of breath and tells me he went to the wrong terminal. He bends over, resting his hand on the back of the chair next to me. In between breaths, he asks me if I am all set for this meeting. I look at him, wondering if he is going die on me before we get on the plane. I tell him that I have been ready since he told me about it, back in March. The Tannoy says that the plane is ready for us to board. I cannot stop thinking about Olivia and Helen. I feel that there is something not quite right with Olivia but nothing has been said. My senses always tell me when something is not right and I get this with Olivia. She has not told me why she went to Miami so quickly when she has not spoken to her friend in years.

During the flight, my agent starts to order drinks and asks if I want one. I look at him wondering why he has an urge to get as many drinks inside him. I nod my head to say not interested and pick a random magazine out from the pocket of the back seat in front of me. My agent is drinking a martini cocktail with a cherry. He asks the stewardess to keep bringing them to him. I am happy looking out of the window at the ground while flicking through a magazine about the airline company. I wonder about how I think the meeting will play out. My predicted thoughts on how a meeting will go is majority of the time right. I have this ability to visualise the future in some important aspects of my life. One of them is Olivia and this meeting. I can picture a large room with a large table and just four of us there, sitting opposite each other.

Once we land and leave the plane, we head towards the exit for the taxi rank. As we come out of the luggage collection, we see a man with our names on it. We look at each other, surprised that they organised someone to collect us. We identify ourselves and follow him to a limousine. I can see my agent looking at the drinks cabinet and I give him a firm nod to say 'do not think about it' so he still has a drink. I have never been in a limousine before and as per usual, it does not impress me. The journey from the airport to the studio is about twenty minutes. When we arrive, someone is outside the building waiting for us. We shake a lady's hand and she introduce herself as the personal assistant and shows us to the tenth floor where the meeting will be.

Once we get in the room, as I sensed, there are two people sat on one side of a massive table that could seat twenty board members. We sit opposite them and we get the pleasantries over with. Five minutes into the business deal, I look at the contract which says that I will get six hundred thousand dollars from the production of my series based on supernatural angels. It is a series of five books about a human who was once an angel. They reckon the sales will equate to around two million dollars and I will get thirty percent of that, equating to the six hundred thousand dollars. We look at each other, pleased with the deal.

Then suddenly Helen's dad, Bill comes in, acting as though he was included and that he wasn't running late. He is in a three-piece blue suit and has a briefcase in toe. He stands behind us and grabs the contract. The two people look at each other wondering who this guy is. My agent and I feel embarrassed and do not know what to say.

Bill perusals the contract while humming to himself with a few murmurs in-between. After he has finished reviewing the terms and conditions, and then tells the producers no. He tells them this is how it is going to play out. He rattles off a load of opportunities such as franchises to be shown around the world, a movie to eventually be made for all five books and finally toys to increase the series' book sales. He says that I am his lawyer and that he is going to do this alone. The producers are open-mouthed as he bamboozles them with terminology that my agent and I did not know existed.

Bill looks at the producers as if they were bubble gum under his shoes. "Sorry I am late. The traffic was hectic. I drove from up town to get here. Phew. Well now I am here, we can start proceedings. This is how it is going to play out. Harvey signs that contract you have drawn up. You give a spiel while he is signing the contract, that it is a gamble that this may not be successful. Then, by some miracle it is a success. Harvey has already signed the contract and so he loses out on money. Does that sound about right?"

Bill does not give either Harvey, his agent or the producers time to answer the rhetorical question.

Bill continues. "Well, this is what is going happen now.

We tear up the old contract. I have a fresh contract here. Harvey is intelligent and his books are off the charts. Or else you wouldn't be here. I have read his books. Spent two solid days without sleep reading all five series. So, this is how it is going to play out. Harvey has full rights to his work. He is not going to sell it. You won't own a cent. Harvey franchises his work out to you. This means that if he feels fit to sell it on some Mexican channel, he can. You say yes to the contract. Harvey gets five percent of sales on all merchandise, the television series and eventually, the movie. Because we all know that series turn in to movies. Look at all the *STAR TREK* movies. Harvey is not bound to you, and so if he wants to franchise it out around the world, you do not have a say. Now, based on my calculations last night and my experience six hundred thousand dollars is a joke. My new contract has a revised figure. I have made four copies on the assumption that your lawyer will be here but I can see that he isn't, which confirms that you thought this would be a steal. You read the new contract at your perusal. I suggest you read it, get your boss to see it and then sign it. I have got all day. Harvey, you will buy me dinner before drive home. I don't care what you do after that. Is everyone clear?"

My agent looks at me and then smiles from ear to ear. "Whatever he said."

I look puzzled as to what has just happened. "Yeah. Whatever he just rattled off to you."

Five hours later, the producer's bosses sign the new contract. Bill gives me a dirty look, like a disapproving dad. Six hundred thousand dollars has turned into ten million dollars over five years. My agent gets five percent of my fee. Bill has written in the contract that I am to peruse the final draft of the script when it is finished. The first draft is planned for the second week of August. I also have the option of living in Atlantic City to oversee the project or get a monthly report on the progress.

When we get down to street level, Bill tells me that his services were free, as a way of saying thanks for looking after his daughter over the last two months. He reminds me that it would have cost me a cool million to get that contract. He must really like me. My agent shakes Bill's hand profusely, thanking him for coming in at the eleventh hour. Bill was joking about the dinner part. He also lied about driving all the way here. He has a private jet that is parked up at Santa Monica Airport. He offers to take us back on his private jet. We think about it and decide to explore Atlantic City to see what it has to offer as a potential home for me. Bill walks away to get a taxi and leaves us to it.

My agent asks about Olivia and what is going on, while waiting for a taxi. I tell him things are good. She is in Miami seeing an old friend she has not seen or heard from in years. My agent looks suspicious and says to me to be weary. He does not explain himself and I just brush it off.

Helen has been able to see for three days now, since she lost her eyesight in October last year. She left the hospital a couple of days after the operation to be housebound for about a week before she can do the most basic tasks, like going for a gentle walk. She is not allowed to go back to work for two weeks. When she does go back to work, it is light duties.

Helen is on a mission to find out who Harvey is. She was dying to meet him when she gained her eyesight back. She assumed that it would have just been her and him. She was bewildered when she saw her relatives crowding her hospital room. She thought her parents would be home the next day. Rob was the last person she expected to see, considering he was only around once a week over the last eight months.

Looking back, Helen cannot believe how eight months has flown by, before having an operation to restore her eyesight. The journey for her seemed long and painful until she met Harvey, the faceless man.

She starts to think about the dates she had with him. That is how she will remember it. She remembers her first date, where Harvey took her to some restaurant that needed a lift. She remembers the conversation of most embarrassing moments. As she thinks back, she remembers her funniest story. The story about him getting an erection over a photocopier, when showing a girl how to use it. As she remembers, she laughs to herself inside.

Helen does not want to wait a week before finding the man who saved her from wanting to kill herself. She did not think that a simple man who was just himself could have made her eight months of pain bearable.

Helen starts off with going round her parents' house.

She is nervous and so decides to walk over. She hopes the ten-minute walk will allow her time to cool her nerves. She has no idea why she is so nervous. She went out with him four times a week over three months. That's sixteen times per month, forty-eight times in total. At least three hours per visit. Her brain is getting frazzled just thinking about it during her walk down her drive and up his drive. During her thoughts she realises she has already arrived in his open space car park. The house looks empty with no cars.

She is surprised how different his house looks. There are no steps leading up to the door. The house has two double doors in mahogany wood with a mirror marble effect. The house looks twice as big as her parents'. They have a water fountain in the centre of their car park, like it is forming a roundabout. It is currently on.

When she rings the doorbell, she expects no one to answer. She has made her mind up to only ring twice, with a minute's wait in between.

Just as she is about to ring the doorbell again someone opens the door, to her surprise. Her gut feeling is that it is not Harvey opening the door. She feels that Harvey is not home.

Helen sees an old lady answering the door. Helen

assumes that it is his mother, even though she has never met his family. Even when she stayed over on Thursday night with Harvey, she did not have a chance to meet any of his family.

The woman gives Helen an inquisitive look, waiting for her to say something. Helen is unsure what to say and blurts out asking if Harvey is home without introducing herself. The lady says no and asks Helen who she is. Helen says that she is a friend of Harvey who looked after her now and again. The lady says that Harvey has gone away for the day. She tells Helen that it is his mom. So, Helen assumed right.

Helen is disappointed. She wishes she had Harvey's cellular number. She did not need it before as it was pointless, being blind. Living around the corner, it was easy for Harvey to come around without relying on phone calls. Now when she wants to see him with her own eyes, he is not around.

Helen tells Harvey's mom that her son looked after her when she lost her sight. His mom is not aware of Harvey's activities, so looks blank when Helen mentions that.

Helen is back at her parents' house, bored and staring at the four walls in the living room. Everyone is at work and so she has no friends that she can go and see.

The rest of the day she spends moping around the house, flicking channels on the television and opening the fridge door in the kitchen every ten minutes.

When her dad gets back from work, the first thing she asks is for Harvey's cellular number. Her dad sends her a text from his cellular contact list.

It is the next day, Tuesday and Helen has been awake since five o'clock. She makes the most of having her eyesight back. She still panics that she is still blind when she wakes up from her sleep. Her bedroom is pitch black at night time and so she feels blind if she wakes up. She naturally grabs for the lamp switch to check that her eyesight is still back. It gives her a kind of panic attack. She feels that it will take days, if not weeks, to overcome this fear. Each morning she thinks it when she becomes conscious but has not opened her eyes yet.

She is anxious to text Harvey at a reasonable time. She does not want to worry him receiving a text at five in the morning. In the meantime, Helen tries to go back to sleep but is struggling to as all she can think about is finding out what Harvey looks like and being able to thank him. She was never given the opportunity to say thank you properly, with her own eyes.

When it has gone nine o'clock, Helen hesitates as to whether to call him or just send a text. With a phone call she will know if he is ignoring her and she can leave a message on his answer phone. If he picks up, she can read his voice but with a text, she cannot know if he is happy to hear from her. Also, she cannot make him answer a text; not that she can make him answer a phone call but she is able to know if he cuts the ring tone short or lets it ring out. All these thoughts that go through her head make her more hesitant. She is also worried what he will think about Helen getting hold of his number without his knowledge. Will he think she is desperate or devious or a complete loser? Her engagement status does not change those thoughts.

She chooses to text him and leave the message as open-ended, so he is expected to reply. She writes a short message to say, 'Hi. I got your number off my dad, Bill. It is Helen. Clearly, I can see now, as I am writing this message. I really want to find a way of thanking you. Do you have anything that I can get you as a way of saying thank you?' After Helen finishes the message and sends it, she suddenly realises that the family won the National Lottery and so why would he need anything? Well, she has already sent the message.

It has been hours since she sent the text. It has now gone three in the afternoon and still no reply. Helen feels that Harvey has become evasive and does not want to see her again. She wonders what she has done wrong for Harvey to disappear.

It is a Wednesday and I have to sign copies of the new book I finished back in March at a local book store down town. I have a queue of about twenty people waiting in a single line. I ask them what they want me to write in the front cover. My body is here but my mind is elsewhere. I am like a conveyor belt just waiting for the next one in line. The people all have sombre faces with no excitement at seeing me and just want my autograph in their book. My agent is not here. The shop owner is panicking that my books are running out and that more and more people are arriving. I watch a woman who looks like a stereotypical librarian try and make her calm down. I am relaxed, without a care in the world. It takes three hours to see each of the people, fans of my books. Not one of them asked anything about me or about the book. After everyone has their book signed, I head straight home.

On the way home, I think about the text that Helen sent and I wish I could reply. But I had a lunch meeting with her fiancé on Tuesday, as well as a few other things to sort out. I had plans to text Helen back after lunch but her fiancé basically told me not to come over ever again as they are working things out. I personally thought he was a cock and I can buy him over a few hundred times. I hold back with the fact that I am worth roughly ten million dollars. I kind of felt sorry for him and for Helen for being with someone like him.

CHAPTER FOURTEEN

Unexpected Proposal

It is the end of June and it is our second barbecue of the year.

It is Friday and I am at home, watching the catering people rushing round getting the barbecue ready. I check that my favourite wine, Latour, is in safe keeping behind the bar. My parents are directing the man power telling them where to put things. While I am in the garden overlooking the chaos, I get a phone call from Olivia and walk to a quiet space to pick up the phone. I have to put my finger against my ear to block out the noise of the chaos. Olivia wants to tell me that she is heading back on Sunday and wants to see me on Monday at my office. She has important news to tell me. It is does not sound good for me. She says how much she loves me and that she cannot wait to see me. As per usual, I am not able to get a word in edgeways to let her know what I have been up to post Helen's operation and about the deal. The noise in the garden is too loud for me to get an understanding of what she was talking about.

My siblings, nephews and nieces are all out at work, school, college or nursery. It is just my parents and me. I had no reason to be in the office today as I have stopped writing and decide to take a break from it. My agent is not expecting another script from me in a long while.

The barbecue starts at seven o'clock. I have my usual routine of grabbing my favourite bottle of wine and a glass hidden behind the bar. I then walk over to the solarium to my favourite spot. I start people watching. This time I do not think about what I will write or think about which people I will have as my characters. I just pause and reflect on what has happened over the last three months. It is almost July and I think about myself flying the coop. I will miss Helen and look forward to spending the rest of my life with Olivia. I am looking forward to telling her my plans and see us living in Atlantic City, New Jersey.

When I am lost in my thoughts, people watching, I hear voices in the solarium. The voices appear to be two women whispering in the distance, in the direction of the door entrance. I feel that some guests have got lost or are thinking of escaping the party in here. I creep towards the whispering to see where the they are. When I can see two people a few feet away, I suddenly realise that the voices I can hear whispering are from my mother and Helen. It is too late to avoid them as my mom has noticed me and I see her pointing at me, as Helen follows where she is pointing. It makes me jump as I did not want them to see me. I thought the darkness had cloaked me but evidently not. I watch Helen walk over to me with a smile forming.

I think of the meeting I had with Rob, not wanting me to hang around with her anymore. I wave at my mom to acknowledge her and then wait for Helen to reach me, before walking her to my spot. We both do not say anything to each other. I am wondering what she is thinking, not replying to her text. She must be angry at me. I do not know why she still looked for me. Not that she sent loads of text messages to hound me. Just the one. She is making me feel guilty now.

Once we reach my favourite spot, we sit next to each other on the ledge.

I wonder how my mom knew I was here and how Helen knew about our barbecues. She has never been to our barbecues, although her parents have. Helen parents must have told her about the barbecue tonight. But I do not know how Mom knew I hung out here.

Once we are sat down, Helen smiles at me and warns me that she is going to feel my face. She almost giggles and goes giddy as she places the palms of her hands on my face and closes her eyes.

Helen recalls how she felt when she went on her second

outing with Harvey. As she remembers, she tries to see if she feels the same way, as a way of trying to verify who he is. This is despite Harvey's mother pointing him out to her. The same touches mimic her first experience of feeling his curves and imperfections. She runs the tips of her fingers over his eyebrows, cheek bones, chin and nose. As her feel duplicates what she felt three months ago, it confirms to her that this is Harvey. She smiles as she recognises him again.

Helen smiles as she opens her eyes and takes her hands away from me. "Hi, Harvey. You are a hard man to find. I had no way to find you. I was too embarrassed to knock your door a second time."

I do not know what to say. "I have been busy. I am taking a break from work."

Helen is giddy with finally seeing what I look like. "You are exactly what I imagined. I came to say thank you for everything. I was upset that you were not there when I opened my eyes."

I quickly explain about feeling claustrophobic. "Your family needed to be there. I felt that I was just in the way."

Helen looks disappointed. "So, this is where you hang out. You don't like parties?"

I look around and walk her to my favourite spot. "I like to people watch. This is not my idea of a party. I don't know anyone."

Helen sees my bottle of wine. "Can I have some? I could do with a drink."

I clean my wine glass with a handkerchief and pour her out a glass. "So, where is Rob?"

Helen looks like she wants to forget him for one night. "I told him to go away. I wanted to spend some time by myself. I also wanted to see you."

I am puzzled. "Why would you want to see me?"

Helen is hesitant. "I wanted to see how you lived. What you do in your spare time. With all this time finding out what I do, I never asked what you like doing. Umm, nice wine. I am guessing a thousand dollars a bottle."

I am amazed how she knows. "Have you drank this before?"

Helen hums to herself. "Not really. The price is on the bottle."

I look and had not noticed that before. "Oh, ah ah. Of course. So, how are the wedding plans going?"

Helen turns away and observes the solarium. "You have a beautiful garden. Did you get this house for your parents?"

I guess she does not want to talk about her wedding. "Yes. My parents don't do much. This keeps them out of mischief. I had this built when we first moved in."

Helen looks fascinated with everything. "I heard that your dad got you a deal. He wouldn't go into detail, client confidentiality."

I do not go into detail. "It was nothing. My family business came into a new venture. He helped to iron out the fine print."

Helen looks like she is no hurry to go anywhere. "I would like you to take me to your party. Introduce me to your family."

I feel uncomfortable with the thought of socialising at my barbecue for the first time. "Can we just stay here?"

Helen will not take no for an answer. "I am your guest so I have a say. Take me to your party."

We leave the solarium to find where my family are sitting. Helen appears to be eager to meet them. When we find them, my siblings look surprised to see me and with a woman.

My siblings and their wives and husbands are sat around one of the many hired garden tables. Like the other guests, they are in dinner suits and dresses. Their children are playing about away from the guests, but inside the perimeter.

It is not surprising how the similar characters sit next to each other around the garden table. All eight of them. Michael, Melissa and Xavier are chilled, calm and laid back, respectively. While Natalia, Montel, Chevalier and Christine are feisty, argumentative, Pessimistic and to the point respectively. That leaves Mercedes, with her happy-go-lucky attitude.

Everyone has plastic cups of spirits and there are beers randomly placed on the table. I grab two empty chairs from the table next to us, for Helen and I to sit on. I feel embarrassed at Helen seeing my family drunk but Helen looks blasé about them being rowdy. Helen finds them amusing and looks like she wants to join in the fun.

Five minutes in, Helen is laughing with them hysterically. She looks like she is getting drunk herself. I feel I am on the outside as I watch Helen enjoying my family. My family. I feel jealous.

Helen confidently mingles. "So, these are your siblings?"

Xavier looks over. "Oh, Harvey is here. This is quite a surprise. You are never here. Did he show you his hideout?"

Mercedes is already aware of Helen. "So, you are Helen. I cannot believe you were blind. Harvey told me all about you. How are you?2

Chevalier tries to say that he had a worst near miss as per usual. "I almost went blind once. There was an oncoming car with its high beam lights on. I had to stop right there and then. Seriously."

The rest of my siblings indistinctly moan at his comment in unison, while Helen finds it amusing and funny. I thought Helen would find Chevalier comment offensive, but she seems to like the banter.

I just observe their conversation. The conversation moves on to how we know each other. Helen says we met through her dad.

My family have no idea that I fancied her since elementary school.

Helen brings up our first outing where we talked about

our embarrassing moments. She mentions about the photocopier incident and made everyone laugh. I get upset with her until she tells them about her embarrassing moment, going to a wedding, then I do not feel that she is being facetious. I still feel a bit annoyed with her, however.

Just as I feel like sloping off without them noticing me, Helen brings up the opera and how much she enjoyed it. My siblings look at me condescendingly. Helen holds my hand as she is telling the story.

They all think she is great and ask me where I have hidden her. They praise her personality saying she is witty and funny. Helen is making them all laugh and I feel that I am being pushed out of the conversation. I feel she has overstepped my boundary by helping herself to my family. I like keeping my relationships separate from my family. I watch them all laughing with Helen and feel that I am losing her to them.

When the guests start vacating, the garden looks sparse. Helen is now ready to go home and asks me to walk her back. I guess back to her parents, as her apartment is in town. Helen thanks my siblings for an enjoyable night. She can sense I am a bit unhappy.

On the way to her parents', we do not say anything to each other. My thoughts are about how I used to fancy her and I how never saw this side to her. When she was blind, she was conservative. Now she appears liberal.

Helen plucks up the courage to start a conversation. "I didn't realise how nice your family were. You have a great family."

I ask her why she came. "What made you come over?"

Helen seems coy. "I wanted to see the man who kept me company all this time."

I am curious to what happens now. "So, now you know, what are you going to do moving forward??

Helen wants to know why I was not at the hospital. "Why weren't you there when I woke up?"

I am honest. "I thought you would rather be with Rob. I assumed you arranged for him to be there. My job was done so I decided to leave."

Helen is honest with me. "I really wanted you to be there. It was you who kept me going and made sure I got to the hospital okay."

I shrug it off. "Nah, I just took you out to distract you. It took a lot of elaboration to makes keep things interesting."

Helen looks like she has something she still wants to tell me. "I… I don't know how to say this. I don't even know why I am struggling. We are mates. We are mates, aren't we, Harvey?"

My eyes move from left to right. "Well, yeah."

Helen takes a deep breath. "Robert and I are going to get married in August this year."

I am open-mouthed. "Wow. That is… fast. Who decided?"

Helen gives a nervous embarrassing smile as she says. "It was my idea. Why bother waiting now? We have been together for over ten years. What do you think?"

I have no opinion. "Why are you asking me?"

"Your opinion matters to me."

"You have already made your mind up. So what difference will my opinion make?"

Helen looks like she is keen to know my thoughts as I see her trying to read me. "If you have any doubts, tell me."

I have a blank expression. "Why would I have any doubts?"

Helen is still trying to read me. "If you had any doubts, I would cancel."

I am a bit annoyed with her assumption now. "You wouldn't. You know it. Besides, it is not my right to pass judgement."

We reach a stalemate and I do not know what to say after that so we do not talk for the rest of the way to her parents' house. It takes about ten minutes to walk her home.

When we get to the front door Helen turns around to thank me for a great evening. She gives me the cutest smile. I see her go in before I turn around and walk back home.

It was odd seeing Helen with her eyesight back. I kind of wish she was still blind so that we could go back to the way things were. I liked our activities and miss Florence, who left the day before Helen's operation. She was funny. I last saw her on the day I was bringing her round to my house. I arranged for a limousine to drive her back to her home, as a thank you for all she done for Helen. I wonder what she is doing with herself now and again. Her husband passed away a few years earlier. I hope she is okay.

It is the next day and everyone is in the kitchen chattering away and the conversation is indistinct, so I do not know what they are talking about. I pour myself coffee before I sit down with them. I sit next to Mercedes and she feels I want to talk, so she says something.

Mercedes leans towards me. "So, she is Helen. She is very pretty. I can't decide who I prefer, Olivia or Helen."

I respond. "Helen I spoken for. So that is the difference. Besides I am with Olivia and we concurred that we… lo… lo… like each other."

Mercedes asks about last night. "So, where was Olivia last night?"

I remind her about Miami. "She went on holiday to Miami a couple of weeks ago so she could not be here. She doesn't fly in until tomorrow."

Mercedes is inquisitive. "Why couldn't she leave a bit earlier and come to the barbecue?"

I am a bit short. "So, both of them are there? We had a proper conversation about it and we both agreed. She wanted me to go to Miami with her and she was upset. I explained to her that I had a few things to sort out myself."

Mercedes asks. "So why did Helen come over?"

Mom suddenly speaks up. "Helen was so nice. Well spoken."

I speak to Mercedes. "She wanted to say thanks for being there."

Chevalier gives his advice. "Not being negative, but I think you're better off with neither of them. They both look dodgy. I wouldn't trust them."

Christine joins in. "Helen has a fiancé and so why are you bothering with her? Why was she at the party instead of with him?"

Montel is his cheery self and says. "I wouldn't bother with Helen, she will only end up breaking your heart."

I remind them. "I am not with Helen. I am with Olivia."

Natalia wants to get her message across. "She has found out you are rich and now wants your money."

Chevalier agrees. "Helen is only after your money. She never noticed you before."

I respond with sarcasm. "She was blind. And she still does not know I am rich."

Michael gets involved. "Does Olivia know that Helen likes you?"

I chuckle. "She does not like me. She is getting married. Assuming in a year's time. If not, this summer. She has waited long enough."

Dad now passes comment. "And what if she likes you? What if she is willing to give up marriage for you. Then what?"

I repeat myself. "I am… with Olivia! What part do you guys not understand?"

Chevalier finishes off. "What will you do when Olivia shoots through?"

I sigh and walk out of the kitchen. My head is foggy with echoes of the individual comments. I go to the lake to get away from everyone.

When I get to the lake I text Olivia, asking when she lands and if she fancies me picking her up. She texts back to say that she is going to find her own way home and that she wants to relax and unpack, so she does not want me to come over. Olivia texts to say that she wants to see me on Monday. I text asking what time she is thinking. She texts back saying late morning.

She has not asked me how my week has been. I have I mentioned Helen and what my plans are. She has not asked how my deal went.

Helen is still eating with her parents for breakfast. Her parents are looking at each other wondering why she is at their house. Helen is oblivious to them looking at her.

Helen was always blind to other people unless they followed the same path. She only saw when she was blind. The reason is because she was forced to listen, really listen. Her dad wants to know what is going on.
Bill touches her wrist to get her attention. "What is your plan, now you are back to normal?"

Helen looks down. "I plan to get married in August. Something simple, immediate family and neighbours only. Neighbours, as in here."

Bill assumes she means next year. "So, that gives you just over twelve months. Do you need any money?"

Helen is abrupt. "Next month."

Martha looks surprised. "But that doesn't leave much time for planning."

Helen sighs. "I have waited long enough. Robert has agreed with me. We do not want to waste any more time."
Martha and Bill look at each other, then look down at their breakfast and nothing more is said. Helen lets them know that she is beginning to look for venues after one o'clock today. Her parents suck their tongues under their breath and continue eating. Helen's first appointment is at one thirty.

Helen needs to have a shower first before she goes to meet Robert. She recalls the places in her head that she wants to go to with him. The venue will be used for both the ceremony and reception afterwards. Helen and Robert want to save time by not having to travel between two venues. The venues that Helen found on the internet, a couple of days ago, are Mountain Gate Country Club, Le Foyer Ballroom, Le Banquets - Legacy Ballroom and Lounge, Le Banquets - Brandview Ballroom, Regency Event Venue, Vatican Banquet Hall & Reception and Taglyan Complex. Helen meets Robert at Mountain Gate Country Club first as it is not that far from her parents' address.

While Helen and Robert are travelling between each venue, Helen cannot stop picturing Harvey's face as she realises that she finds him handsome. She wonders how her dad found him. Helen knows that only her mom has attended Harvey's barbecues. Helen has taken notice of her parents' conversation.

It takes the whole afternoon to visit all seven venues, collecting brochures with prices and getting a feel for the places. Helen felt that she had a favourite while Robert was too bamboozled to make a decision. He is leaving it to Helen to choose a venue.

When Helen and Robert finally get home after seven o'clock, Robert feels the urge to get frisky. He looks at Helen's bum as she walks into their apartment first. He decides to grab her waist and pull her towards him so he can press his crotch against her sexy bum. Helen responds by grabbing his hands and moving them to her boobs. Robert starts kissing her neck before turning her around and pushing her against the hallway wall. They then start to breathe heavily while passionately kissing full on the lips. Robert presses his body hard against hers. She says in between deep breaths that she has missed this.

They do not make it to the bedroom and instead move to the floor in the living room. He fights to pull her jeans off, as she helps him. They continue to heavily kiss each other.

Eventually both their bottom halves are naked and they make love. She gasps as she feels him going inside. It is not the action, it is from not having sex for a year. For

Helen it is like not having chocolate for a month. She closes her eyes to savour the moment. Because she has not had her man inside her all that time, it is not long before she feels a bolt of electricity through her. Her body shudders underneath Robert's. Her muscles contract around his cock which stimulates him and soon after, he reaches a climax. He hugs her tightly as he releases himself.

They start to giggle together, and Helen is out of breath. It is like she ran five kilometres. Robert is panting as well, with a huge smile of relief.

After they get their breath back, Harvey pops into her head for a brief moment, and she imagines it was him making love to her. She feels unnerved as she is still recovering from her orgasm and because she is comfortable with visualising Harvey giving her the orgasm. She does not know why she has Harvey on the brain, literally.

It is Monday morning and I am in the office downtown, pondering about going to Atlantic City. It is the start of July and I have been with Olivia for three months now. We realised that we were in love with each other a month ago. Since losing my virginity to Olivia we have been inseparable. It has been hard not seeing her for the last two weeks. We spoke on the phone every night and texted each other during the day. She came back on Sunday and we agreed to see each other today.

Five weeks ago, Olivia first mentioned her friend and it seemed like a matter of fact and nothing more to it. The next thing her old friend invited her to Miami for two weeks. Now Olivia has something ominous to tell me since coming home from Miami. She asked if I wanted to go but the following Thursday and Friday, I had to be with Helen. Then in the second week was my business deal, book signing and barbecue so it was not practical to go with her.

Now she is back and she has taken the Monday off

work. Olivia wanted to come to my office rather than wait till tonight or meet up for lunch.

I am expecting her to arrive in the next few minutes. While I have been waiting for her I have a sense that Olivia has made plans that do not involve me. Or she is deciding to tell me once her plans are in place, that involve both of us.

I am considering how to juggle seeing Olivia here in Los Angeles and going to Atlantic City to oversee the production of my book. I can look at commuting there a couple of times a week or month. I can see myself spending the rest of my life with Olivia and so I want to stick around. Olivia has not hinted that she may be doing something that does not involve both of us.

She told me that a friend called her out of the blue five weeks ago when she picked me up from the hospital. It was a week later that I first made love to a woman. Then two weeks later she went to Miami to meet up with her friend. I did find it weird how, out of the blue, she heard from someone she had not heard from in ten years, then she spent two weeks with them. I am suspicious and my gut feelings are always right. I feel that she will have something bad to say.

Olivia walks into my office and says, in a nervous, soft voice. "We need to talk." I sense that the trip to Miami was not a friendly visit. "I guessed."

Olivia is standoffish. "I have this opportunity to run my own business. I have given this a lot of thought. A lot of thought. Seeing how you are, you have made me realise where I want to be."

I knew it. "Miami wasn't a holiday, was it?"

Olivia looks guilty. "It was at first. I asked you to come."

I feel that our relationship is ending. "So, where are you going to set up shop?"

Olivia is hesitant. "When we first met, I was happy where we were. But you changed me. You made me have ambition. And I can't change that. You made me this way."

I wish I had not told her what I had. "I wish that I never told you about me but you recognised me anyway. The money does not make you successful. That is an illusion. Success is finding happiness. I have found that in you."

Olivia walks up to me. "I look at you. I do not feel comfortable with you paying my way when I have a career. I feel like I have a low paid job next to you."

I do not know how to come back from that. "You pay for everything. We go to the places you can pay for."

Olivia kisses me on the lips to shut me up. "I was afraid to ask how you deal went because I knew that it would make me jealous. How did it go?"

I want to lie. "A ten-million-dollar agreement."

Olivia is open-mouthed and says, with a smile. "You see. I knew it. That is why I did not ask. That is what I want and I need to do this by myself."

I understand. "So, the love thing was not real?"

Olivia is quick to disagree. "No, no. I love you. This is why I spent two weeks agonising over this. I am still in love with you. And meant it when I said you are the best sex I have ever had."

I am almost tearful. "So, it is my fault you are leaving."

Olivia is close to tears as well. "No. It is no one's fault. It's just that you inspired me. It is one of the reasons why I fell in love with you. I am scared that if we are still together, you will hold me back. I need to do this by myself."

I get it now. "So, if I am around, I will offer you money, and my money will not give you the motivation to get your business off the ground."

Olivia nods her head. "Like I said, you have a gift, Harvey Spade."

After we stop getting emotional, Olivia leaves to go and prepare to move to Miami to start her new life. I agree to see her off at her place, this Friday. She plans to continue to pay for her flat until the lease runs up so she does not waste time leaving to take over the business. She asks if she can use my accountant and I give her his number. I advise her to give my accountant the books for him to check things are above board. Olivia appreciates that.

It has not sunk in that it is over between Olivia and I. I am alone again. I have done nothing wrong to cause us to break up. My life as an author has given her motivation to do something with her life. I wish I stayed as an underwriter. I could still afford a shrink and our paths would have still crossed.

It is no longer necessary for me to stay in Los Angeles to be with Olivia. Helen has fully recovered and is planning her wedding. I am back to square one with no one in life, except for my family. But that is not enough for me anymore.

I sit at my desk and take one more look around as I do not plan on coming back into the office. I never did send my clothes to the charity shop. I feel that my flashy clothes no longer do it for me. I decide to start wearing my old clothes again and get back my shitty blue Chevy. I still cannot let go of it. I have made my mind up to go back to the Mercedes dealership and buy my old blue Chevy back. I will look to go to the dealership on Saturday. I will give my Mercedes CLS to one of my siblings. It will be no good to me anymore. I guess it is time to fly the coop.

CHAPTER FIFTEEN

Returning the Favour

It is the end of the first week in July and Olivia is now ready to move to Miami.

It is after five o'clock on Friday afternoon. Olivia has her flight booked for eight o'clock. She is bound for Miami to start her new life. She has to leave by five thirty to allow time for her to check in before the flight.

I am at Olivia's place, watching her pack the last of her belongings. As she is packing her life in her suitcase, I am sat on her bed next to her. I watch as she aimlessly chucks her clothes in her suitcase, with no particular order. I look around her bedroom seeing it as an empty shell. Her furniture has already been packed in a removal van and is heading to Miami by road. It left yesterday with over a day's drive ahead of it. Olivia's new business partner is dealing with the other end, watching her furniture being unloaded in her new rental apartment.

You can see on the carpet in the bedroom as well the living room, the dust marking the outline of where her furniture used to be. The rooms look like a crime scene, outlining the furniture shape. You can see the outline of where her chest of drawer and bedside cabinet used to be against the wall. There are light patches of wall paint where furniture preserved the colour.

The bed is staying, as it came with the apartment originally. She is leaving the original mattress as well because it did not belong to her. I arranged for a new luxurious mattress as a present. I would not take no for an answer. Olivia swallowed her pride and accepted my gift. It was the least I could do.

The atmosphere in the apartment, particularly the bedroom, is quiet and sombre. I am slowly coming to terms that she is leaving to start a new life in another city. It feels like she is going away and she will be coming back in a month. Olivia looks like she is prolonging her packing and keeps looking over at me while sniffling. I do not know if she is having second thoughts, regrets or wants me to go with her.

I have no expression on my face but I feel sad and numb inside. I try to think of a reason for her to make us work. I want to give her a loan and use a lawyer to make it above board but I am too shy to suggest it. I also do not want to make it awkward for the remaining time I have with her.

I start to reminisce what we did here, such as ordering pizza and watching a romantic DVD. I visualise what used to be in her apartment. It makes it hard to let go and accept that I will no longer be coming back here.

Olivia finally finishes packing her life away and I hear the zip closing the suitcase. She then sits next to me on the bed.

We just stare at each other without exchanging words. I want to kiss her but our natural intimacy has gone. She feels like a stranger to me now.

I suddenly say to her. "I don't have any regrets. I don't regret responding to your message on the dating site. I don't regret going on our first date. I don't regret having my health check on your say so. I don't regret… falling in love with you. I especially don't regret losing my virginity to you."

Olivia sheds a tear as she listens to me. "I wish you weren't a millionaire. I wish you didn't have an influence on me. But I don't wish I didn't fall in love with you."

I smile at her. "If you need anything… someone to listen, a friend, a business partner. Just ask and… I'll be there."

Olivia tries not to smirk as she wipes her tears away. "I will miss you, Harvey. I promise I will buy your book.

And each one after that."

We linger into each other's eyes and I feel myself naturally gravitating towards her again. I go to kiss her and she reciprocates. As we go to kiss, the sound of a car horn beeps outside. The noise interrupts us and we lose the moment. Before walking out of her apartment for the last time I take one long look around, knowing I will never be coming back here again. Someone else will be living here. It is bare, lifeless and drab. It does not look like Olivia lived here. There is no trace of her presence.

I walk her out of the apartment for the last time, on to the street. I carry her suitcase with her life inside. The taxi driver is standing by his trunk to take her suitcase from me.

I want to go with her to the airport, but she wants to say goodbye on the kerb. She admitted to me that she would find it too hard to say goodbye to me at the airport. She would want to prise the doors open of the plane to stay with me.

When the taxi driver puts her suitcase inside the trunk, we stand there not knowing how to say goodbye. She shrugs her shoulder before uncontrollably hugging me. She hugs me for dear life. I respond, surprised, before I hug her with all my might. As we hug, I do not want to let go, just savour every second we hug. I do not want this moment to end. I hug her like I am a mayfly and I have to make the most of now before tomorrow never comes. I try to gain as much memory of her, such as the way she smells and her smile. I do not want the smell of her body to leave my clothes.

I feel Olivia is hesitantly letting go. I release her from my clutches for the last time. I watch her get into the back of the taxi.

Olivia cannot look at Harvey as she will want to pull the door apart. She did not realise how hard it would be to see him for the last time. She knows she is leaving for the right reason.

She starts to fight the tears back as the taxi drives away from the kerb. She rests her head against the door window, with her knees to her chest, uncontrollably crying. She cannot believe that she is leaving the first love of her life. She never told him that he is her first love.

Olivia knows that she needs to take the opportunity as she does not want to look back and think 'what if'. At first, she thought she could be a kept woman and live on her current salary. But Harvey showed her a glimpse of what life could be. She is too independent not to take the opportunity.

I do not take my eyes off Olivia's taxi as it drives down the road. There is a T junction at the bottom of the road. I wait for the taxi to reach the end of the road, see it stop to check for traffic, then turn left.

I find it hard to accept that I will never see her again. I just want to buy a private jet and fly to Miami. I feel that she has died and I am mourning for her. It is a strange feeling, knowing that she is still alive. My heart is pounding fast, like it wants to rip through my skin.

I find myself having to sit on the steps of her old apartment. I have an over whelming feeling of pain as I cry. My body gives way lets out all my emotions. I cannot stop crying, no matter how much I try and compose myself.

Olivia is still crying as she motions the taxi driver to keep going. She feels like Harvey has died and she is mourning him. Her body cannot contain her emotions, and she feels limp. For a brief moment, she thinks she has made a mistake.

I look down at the sidewalk wondering what I am going to do with my life now. I am single again and I feel that I have had a drug taken away from me; I am feeling the symptoms of withdrawal from being in a relationship. The drug is the relationship. I feel I need another fix in order to go back to how it felt having a girlfriend to share my life with. Someone to go home to every night.

I have the urge to go to the lake and sit under my tree again. I just want to be there now. I just want to teleport myself there.

I get in my car and drive fast with the image in my mind of the tree. I am surprised the groove of my bum is not on the trunk of the tree that protrudes from the dried dusty earth. I find myself driving faster the more I visualise the lake and the feeling I get when I am sat there. Once I get to the lake, I breathe a huge sigh of relief. I find myself uncontrollably crying as I wonder where Olivia could be. She does not want me to call her or text her as she wants to try to get over me. She said that just thinking of not seeing me ever again made her want to cry. I just want the pain to go away. I keep thinking about getting in the car and driving all the way to her new place and just making love to her and telling her that I am fine with giving up potential millions from the contract. But I also know that she would tell me off.

I sit at the lake for two hours just staring into the still calm water while I re-evaluate my life and picture how I think I want it to be. Can I really see myself living in Atlantic City and watching my book being turned into a live picture? Being there by myself, knowing no one and having no family close by. At the same time, I realise that I cannot be here. I have too many memories of Olivia and am reminded of her presence when I walk by the places we been together. I want the dull pain in the pit of my heart and stomach to go. I suddenly think about killing myself to get away from it all. I do not have Olivia, Helen was never to be and my family are content with their lives. The house is bought and paid for so I will not leave them with any debt, even though the mortgage would have been paid off after my death. I feel I have gone backwards now I am back by myself. I am no longer looking after Helen, so I cannot even use her as a distraction or a way of healing, emotionally.

I think about my financial affairs as I start to mentally plan my suicide. While I am thinking about it, I realise that all those months of sessions with the shrink were a waste of money. I still feel the same way as I did before I started therapy.

I consider walking into the lake and drowning myself. No one walks by there and so no one will try to save me or find my body anytime soon.

I suddenly think of getting my favourite bottle of wine before going to the lake. I can quickly go in to the house and grab my favourite expensive bottle of red Latour. I can relax and drink the bottle, taking my time to become drowsy. I can then walk into the lake and let myself drift off to sleep. I will not be able to take my own life sober. Also, I need to grab some pills from the pharmacist to make sure I do a good job.

As I plan my suicide, I think of my family's reaction, Olivia's and Helen's. Olivia will find out somehow. I will have to assume that Olivia will know that it is nothing she did. I do not want Olivia blaming herself unnecessarily. I will not be able to live with myself in the next world.

After going to the pharmacy and parking up outside the house, I go to the pool house for my wine. On the way, I see the gardener who saw me wanking off. We both startle each other, with me almost slipping up on the driveway's gravel. The gardener bolts off in a different direction to avoid me, almost walking into the hedge, head first.

Of all the things that could happen, while planning my suicide, I see the gardener. I imagine him at the lake watching me take my own life.

Once I get my bottle, I take my time walking to the lake. All I can think of is my past life, when I was bullied at school for being different and not being good at anything. It resonates as I feel I have found another thing I am not good at.

When I get to the lake, I sit by my favourite tree. I drink my wine direct from the bottle. I start to think about ending my life while I get through half the bottle. I start to feel drowsy but conscious of what I am thinking. I eventually finish the bottle, then stand close to the edge of the embankment. The ground is bone dry with brown dirt. I do not want to take my own life. I now know that my therapy has worked. Despite how bleak my life looks, I do not want to end it.

As I turn around to walk away from the edge, I slip and slide down the dry, dusty embankment into the water. I am fully submerged, gulping some of the lake water. I start coughing and spluttering as I reach the surface. I cling on to the exposed tree roots on the embankment. The tree roots are scraggly, long and thin. Luckily, the handful of roots I can grab are enough to hold my weight. I start to pull myself up, using my elbows to prevent myself from sliding back in. I am frantic as I struggle to get to the top.

I am soaked through and my two-hundred-dollar designer jeans are covered in a film of dirty, muddy, slimy water.
After getting over the shock, I briskly walk back home, feeling the sludge of water turning my legs, chest and back cold. I am just glad that I only live close by and can quickly run home. I decide to shower in the pool house so no one can see me. My clothes look like they are in disrepair so I decide to chuck them away. It feels good watching the mud flow down the plug hole. I shower three times, washing my face, ears and hair.

It is around nine o'clock and I feel achy and exhausted. I decide to go to bed without telling anyone. I feel a fever coming on. I lie in bed shivering but covered in sweat.

It has gone eleven o'clock the next morning, Saturday. Everyone is downstairs, either in the living room or kitchen, chilling out. Everyone has already eaten breakfast and is now allowing the food to settle. No one realises that Harvey has not come down. Harvey's mom asks if anyone has seen him and no one remembers. Harvey's mom, Lyra, goes to look for him in his bedroom to see if he has woken up. When she goes into Harvey's bedroom she sees her son under the duvet. She panics, thinking he is dead as his body looks lifeless. She rushes out and catches Chevalier walking in the corridor to his bedroom. She grabs him and goes back to Harvey's bedroom. Chevalier looks puzzled as he is grabbed, then fazed at what he is meant to be looking at in Harvey's bedroom.

Lyra's voice quivers. "Is he dead?"

Chevalier is not sympathetic. "Has he written a will? Bagsy I have his car."

Lyra looks at him with a screwed-up face. "Don't be so silly. Check he is alive. Prod him."

Chevalier hesitates at first and then gently moves the duvet away. I stir from my sleep as I feel my duvet moving.

I hear a loud voice say. "Aaaahhh! Damn it!"

It makes me jolt and I turn over, under the duvet and glare at Chevalier.

I still feel very ill and vaguely pick up on his comment about my car. "No, you will not have my car. I am ill. Think I am dying."

Chevalier recovers from the shock, breathing heavily. "Bloody hell. You scared the shit out of me."

Lyra asks me. "Are you feeling okay? I thought you were dead."

I quickly grab the bin by my bed and throw up ferociously. "I need the doctor. I think I am in a bad way."

Lyra thinks of Helen. "I will get Helen."

She is the last person I want. "No! No. Get me an ambulance."

Lyra sucks her tongue. "You are not dying. I will get Helen. She is a black doctor so I trust her."

I am too weak to argue back. "Whatever. Just get someone here now." I suddenly throw up again in the bin and then groan in pain.

Helen is at her parents' house still, as she has one more week before she goes back to work. She is in her childhood bedroom lying on the bed, drifting in between sleep and daydreaming about her wedding. She hears the doorbell go but does not move. She tries to listen in to her butler opening the door. All she can hear between her closed door and the floor boards, are two very faint muffling indistinct voices. She can make out her butler's voice, but she cannot work out what is being said. After a few seconds, she can hear her mother's faint muffled voice, but again cannot make out the conversation. Helen holds her breath so can hear the conversation more clearly but this does not make it easier. She is now intrigued as to who could be downstairs talking to her mom.

After a couple of minutes, Helen hears someone walk up the stairs and then knock on her door. Helen tells them to come in and sees that it is her mom. Her mom looks concerned and tells Helen that it is Harvey. Helen looks worried, thinking that something bad has happened to him. Martha tells her that Harvey's mom is downstairs and is asking for Helen to come over to check that Harvey is okay. Helen nods her head as if to say 'of course'. She quickly looks around for her medical bag that she keeps with her outside of work in case of emergencies like this.

I am drifting in and out of consciousness while intermittently throwing up and feeling that the only thing that can come out now is my intestine. I still have the shakes and sweats. I know I have a fever and I this is not good. Whatever I drank in the lake is disagreeing with my stomach. I would hate to think what is inside that lake.

When I am almost asleep, I sense that I am not alone in my room and suddenly jolt when I see four blurry bodies standing by the door. I wait for my vision to come into focus, before I can make out who they are. I eventually make out my mom, dad, Chevalier, Xavier and Helen. I am guessing Chevalier wants to see if his windfall has come in yet. Helen sits next to me as she puts her medical bag on the floor next to my bin full of sick. She glances at my bin as she tries not to gag and then looks at me. She smiles at me like I am a lost puppy and puts the back of her hand on my forehead. She frowns as she feels my forehead, as if I am one of her child patients. As she puts the thermometer in my mouth that she has got from her bag, I struggle to keep my eyes open as I am so sleep-deprived. I hear Helen ask that my parents and my brothers to leave the room. It does not sound good.

Helen has a worrying look on her face. "Harvey, I am not going to lie. You have a fever and your temperature is about hundred and twenty-five."

I shiver while asking. "Is that bad?"

Helen strokes my cheek with her index finger. "You could say that."

I stare at her with a quizzical look as to why she is stroking my face. "So, are you going to leave now?"

Helen has a sombre look while still stroking my face and in a quiet voice says. "No. You are sick. How can I leave you now? The first thing to do is get your temperature down. This is serious, if we don't get your temperature down, you could go into respiratory arrest. You could…die."

I feel my life is slipping away as I struggle to breathe normally. I try to keep my eyes open by focusing on Helen's beautiful face. I feel myself having shorter breathes as I say. "I am not afraid. I… I have nothing else that I want to achieve."

Helen looks right into my eyes, really into my eyes and can see where I am coming from. "Not on my shift. Now let me get to work."

Helen is almost tearful knowing that Harvey is in a bad way. This is not some flu or bug.
Helen stands up and walks out of his bedroom, where his family are waiting outside.

Helen tells Harvey family that she has to make a quick phone call about something she forgot. She tells them that she will be downstairs for a brief moment. She says this as she does not want to alarm them of Harvey potential life threatening illness, without a second opinion.

She is really calling her boss for an opinion based on her observations. She wants to have a private conversation without Harvey family over hearing.

Once she knows she is alone and away from prying ears, her hands start to shake as she calmly dials her boss's cellular phone. She whispers to herself, telling her boss to pick up. Just as she thinks the dial will ring out, her boss picks up her cellular phone. Under her breath, she thanks God. Her boss has a quizzical voice, wondering why Helen is calling.

Helen quickly tells her boss about Harvey's temperature and his irregular shallow breathing which gives her concern for his life. Her boss takes in what she is saying and concurs that she is not overexaggerating and was right to call. Her boss suggests calling an ambulance to bring him in and they will get a crash team ready if he arrests. The realisation suddenly kicks in when she gets a second opinion from her boss.

The sound of the sirens from the ambulance can be heard in the distance. Helen has already briefed Harvey's family who went from finding it humorous that Harvey was sick, to seeing that his illness is life-threatening. His mom is struggling to take it in. She saw her son just being sick and thought a simple prescription would sort the matter out. Now it has gone beyond ordering a simple prescription.

When the ambulance finally arrives, Helen briefs them with Harvey's latest vitals, as they get Harvey out of bed and on to a stretcher. They put a breathing mask on to help with his breathing. Helen gets into the back of the ambulance with Harvey and talks through with him what is happening.

Helen is worried now as it is starting to sink in that this is serious.

When they arrive at the hospital where she works, she helps the paramedics get Harvey out of the back of the ambulance and rush him inside. Her boss is already there, expecting Helen to be with the paramedics. Once the handover is made, her boss checks Harvey's pupils and then suggests putting in a cannula to add fluids. Her boss thinks there is more to it and suggests running a few tests to see if there is more to it than a simple fever. Helen goes along with her boss and says that she will organise that.

Harvey became unconscious during the journey to the hospital.

A few hours later, the test results come back and Helen's boss walks into Harvey's room where Helen has been sat by his bedside all this time. She has been dozing in and out of sleep, trying to stay awake to see if there is any change in him. Helen hears her boss walk into the room and quickly sits up. As her boss is about to tell her something, she stands up and walks around Harvey's bed to stand next to her. Her boss tells her that from the blood tests, that Harvey has an amoeba, which is a shape-changing cell. Harvey will have to take nitroimidazole drugs by mouth or directly into his veins. As Harvey is still unconscious, it will have to be injected directly into his veins. The drug will kill the amoeba in his blood, the wall of his intestine and his liver abscesses. Helen is told that he is very lucky to catch it in time as it could have travelled to his brain and caused brain damage and even death.

Helen is in shock and does not know what to think. She turns around to look at Harvey thinking that she could have lost him. Her boss already has the drug with her and injects it into his vein. This has to be given for ten days so Harvey will have to stay in hospital until the course of injections is complete. It will take no less than ten days to recover.

Helen chooses to stay by his bedside for the next ten days. Harvey's family came soon after he was admitted to hospital. Visiting hours finished at seven o'clock in the evening and so his family have already gone home. Helen has privileges and so the visiting hours do not apply. She wants to be here so Harvey has someone to wake up to.

Two days later, Harvey finally comes around to find himself alone. He rubs his eyes feeling slightly weak. Helen soon walks into the room with a hot drink. Helen is upset that she was not there when he woke up.

I am glad to see someone. "How did I get here?"

Helen sits in the chair next to my bed. "I wanted to be here when you woke up."

I don't think she heard my question. "How did I get here?"

Helen recaps. "You were burning up and I called for a second opinion. The next thing, I called for an ambulance. You had passed out by then."

I wonder how long I have been asleep. "How long was I out for?"

Helen thinks back. "About two days. You were lucky. You had an amoeba. If we hadn't caught it in time, it would have travelled to your brain and you would have died."

I am not fazed by her story. "Interesting. So why are you here?"

Helen asks me a question. "Where is Olivia? Does she know you are here?"

I feel embarrassed. "We finished."

Helen feels awkward. "What? When did this happen?"

I cannot look at her. "A week ago. She left town last Friday."

Helen cannot believe it. "But you were so good together. I assumed she was the one."

I change the subject. "So why are you here? Don't you have a wedding to plan?"

Helen is still thinking of Olivia. "You spent all that time looking after me. It is time to return the favour."

I do not like being fussed over. "You do not have to do this. You should be resting yourself from your operation."

Helen leans forward and puts her fingers on my lips. "Shut up. My wedding is already sorted. I thought I was going to lose you."

I wish I was somewhere else. "I don't know what the fuss is about. It is not like I have someone waiting for me."

Helen remembers what I said two days ago. "What about your family?"

I think of them having their own families. "They have each other."

Helen cannot imagine not having Harvey in her life. "What about me?"

I look at her. "Once you are married, you will be too busy to see me. So, you would not notice if I was not around."

Helen thinks about what I just said and does not want to believe me. She wants both Rob and Harvey in her life. She can see the pain behind Harvey's eyes as she watches him turn over to face away from her. She feels affected by his behaviour and reminded of what she went through when she was blind.

I feel like crying, because I have no one to care for me. I am dreading spending the rest of my life alone. I should have let myself drown in that lake.
Over the next few days in hospital, my strength gradually comes back. Helen did not leave my bedside, despite my moans and groans. I tried to make myself hate her, but her kindness overshadows this. I want to hate her because I am falling in love with her all over again.

She always tucks me in at night time and is not shy brushing herself against me. I cannot help smelling her body each time she brushes past me. I find her more attractive than before I met Olivia.

I feel guilty fancying someone else just a week after

finishing with Olivia but Helen is not a new person that I love. I have loved her all my life. She has no idea how much she means to me.

It is my last day in hospital. I feel a lot better. I have had my last blood test and the amoeba has completely left my body. As I finish changing into my clothes, Helen comes in.

She signs my bill of health and seems to want to hang around. I ask if she is looking forward to getting married, as it is just around the corner. She does not have any excitement behind her eyes. Not the excitement when I took her to the opera. I do not question her or make her feel uncomfortable.

I now realise that it is time I left Los Angeles and start a new life in Atlantic City so I will savour every last moment until I leave. I have decided to just leave quietly. No party or big band send off. I just want to leave before anyone knows I left. I will properly say goodbye to my shrink and my sister, Mercedes.

CHAPTER SIXTEEN

Flying the Coop

It is the second week of July. I plan on leaving the city at the end of next week, spending two weeks travelling and staying in Lake Tahoe. Then after the first week of August, I will spend a week in Atlantic City to oversee the final draft of the television script.

I have another appointment with my shrink. I turn up to see my shrink for the last time. When he opens the door, he can see it in my eyes. He smiles, almost chuckling to himself, before letting me walk into his office.

Before I sit down, I slowly spin round, taking one last look. My shrink is already sat in his chair.

I calmly tear up and say. "I broke up with Olivia. I went to the lake on the intention of killing myself. But for a brief second."

My shrink asks. "So, what happened?"

I tell him. "I turn around and fall backwards into the lake anyway. Caught a bug. But I was ready to die. I was not afraid. I am not suicidal anymore. You fixed me."

My shrink has a sombre look. "I know… I know. What have you been up to since I last saw you?"

I start from the beginning. "Helen got her eyesight back. Olivia has moved to Miami to achieve what she always wanted to do – run her own practice. Oh, and I nearly forgot, I nearly died, twice. Falling in the lake and getting a life-threatening illness."

My shrink is open-mouthed as he listens. "Huh, so you have been busy. How are you holding up?"

I scoff. "Under the circumstances, I am bearing up. I realise I am still in love with Helen. She forced herself on me. NOT like that. She helped me to recovery. She came over every day, without fail. I even risked showing her my erection a couple of times, when I found myself getting aroused by presence and bedside manner."

My shrink smirks. "That's the tapestry of life. You are now living it. What will you do now?"

I clear my throat. "I am going to take that deal. One more mill won't hurt. Helen's dad interfered and turned my deal from six hundred thousand to ten million. Over five years. I was upset at first."

My shrink's jaw drops. "Can you spare me some I helped indirectly… seriously, good for you… good for you. So, are you going to tell Helen?"

I have a blank face. "What, tell her I love her? No way."

My shrink's face is deadpan. "Closure, Harvey. I will tell you, you will regret it."

I think about it. "Maybe."

My shrink changes the subject. "So, for our final meeting, what do you want to talk about? It can be anything."

I wonder why some people find it easy to fall into a relationship whenever it suits them. "I don't understand why people can just easily meet a girlfriend or boyfriend. Why can't everyone meet their partner just like that?"

My shrink is honest. "I don't have the answer."

I am frustrated. "Why can't I have what they have? Why can't I be like them? Find it easy to meet that person."

My shrink shrugs his shoulders. "Again, I don't have the answer. You will meet someone. I promise."

I use examples. "I see poor people, ill people, addicted people all in relationships. Do I have to be like them to get a relationship? I would give up everything I have just to be with someone. All I wanted in this world was to be in a relationship. I did not work to own my house outright, become rich. I only do what I do because I enjoy it. It is a hobby. I did not do it to try to get a girlfriend."

My shrink looks unable to give me an answer. "You

think that a person who falls in and out of love is happy? Listen to Ivan Neville. He says it best. When you next see a couple, focus on their flaws. You will realise that no one is happy. Unless you choose to work at it. Do you think drug abusers are working at their relationship?"

The penny drops. "So, what about people like Rob. They sleep around and still have their girl."

My shrink cuts me short. "No. She had to go to you for help. Have you thought about how that made her feel? She has this wonderful man, but he can't change a few shifts to be by her side. Trust me, his employer would have given him all the time in the world to be with Helen. Rob chose to stay away from her."

I question. "So, do you think he will eventually change?"

My shrink pauses. "You have heard the story about the frog and the scorpion."

I give a curious look. "Yeah?"

My shrink still tells the story. "A scorpion's nature is to sting anyone in his sight. It is the way God made them. Now the scorpion thinks he can change if he is out of his surroundings and needs help. Well, let's say Rob is the scorpion. The frog is Helen. Helen has reached a junction in her life. Rob is the same, hence the proposal. The frog is at the edge of this huge pond. There are no other routes to get round the pound. So, the frog has to go across the pond to get to the other side. Helen has no choice but to commit to Rob, as there is nothing else to fall back on. Rob is like the scorpion; no one else wants him. Every whore in town has been with him, and you think these women don't talk. So, the scorpion turns to the frog for a piggyback. The frog says, 'You must be joking. Halfway across, you will sting me'. The scorpion says, 'You are the only person I have. I am not going to screw that up'. The frog thinks about it and knows both will drown. The scorpion even says, 'I will not allow myself to drown'. So, Helen says yes to marriage. Halfway into the marriage – pond – Rob cheats on her. Helen screams, 'Why? You asked me to marry you'. Rob turns around. 'I am sorry, it is in my nature'."

I get it now. "So, Rob is not aware of his nature."

My shrink smiles. "Exactly. He can't change just because he is married. Just like the scorpion being on the pond. Time's up. You are now free. When do you have to leave?"

I think about my itinerary. "I head to Atlantic City. I always wanted to go to Lake Tahoe. It's on the way. Thought I would cruise the motels along the way. I will spend four weeks travelling. A week in Lake Tahoe."

My shrink has a curious look on his face. "Why Lake Tahoe?"

I think about a film I saw with Meg Ryan. "I saw a film once."

My shrink is ready to let me go. "So. If you need anything. Someone to spend your millions on, here is my card. You can call anytime. And I will be there."

I stand up and go over to shake his hand. The shrink stands up to meet me in the middle and looks at my hand, then at eye level, back to my hand and hugs me. In a quiet and comforting voice, he says. "You're welcome. You're welcome. You're welcome."

I cannot stop crying. "Thank you. Thank you."

It takes me a while to compose myself and finish off the details of what my plans are. The shrink wants to come and see me once I settle there and have a tour around the studio where my book will be adapted for television and eventually, into a film. I tell him about the access I will be allowed at the studio and that I will be treated like royalty. The shrink looks amazed and impressed with what I tell him.

The shrink has his next appointment and so he shakes my hand. "You didn't give me time to get a cake and balloons."

I chuckle at his comment. "Maybe next time. Oh, by the way I hope you don't mind but I gave a friend called Helen your card. She totally recovered from her car accident but she has no memory as to why she was out driving that night. I said that you would be able to do hypnotism to recall her memory."

The shrink is more than happy. "No problem. What is her name again?"

I quickly tell him. "Helen. She is the doctor who I was looking after for three months. The one I fancied for years."

The shrink frowns. "Ah, yes. The one you still fancy. The one you won't tell that you still fancy."

I laugh off his last comment and leave his office. As I walk out of the door, his next client walks in and the door is shut. I overhear the client gasping and asking if 'that is the author'. I can guess the shrink is nodding his head with a sigh. I take one more look at his reception before leaving for the last time. It feels like this place was my second home. A year and half later, I am now fixed. I am ready to go out into the big wide world.

My next point of call is to see Helen at her place of work, where she looked after me. I feel anxious as I do not know what to say and without her knowing I am leaving tonight.

I do want to make an announcement that I am leaving. I just want to slope off, undetected.

When I have seen Helen, I will get my car back and drive to Atlantic City. I will leave my new car at the house, for anyone to have. I will keep my designer clothes, now I am used to wearing them and they were not cheap.

When I get to the Ronald Reagan UCLA Medical Centre, I ask at reception which floor Helen Simms works on. I then go to look for her.

After about ten minutes, I spot her doing her ward rounds. I get her attention where her eyes light up with joy to see me.

Once she has finished her round, she smiles at me as she walks over to me.

I feel nervous as I say. "I came to see how you are. I have been a little busy. I just wanted to say that I am going away for a few days. A short break."

Helen looks taken aback. "How long are you going away for? Where are you going? Who are you taking?"

I feel like I am being judged and so I am defensive. "I am just going away for a short break. I haven't had a proper break this year. Nothing exciting. I am going across state."

Helen is really pushy. "How long you going away for? I can't believe you did not mention to me first. You are going to be back in time for my wedding next month? First Saturday in August."

I feel like we are boyfriend and girlfriend. "I didn't think you would be interested in knowing what my whereabouts are. Yes, of course I will be back in time for that. I am only going away for a couple of weeks."

Helen is focused on her wedding day. "You are going to be back in time for my wedding, right" So, that leaves only a couple of days before my wedding."

I am flustered and lie. "It is just a couple of weeks. I will be back Friday day."

Helen relaxes. "That's cool. I cannot imagine you not being there."

I do not feel that my presence will make her day any different. "Don't panic. I will be there."

Helen looks relieved. "Good. Because… you mean something to me… not like that obviously… but I feel that we have formed more than just a normal relationship. I consider you my best friend. You almost gave me a panic attack."

I have no idea why she is being like this. "I guess I had better get going. I haven't seen you in days and so I thought I would come in to let you know… before you get married. Because you are going to be… really busy, what with the honeymoon and then settling into married life."

Helen is quick to reassure me. "You do know that

nothing will change between us. We will still hang out on a regular basis. You are not going to get rid of me that quickly."

As we both look at each other, I study her face as I know this will be the last time I see her. I want to remember her face in detail as I am scared I will forget her. She looks at me anxiously. She has to hurry back to her work. I wait till she is out of sight, so I can just savour one more look at her. I do not plan on seeing her ever again.

My next stop is to get my old car back. When I get to the dealership, I look around to see if it is on their forecourt and cannot find it. I am nervous walking in and wondering what they will think of me asking for my car back. I see the same salesman who sold me the Mercedes and thought I was broke.

I walk up to his desk and stand there, waiting to get his attention. He is looking at his paperwork before he notices that I am standing in front of his desk. When he looks up, I see he recognises me and I can see that his mind is wondering how he knows me. Then the penny drops when his face lights up, then slumps. He must be thinking that I am returning the car or going to make a complaint. I explain to him that everything is fine and ask if the car is still here or auctioned or sent to the junk yard. He says that they have been busy and have not had a chance to dispose of it. It is round the back, parked outside their service garage. I explain to him that I want the car back, despite having the Mercedes and he does not find it weird. I am surprised by his reaction.

He walks me round the back and we make idle chat. He mentions that he has started reading one the early books I wrote as a child, then tweaked in adulthood. He asks if I would sign the book and I naturally say yes. The book happens to be in his desk drawer. Once I have a look over the car I notice they have cleaned and valeted it in preparation of selling it. I am pleased with the finish.

We go inside to sort out the paperwork and he says that

it will not selling it back to me. His reason is because I had spent so much money on the new car. I check with him to make sure he is okay with that. He says it is fine, if I sign his book. I wait for him to get it out and I ask what he wants me to write. Once he tells me, I write down word for word what he asked and sign it with a different signature, for security reasons. I ask if one of his staff could drive my Mercedes back to my house while I drive my Chevy back home.

On the way home, I am reminded quite quickly how uncomfortable this car is as I go over the bumps in the road. It is not that comfortable after having driven my new car for almost four months. However, this is my first car and I will just keep safe somewhere once I arrive in Atlantic City. I will have to arrange somehow to get my other car over at a later date. I feel that I need to drive Chevy down to Atlantic City as that is my gut feeling.

While driving back, I think about when the production will start. I was told that they will start filming sometime in August. At the moment, they are getting the scripts finalised for me to review and then the actors will start reading to familiarise themselves with the story. I want to be there for that. I then start thinking what I have to pack and how many suitcases I will have to take with me. When I get there, I have to find a place to rent, or even buy. What with waiting for Olivia to leave and getting ill, I have not had time to properly plan a place to stay. The people at the studio are not going to lay out a red carpet for me, with a lavish apartment and chauffeur driven car. Not after what Bill did tearing up their original contract.

As I drive into Groveton Place, I remember that I want to give Helen's mom a letter. I did not want to give the letter to Helen at the hospital, because if she wanted to read it in front of me I would have been embarrassed. I will give her mom the letter on the way out to Atlantic City.

Under the circumstances, I feel upbeat and happy. I

think it is to do with getting my book made into a television series and that will be a huge distraction from breaking up with Olivia and realising I am still in love with Helen. I feel on a high.

As I approach my home, I see that everyone is home and wonder where everyone is in the house. I plan on going straight upstairs to my room to start packing. I will then sneak out without anyone noticing. When I get to my first stop off, I will text one of my brothers that I have left.

After parking up and getting to the front door, I quietly let myself in and see if anyone is walking by in the reception area between the kitchen and the stairs. No one is around and so I quickly run upstairs to my bedroom and shut the door behind me. Phew, I did not run into any of my family.

I grab a suitcase from on top of my wardrobe and chuck it on the bed. I then think about what I need to pack, such as toiletry and underwear. I then think about how I am going to fit in all my clothes that I bought back in April. I hear the bedroom door open as I finish packing my suitcase. It is my sister, Mercedes, who goes to sit on the end of my bed. I start to feel solemn and it suddenly hits me. I have nothing here to keep me. If this business deal did not happen, I would be here, reminded of Olivia not living here anymore and Helen being married. I start to feel sad again, wondering if I will ever meet anyone. I stare at my sister, wondering why she has come into my room.

Mercedes looks like she is worried for me. "Are you going somewhere?"

I am honest. "I got a business deal a few weeks ago. It is in Atlantic City."

Mercedes asks what the deal was. "To write more books?"

I casually say. "To turn one of my series of books into a television series. Worth around ten mills."

Mercedes' jaw drops. "You made a deal for ten million

dollars?"

I do not feel remotely excited. "Yeah. It does not mean anything now. I do not have anyone to share it with."

Mercedes does not know how to respond so she looks inside my suitcase. "Is that all you are packing? It doesn't seem a lot."

I am a bit snappy. "I have money! Sorry. I can buy new things when I get there."

Mercedes is intrigued as to how long I am staying in Atlantic City. "So, how long are you going away for? You are going to come back for Helen's wedding, right? We got our invitation through today. You got a separate one to the rest of us. You must have made an impression."

I tell her, 2I am not going. I... the thought of watching her get married..."

Mercedes suddenly gets it. "You are in love with her. That is why you are leaving."

I look at my sister and she can see in my eyes how much I love Helen. "Once the books are turned into a television series I think I will go for a walk about. I am thinking New York."

Mercedes can see that I do not plan on coming back. "So, do you think you will ever come back?"

I check my gut feelings. "Probably not. There is nothing for me here."

Once I zip up my suitcase, I am ready to leave. Mercedes walks with me downstairs where I see everyone by the door. They are all looking at me as I walk down the stairs. I wonder why they are all huddled in the reception area by the front door. I feel like I am being ambushed. I try to ignore my family while I walk to the door to leave. My mom goes to say something.

My mom gives me a concerned look. "I know things have not gone right. You are the only one who never flew the coop. I don't want you to come back. Not until you find happiness."

I ask my mom. "Do you see me getting married?"

My mom is honest. "You will come home one day,

married with a child."

I wish I could believe her. I look at everyone else and then take my time to leave the house to go to my shitty blue Chevy. I have my life in one suitcase. I think of everyone in my life, having what I always wanted. I thought writing stories to entertain people's minds, would be enough. But a career, money is not enough. A career and money do not give you comfort or make you feel loved. I would give up all my millions if I could be guaranteed love for eternity.

Before I head out of town I stop off at Martha and Bill's house to give the letter. I decided to write a letter to let Helen know my true feelings. It is my way of having closure and her finally realising I love her. I know it will make no difference, not that I am hoping for anything.

I ring the doorbell for the last time and the butler answers. He calls for Martha and asks how I am. I play it down, saying that work is busy.

I have the letter in my jean pocket. I feel comfortable and confident passing over the letter. I have it sealed in an envelope clearly marked for Helen.

Martha comes out to reception. She smiles when she sees me. I smile back, waiting for the right time to give the letter. She naturally tells me that Helen is not here. I tell her that I know and I am here to see her. She looks curious to why and that is then that I give her the letter.

Martha looks confused as to why I am giving her a letter. I explain that it is something I want Helen to know. I explain that I want her to read it later. She questions why I am giving it to her. I lie by telling her that I am leaving town for a couple of weeks, in case Helen mentions it to her mother. I do not explain that it says I will not be coming back. She takes it and tells me she will leave it in Helen's bedroom. She asks me if it is something that she should be worried about. I reassure her it that it is nothing exciting.

Bill comes out into reception to see me. I feel that

something is not quite right. They ask me to come into the living room and offer me a drink. As I have a long drive ahead of me, I tell them that I will have a coffee.

Bill tells me to take a seat. "How have you been?"

I look at them both opposite me. "Okay?"

Bill rests his back against the sofa. "You and my daughter have got quite close these past couple of months. You have been treating my daughter better than her boyfriend. Sorry, fiancé."

Martha looks serious. "I sense that you care about our daughter very much."

I feel like they are warning me off her. "I am actually moving away. I am leaving tonight. I am looking at starting a new life in… actually, New York."

Bill is shocked. "I thought you were heading to Atlantic City? You have your production."

I am planning to stay in Atlantic city to review the script and once I am happy, then shoot down to New York. "I am going to Atlantic City to see that they get the script right. Once the script is finalised, there is no need to be in Atlantic City."

Martha looks worried. "But you are going to be at the wedding? We were hoping to interject."

I am confused now, as I thought they wanted me to stay away from the wedding. "You want to stop the wedding?"

Bill has cool, calm and collected body language. "We can't stand the man. Since you arrived on the scene, alarm bells started going off. Helen has been at her happiest since you came on the scene. You were just meant to help her see through the last three months before the operation. You did more than that. You made her smile, which she has not done in a long time."

Martha jumps in. "What my husband is trying to say is that we would rather have you as our son-in-law. Bill, I can see it now. Can you?"

I have no idea what they see that I cannot. "I don't know what you mean."

Bill smiles. "Yes, I can."

Martha is frank. "You are in love with her. You love our daughter. I can see it in your eyes. Each time we mention her name, your eyes light up."

I feel my throat going dry and swallow. "Ah ah ah. Yeah, right. Don't get me wrong, she is sweet, but no. I have just finished with Olivia."

Bill leans forward. "You have been in love with her long before you met Olivia. You and Olivia belonged to each other but she is out of the picture now. Your feelings for Helen are not new or abnormally formed within days of losing Olivia. You have buried them and just forgotten they existed."

I feel I have been caught with my hands in the cookie jar. "Hypothetically, if I did have feelings for Helen, I cannot get involved in stopping her getting married. I would always be wondering 'what if'. Did I do the right thing? I am really better than him? I would feel I was no better than him."

Bill looks disappointed. "What if we interject? We leave you out of it. Would you consider being her partner? We are not saying marriage. We are open-minded. Just so long as she is with someone that will make her happy."

I do not feel comfortable with the whole idea. "Helen has my cellular. She has her own mind. If she wants to be with me, she will naturally find me. The truth is, I liked your daughter since elementary school. She never noticed me all the way up to university. It took her to go blind to notice me. Even then, you intervened. She would never have met me. And why now? At what point were you going to have this conversation?"

Bill stands up and paces around. "We were going to come over to your house tomorrow. It is just as well you came over here, as we would have missed you. Look, this guy is the only man she has ever been with. She doesn't know any better."

I mention my suspicions. "Helen cannot remember why she was driving that night. She was meant to be doing a normal night shift. She cannot understand why she would leave in the middle of her shift. Laterally thinking, you would only leave your job for three reasons and one them is a bit farfetched."

Martha is keen to know. "So, why did she have that accident?"

I reluctantly say. "The first is a family emergency. Now, from what I have gathered, there was no family emergency. The second is a daughter or son in trouble. She does not have kids… yet. The third… the third is if you were prewarned that your partner was having an affair and you wanted to catch them in the act."

Bill is still pacing about when he looks at Martha. "Being a lawyer, reading people is part of the job. He looks guilty as hell. I told you, Martha, that I thought it was odd him suddenly wanting to get married. It was guilt. It was a panic reaction."

Martha asks me. "Can you prove that he has been cheating on our daughter? So, we can show her?"

I have one suggestion. "In that envelope is a card. That card is to a shrink that I used to see. He does hypnotherapy. If anyone can tell her what happened that night, he can. Now I have a three-hour drive before I hit the first motel."

Martha thanks me in person for everything I have done for Helen. Bill says that if I need anything not to hesitate to call him. Bill and Martha end up hugging me and I feel that they see me as family now.

As I am driving through Los Angeles for the last time, heading towards Route 395, I find myself tearing up, knowing that Helen's family wanted me to be their son-in-law. They like me that much. I suddenly have a song playing in my head that sums up how I am feeling right now.

The song is about a person who is sitting in a corner of a night club. The person has feelings for someone who they can see on the dance floor. The person on the dance floor is with someone else and they are kissing each other.

I am the person sitting in the corner looking at a woman on the dance floor. I am watching her kissing another man. I can be clearly seen but I cannot understand why she cannot see me. I am able to give her all I have and what she wants but I am not the guy she wants. I find myself dancing on my own. The dance floor is Los Angeles. The corner of Los Angeles is my house.

It is a seven and half hour drive to Lake Tahoe. I left Helen parents' house just after seven o'clock in the evening and so I will find a motel or hotel when it is close to ten o'clock. That will leave four and a half hours left of driving tomorrow. I will look to get to Lake Tahoe by lunchtime. I will take the risk of finding accommodation when I get there.

CHAPTER SEVENTEEN

Regrets

Helen finishes her last night shift at seven o'clock in the morning on Tuesday, four days before her wedding day. She goes straight home, showers and then goes to bed. She is struggling to go to sleep as her mind is swimming with thoughts of her wedding day and keeps thinking she is missing something. She lies awake staring at the ceiling.

It has been almost two weeks since Harvey left. Helen has been counting the days when Harvey comes back from his break away. She has been wanting to text or call him, but she did not want to disturb his time away. She has not stopped thinking of him since he left. She cannot understand why he keeps popping into her head so often. She still cannot believe that she pictured him when she made love to Robert on the living room floor that day. She feels like a school kid, embarrassingly giggling to herself about it. To her, it feels like he has passed away and she is remembering the good times she had with him. She keeps reminding herself that he has only gone away for two weeks.

Helen and Robert finished all the wedding plans last week and she has done everything by herself. The only thing Robert was involved in was the wedding venue for the ceremony and reception. He seemed to lose interest in the wedding cake and catering. She could understand about the flower arrangements and invitation cards as that is too girlie for a man but she thought about what Harvey would have been like. She could imagine Harvey getting involved in everything, including being present for everything. She hates herself for comparing Robert to Harvey, as if she is putting Robert down.

Helen looks at the time and it is now ten o'clock in the morning. She went to bed at eight thirty. She decides to get out of bed and go into the living room to watch junk television. She remembers that her carer is coming to the wedding as well. She sent her an invitation. She couldn't not have Florence there, after all she has done for her. Helen is glad that Florence can make the wedding. Florence phoned her soon after getting the invitation and asked Helen how she has been since getting her eyesight back and how Harvey has been. Helen felt embarrassed having to say that she has not seen much of Harvey since getting her eyesight back. Florence jokes, saying that she saw more of him when she was blind than when she regained her eyesight. Helen found the comment funny but at the same time it made her feel guilty. Helen knows that Florence was right about abandoning him once she gained her eyesight back but to be fair, he had Olivia at the time and she did not want to cause any trouble.

While switching channels, she gets bored and cannot find a channel of interest. She cannot stop thinking about Harvey and decides to go to his office see if he has come back. She does not want to phone or text him as she does not know if he is still on his break away. If she sees him at the office, then she knows that he is back from holiday. Also, if she saw him she could ask him what he did when he was away. She would rather see him in person instead of talking on the cellular. She does not want to go to his house as she feels that his family will get suspicious, her coming round to see him when she is meant to be focused on her wedding so she goes to 5900 Wilshire Building where she knows his office is.

Once she arrives at the office, she goes to reception to find out which floor his office is on. She has never had a reason to go to his office before. The man at reception, who looks like a security guard, looks on his computer to see what floor his office is on. He then tells Helen to take the lift to the twenty-fifth floor. Once she gets to the twenty-fifth floor, she sees a female receptionist sat there. She walks up to her to ask where Harvey's office is. As she is about to approach the desk, Chevalier notices her and gets her attention. Helen hears her name and looks in the direction of the voice and sees Chevalier. She smiles at him with delight in her eyes and goes over to him to ask where Harvey is, instead of asking the receptionist. Chevalier looks confused as he assumed that Harvey told her that he was leaving town. He is wondering why she has come to his office.

Chevalier does not know how to react. "Hi, Helen. What are you doing here?"

Helen remembers Chevalier from the barbecue. "Oh, hi. Where is Harvey's office? I wanted to see if he is back from his two-week break."

Chevalier looks perplexed. "Harvey has left. I assumed that he told you."

Helen is shocked. "He came to the hospital to tell me that he was going away for a couple of weeks. He said he would be back day or so before my wedding."

Chevalier feels awkward. "He did not go on break."

Helen suddenly feels lost. "But he told me he was only going away for a few weeks."

Chevalier walks her to Harvey's old office to show that it is empty apart from his desk and chair. Also, to sit her down while he goes away to get her coffee. "There you go. He said to us that he was going to go away and that he would text us when he was settled. We were expecting a text by now. Haven't you texted or called him?"

Helen says. "I didn't want to disturb his vacation. I thought that he was having his break away. I think I need to call him now. He said he was going to be at my wedding. He has to be there."

Chevalier sees Helen welling up. "Are you okay? Is everything okay… at… home?"

Helen looks up and back at Chevalier. "It is okay. I think all the wedding planning and work is getting to me.

It is nothing. It's just I was looking forward to seeing him. Find out how his trip away went."

Chevalier finds it strange that she is like this over a friend. "Is there someone I can call? Do you want me to drive you home?"

Helen stands up, not touching her coffee. She eventually says no. Before she leaves, she notices how bare Harvey's office looks. There is nothing in the office like paperwork, telephone, computer or pictures. The look of his office makes her realise that Chevalier is right. There is no sign of his life in the office. It looks clinical. Helen eventually leaves, thanking Chevalier for his assistance and decides to go back home.

While Helen is driving home, the thought of being in the apartment alone does not comfort her. For some reason, she feels that she needs to go to her parents' house. She phones her mom to ask if she can speak to her and tells her that she is on her way to their house. Her mom is at work and feels that Helen sounds upset on the phone. Her mom arranges to meet her at their house as soon as she can leave work. Luckily, her day is not back to back with patients and so she finishes work early.

Helen is keen to speak to her mom and so she wants to get to her parents' house as quick as possible.

She does not know why Harvey has such an effect on her. She does not see him as anything else other than a friend. But she cannot stop thinking about him and the thought of never seeing him again. She feels that she needs to speak to her mom Martha to work out why she has these weird feelings. She does not have any friends that she can comfortably discuss this with. She cannot understand either why she is tearful about it and does not know where it is coming from.

When she gets to her parents' house, she decides to wait in the car until her mom comes home. She does not feel comfortable alone in the house and would rather be sat in the car.

Eventually, Martha drives up to the house and Helen gets out of her car to walk over to her car. She waits for her mom to get out of her car and then she starts to cry and Martha is worried for her. Her mom quickly gives her a hug as Helen cries into her shoulder. After a few minutes, Martha takes her inside and gets her a drink, a spirit, and they sit in the living room. Helen finally talks to her.

She looks at her mom with lost eyes. "I found out that Harvey has left town. I don't know what is wrong with me. I went to his office thinking that he would be back by now. I saw his brother Chevalier and when he told me he is not coming back, I had this overwhelming feeling of upset. I don't get it."

Martha knows that her daughter has feelings for Harvey. "He came around to the house the day he was leaving. He gave me a letter to give to you. He felt he couldn't give it to you as you were at work."

Helen looks bewildered. "Where is the letter?"

Martha remembers putting it in her bedroom. "I put it on your bedside drawer. I totally forgot about it. I was expecting you to come over in the next few days."

Helen is anxious to read it. "Can I go and get it?"

Martha says. "Of course. It is your letter. I'll walk up with you."

They both walk up the stairs together to her bedroom to retrieve the letter. When they go inside her bedroom, Helen feels that she wants to read the letter alone. She asks her mom to go outside so she can be alone when reading what he has written. Martha walks out and closes the door behind her, but she stays by the door. She tries to listen through the door for her daughter's reaction to the letter.

Helen sits on the side of her bed before she picks up the envelope. She sits there for a moment just staring at it, frozen. As she is staring at the envelope she notices it is a peachy cream colour. Her name is written in the centre, scribbled on. She picks it up and smells the envelope first, as a way of determining if there is some kind of expectation of a scent. She closes her eyes to get a better idea if there is a scent on the envelope. She cannot smell anything. She then nervously opens the envelope carefully, so as not to ruin the envelope itself.

Once she gets the letter out, she notices that the letter is folded three ways, width wise like a business letter. It is a A4 printed letter. When she unfolds it, she notices that there are two A4 sheets and a business card falls out. She picks it up and sees that it has a name and the word 'psychotherapist' on it. Her mind goes blank and ignores it by putting on the bedside drawer. There are two and half sides of typed lettering. Helen scans the letter at first to see if he gave an address of where he is living now. She cannot find any known address and he did not even put his old address at the top of the letter. Now she is ready to read the letter, she starts having palpitations as she psyches herself up to read it. She cannot understand why she is so nervous. It is only a letter from one friend to another.

She starts to read the letter.

"Dear Helen

Where do I start? By the time you read this letter, I will have left the city to start a new life. I did not want to tell you face to face that I am leaving for good. I did not want to be talked out of leaving. I wanted to see your face one last time before I left. I did not want to tell you that I was leaving at the hospital, because I knew you would be rushed off your feet and I did not want to make a scene.

I want to wish you every bit of happiness in your marriage. I hope that you have a great day. Thank you for inviting my family on your special day. I received the invitation while writing this letter in my office at home. As you well know, I finished with Olivia a little after a week after you gained your eyesight back. As a result, I came to realise that I have no reason to stay in Los Angeles. You no longer need looking after and you are marrying your long-term sweet heart. As for me, I have nothing left here to stay for.

I managed to sign a television deal, thanks to your dad who came in the eleventh hour. It is a real great deal. A deal that I could not turn down. So, by the time you read this letter, I will have driven to my new life, watching my series of books get turned into TV. I never told you what I did for a living.

The second thing is that I never explained why I fell in the lake. I was going there to end my life when I suddenly realised that I was no longer suicidal. Thanks to a man I was seeing for help. That is why you see a card with the name of my shrink. I would like you to go and see him to find out what happened on the night of your car accident. I have good faith that he will be able to perform hypnotherapy to answer the burning question you have been asking yourself all these months. He is good. He is expecting your phone call as I told him all about you.

When the time is right, I will drop in from time to time to see how you and married life is going. I will see if there are any kids on the horizon. I think you will be a great mother. I will be thinking of you on your wedding day. I have bought a present and have sent it to my house. I have left a note with it to say that it is for your wedding. I hope you like it. You will get why I bought it when you see it. Please place it in the living room as I think it will go better there than anywhere else in your apartment.

There is another reason why I have to leave. I cannot say goodbye without you knowing about how I feel about you. It would hurt me more you not knowing. What I am about to tell you is just a matter of fact. I have not written this letter to somehow guilt trip you into liking me. Nor have I written this letter to get some kind of reaction out of you. Neither have I written this letter with expectation that you will suddenly want to be with me. I just want to tell you by way of closure. Please do not read anything into this as I would have stayed if I expected anything to come from this.

The real reason why I have left is because I now realise that I have been in love with you before you even noticed me. I did not realise until Olivia showed me what love was. I really saw me and Olivia marrying one day and having children. She made me realise that I want a family, not just a wife. But I guess it was not meant to be. My time with Olivia made me realise how much I am in love with you.

The pain would have been too unbearable to see you every day married to another man. I would rather move on and start a new life in another town rather than reminded everyday what I really wanted. You. So, there I have said it. I am in love with you. In a selfish way, I wish you were still blind. It was the only time you noticed me, when you couldn't see me. When you got your eyesight back, you never noticed me again. Isn't it ironic that you had to be blind to see who I really was?

As I am writing this, I find myself trying to fight the tears to be able to finish this letter…"

As she reads the first few lines, she slides down the side of the bed and starts crying uncontrollably. She has the letter in her left hand and her right hand is resting on her forehead, with her elbow resting on her raised knee. She is trying to continue reading the letter through her tears, but struggles. She wipes her tears away with the back of her hand profusely, so she continues reading.

Her mom is already in the bedroom as she goes to sit next to her daughter, wishing that she could make the pain go away. She puts her arms around her as some way of comforting her. Martha can now see how much she really cares for Harvey and that the tears she is crying are for more than friendship.

Martha carefully takes the letter out of her daughters' hand and starts to finish reading the letter on her behalf.

As she peruses the letter, she finds it hard not to cry herself. Helen looks at the letter in her mother's hand, waiting for her to continue reading it. Martha clears her throat as she feels herself welling up.

Martha starts to read the letter from "I find myself trying to fight the tears to be able to finish this letter. I have to confess that I use…" As Martha reads it, she has to clear her throat again, pretending there is something else when she is really fighting the tears. She composes herself once again and Helen finds her mother's voice soothing as she reads on.

"I have to confess that I used to fancy you since we were in elementary school. I did not bother to make myself noticeable as I was too shy back then; not that you would have fancied me. If you had fancied me, then you would have noticed me and you would have said that you remembered me when I first came over to see you. I did not expect to see you ever again since seeing you at university in our first year, which was a pure coincidence. I chose the university because that is where I wanted to go to, not because you went there. I thought I could deal with being friends with you, after l taking care of you but I now realise that I cannot do that anymore. Each time I see you, I am reminded how much I love you and wish that it was me you were with instead of Robert. It is hard watching you move on with your life to eventually marry Rob. Now I realise that I was kidding myself and my shrink advised me that I should move on.

Before I started looking after you, I had an offer which would have meant moving away. I was not going to take the offer as I had no plans to take my work further. Money does not motivate me. I didn't tell you what I did for a living, did I? I write books for a living. There, I said it. I am an author.

I found it a lot easier talking about love rather than experiencing it. When that guy came over to the house when you were there, he was not a friend. He is my agent.

He came over to push me to sign the contract to have one of my book series turned into a mini television series. I think it was a sign for me to move on and so I am leaving to see my book turned into a television show. When I read different books to you, it was my work I was reading to you. It was nice to hear you say how much you enjoyed my books. It made me fall for you even more. When you asked what Florence and I were talking about, it was not to do with thinking I was a dodgy person. It was to do with asking for my autograph in one of her favourite books. You can blame your dad for that.

Also, my parents did not win the lottery. I bought the house with the sale of my books. If I am going to confess, it was me who paid for your operation when I found out that you could have an operation to get you eyesight back. The surgeon is one of my fans and so I was able to persuade him to come into town to perform the surgery. I found out about the surgery when I heard your mom talking about it at our winter barbecue, from the solarium. One last confession, I happen to live next to you because I loved the fact that the house back on to my favourite lake. The lake I found when I followed you home one day from high school. That's it. No other confessions to make.

If the operation did not work, I would have been happy to look after you for the rest of your life, even though my feelings would be there. The difference is that you would never have seen how upset I would have been.

Like I said, this letter is my way of unloading all my thoughts, rather than thinking that you would suddenly like me and leave Robert for me. Not that I would be arrogant enough to think that you would do that. Again, I am writing this letter on the advice of my shrink. I think that is everything. This is my closure.

Even though it is obvious you won't, please do not try to contact me as I will find it hard seeing you standing there in front of me. Well, that is all I wanted to say. I wish you the best for the future and hope that you enjoy your wedding.

I hope this letter finds you well. Your dear friend, H.

Goodbye, my lovely."

Martha is in tears by now and both struggle to compose themselves. "Oh, he really knows how to write a letter."

Helen laughs through her tears. "I guess that is why he is an author. He cheated. He knew that we would get this reaction."

Martha folds the letter up and puts it back into the envelope. "So, what are you going to do about it?"

Helen has a blank face. "Well, I am going to marry Robert. I am in love with him. Harvey has left. This is the first time I am hearing of this."

Martha looks disappointed. "It is your life. If you wanted to stop the wedding, me and your father will be behind you all the way."

Nothing more is said. Helen clears up her tears and leaves to go home. Martha was hoping that the letter would change her mind about marrying Robert. The business card is almost forgotten until Helen grabs it and puts it with the letter inside the envelope. She takes the letter with her and puts it in her handbag. She says goodbye to her mom and thanks her for letting her know about the letter.

When Helen is back at work on dayshifts, it is Thursday. She is on full duty now and has to perform her first surgery since she last operated in October last year. She feels that she is back into the swing of things and her boss assists her for reassurance. Her operation is a simple appendix procedure and so nothing heavy.

As she is carrying out the work, she thinks about the letter Harvey wrote and cannot get it out of her head. She realises that Harvey now takes over her thoughts about Robert and the wedding. She looks on at the work she is doing, taking out the appendix, and finds herself staring into space as she operates. She finds herself having to snap out of it, knowing that her patient is in safe hands. Her boss, Dr Faye, looks on at Helen and is totally happy with the way she is handling the operation, not noticing that Helen is in a trance and thinking about other things.

The operation goes well and the patient is fine. After Helen and Dr Faye are finished in theatre, they decide to go for lunch together. They eat in the hospital cafeteria for staff. Helen is glad of the company and wants to ask Dr Faye's advice, after they get their tray of salad and diet coke from the canteen.

Doctor Faye goes to start the conversation as they sit down. "That surgery is the best I have seen yet. How have you been since starting back?"

Helen replies. "Thanks. I have been okay. I thought it would take me longer to settle back in."

Doctor Faye wants to know what is bothering her. "Do you want to talk about it?"

Helen is relieved that she can talk about Robert. "I don't know what it is. I am getting married in two days and I should be excited. But..."

Doctor Faye is sympathetic. "You have been with Robert for what, twelve years. You are not going to necessarily get all giddy. You two have done everything, apart from start a family."

Helen finds that the answer is not what she is looking for. "But what about you and John? Weren't you excited when you got married?"

Doctor Faye ponders her question. "We were only together for two years before we got married. We did not live together. So, we had something to look forward to. If we had been together twelve years, then I guess I would think the same. But you have starting a family to look forward to. That would make things exciting."

Helen thinks about what she said. "I guess so. But we have never discussed having children so I cannot look forward to that."

Doctor Faye is curious as to why. "Haven't you two

discussed anything for the future? Like getting a proper house or where you two see each other in the next twelve years?"

Helen feels awkward. "No. We are not like that."

Doctor Faye sees alarm bells going off. "So, why did you two see decide to get married?"

Helen explains. "It was because of my accident; he proposed."

Doctor Faye looks concerned for Helen's marriage. "I am not being funny, but that is not an excuse to get married."

Helen starts to become tearful. "That isn't the only thing. Here, I got a letter. Read it."

Doctor Faye opens the letter, not knowing what it is and then is open-mouthed and looks at Helen. "Do you mind if I read it?"

Helen motions her to go ahead. Dr Faye puts her hand on her mouth as she reads it and has the same reaction as Helen and her mom. She looks up at Helen part way through and then continues reading. Dr Faye now understands why Helen is asking the questions.

Doctor Faye is shocked. "So, do you have feelings for him?"

Helen is confused. "I don't know. I never saw him as anything else except a friend. But I have found myself thinking about him a lot."

Doctor Faye sees her answer. "So, you already know the answer. Harvey was the one who was admitted to hospital for a life-threatening bug."

Helen confirms. "Yeah. That scared me. I thought I was going to lose him. I couldn't see him not in my life."

Doctor Faye has her question answered. "If it was Rob, could you see him out of your life?"

Helen struggles with the question as she cannot face the truth. She has already set the wedding and she cannot go on a hunch, even though the truth is staring her in the face. Dr Faye can see in Helen's eyes that she is not in love with Robert. Helen does not give Dr Faye an answer and just looks blankly at her. They both finish their lunch and then Dr Faye wishes Helen a great wedding. Helen thanks her and then goes back to work. She is in theatre again this afternoon.

When Helen finishes her second surgery she is ready to go home.

While she is in the changing room, she gets out the card that was in the letter. Helen ponders whether to call the shrink and get herself hypnotised. She is scared to find the truth out. She flicks the business card between her fingers. She finds the courage to call the number. It is not five o'clock yet and so she should get through on his land line. She types the number into her cellular, then clears it. She types it in again and calls the number, then cancels it. She puts the number in a third time and dials, letting the phone ring. She after five rings, she is about to cancel and the shrink picks up. She gets flustered on the phone and doesn't know how to respond. The shrink says hello twice before Helen plucks up the courage to talk. Helen explains who she is but the shrink remembers straight away and interrupts her introduction. She feels relieved as to her, it is half the battle won.

She asks the shrink how soon he can fit her in as she is conscious of her wedding day being in two days' time. She does not want to find out the cause of the accident after getting married. She explains this to the shrink. The shrink is very accommodating and asks to her last thing tonight. His last appointment finishes at five o'clock and he is happy to see her at five. Helen is overwhelmed and accepts. After they get off the phone, she cannot believe that one phone call has given her an appointment today.

CHAPTER EIGHTEEN

Truth Comes Out

As soon as Helen finishes changing at the hospital, she leaves the changing room to go straight to the appointment as it is now quarter past four o'clock. She does not have time to go home beforehand and so gets to her car and rushes over to the shrink's office.

While she is sat in the waiting room, Helen starts to wonder how Harvey is. She wishes that she could just pick up the phone to Harvey and ask how he is. She wants to tell Harvey that she is seeing the shrink. She wants to say she understands why he left. But she can't. It bothers her that she cannot contact him.

Helen does not want to think about the outcome. She just wants to find out the truth once and for all. While she is pondering about Harvey the door abruptly opens and a man leaves his office. The man is in his mid-thirties and gives a slight smile to Helen before walking away. The shrink motions her to come in with a smile which makes her feel relaxed. He notices that she appears a bit nervous even though she comes across as calm. He stays by the door as Helen walks in and closes the door behind them.

The shrink starts the conversation. "You said on the phone you were in an accident."

Helen agrees. "Yes. I only know about the accident because of what the hospital said. I don't remember anything that night. I don't remember leaving the hospital."

The shrink puts Helen at ease. "Before we start, the process is to make you relax. That will allow your memory to flood back. You will feel sleepy, falling in and out of consciousness."

Helen wants to know how she should be. "Where do you want me?"

The shrink asks. "Can you lay down and make yourself comfortable. Upright, please. I am going to talk in a quiet voice with soothing music in the background. Once you are relaxed, I will attempt to help you remember the day and hours leading up to the accident."

Helen listens to the shrink and makes herself comfortable and relaxed. The music comes on and makes her feel sleepy. The shrink is talking to her as she is trying to stay awake. While Helen is listening to him, she starts to think about how things were before the accident. It is like she is daydreaming about what it was like. She thinks about the day-to-day routine of her relationship with Robert. She starts to remember that she was working the same shifts as she works now. She thinks about what had happened in her shifts, as the shrink keeps talking her over the ambient music. Suddenly she remembers a text from a friend she received two days earlier before the car crash. The friend was someone from university she stayed in contact with and met up with now and again. She had not seen that friend for some time before the car accident.

Helen then remembers that the text was about an accusation that Robert was having numerous affairs. She is still under hypnosis with the shrink still talking to her. As her memory starts to return some more, she remembers asking her friend how she knew about Robert having the affairs. Her memories of the texts received and sent are vivid and all of a sudden, her memory moves on to the night, and following Robert in the car. Helen is struggling to stay hypnotised as she shudders while retrieving memories of following Robert to a restaurant where he was with another woman. The shrink talks to her, calming her down and reassuring her that it is her memories fighting to reach the surface and not to fight it. Helen responds to the shrink and soon stops shuddering and relaxes. The next thing she remembers is being in the car again driving towards an intersection. The next thing is she jumps up as she remembers the impact of the truck slamming into her. She bolts up and starts to cry as her memories come flooding all back, leading up to the car accident.

The shrink puts his hand out to reassure her that everything is fine. He places his hand on her knee for comfort. He does not ask what she remembered. He just asked her if she got what she wanted from this. Helen says thank you to him and wipes her tears away and composes herself. After a few minutes, she thanks him and goes to pay. The shrink waves his hand and says that the fee is taken care of. Helen cannot believe that Harvey had anticipated her going and already paid the fee on her behalf. Helen checks her watch to see if Robert will be home now. It is now quarter to six so he should be home by now. It will take Helen five minutes by car to get home from the shrink's office to her apartment.

In the car on her way home she texts her friend Claire to arrange to meet up. She is the friend she remembered about in therapy session who she received a text from two days before the crash. She hopes that her friend will reply before she gets home. She is five minutes from home. She keeps checking her phone every few seconds.

When Helen gets home just after six o'clock she can hear the shower running, so Robert must be in there. Claire has still not replied. Her text suggested meeting up for lunch tomorrow at a cafe of her choice.

Helen remembers everything so clearly now, after the shrink unlocked her mind. She goes into the bedroom and starts to cry. She tries to control her voice so Robert cannot hear her crying. She is meant to be getting married in two days' time and she now finds out that he has been cheating on her. Her next thought is whether she has had any STI's transferred, due to his infidelity or infidelities. She has to worry about having a sexual health check now, on top getting married. The only person she wants to be with right now is Harvey but she cannot have that.

She hears the shower being turned off and she controls

her crying, wiping her tears away, trying to hide the evidence. She composes herself before walking out of the bedroom to the living room, knowing that she will pass him on the way.

When she walks to the living room, Robert opens the bathroom door and smiles at her with only a towel around his waist. Helen nervously smiles back at him, pretending that everything is fine. He goes into their bedroom to change while she sits down in the living room. Helen switches on the television for distraction.

While watching the television, she keeps checking for Claire's text. She is paranoid that it did not send and so checks to see if her cellular says sent. Eventually, Robert comes into the living room and sits next to her. She is now worried that when the text comes through, he will hear it and ask who it is. She also finds it hard to check her cellular without attracting his attention.

She casually looks at her cellular and says to Robert that she is expecting a text from a work colleague on a case. Robert asks what the case is about and I tell him that I am waiting for results. As she checks, Claire finally replies and she is fine with meeting up. The text asks Helen to decide where to meet as Claire is not bothered. Helen suggests that they meet up at a cafe called Mary and Robbs Westwood for one o'clock. This is where Helen remembers going when she was spying on Robert's date with that woman. Robert asks if that text is the results of her case. As she is texting Claire back, she tells Robert that the patient is okay.

While they are watching television together, Helen finds it strange sitting next to him now she remembers again that he has been cheating on her. She feels that she does not know Robert anymore. He is now a stranger to her. She wonders how many women he has been with since they first dated ten years ago. Robert is sat next to her without a care in the world as if his sexual activities never existed. A tear falls down the side of her left cheek, with Robert sat on her right and so he can't see. She quickly wipes the tear away discretely, in case he notices.

When they are ready to go to bed, Helen says that she wants to finish watching what is on television and that she will meet him in there when it finishes. The show finishes in ten minutes but she waits half an hour, until she thinks he is asleep. After waiting half an hour, she creeps into bed with him, thinking about that night she caught him. As she lies in bed under the duvet with him, she cannot help herself quietly crying herself to sleep.

The next day Helen goes to meet Claire at the cafe they arranged to meet at. She walks there as it is only a ten-minute walk from her apartment in Wellworth Avenue. When she arrives at the cafe, Claire is already sat in the cafe. Helen gets herself a coffee and motions to ask if she wants another one. Claire lifts up her cup to say that she is still drinking hers. After Helen gets her coffee, she sits with her and wonders how to start the conversation.

Claire starts the conversation first.

Claire is Caucasian, athletic and blonde. "What have you been up to?"

Helen thinks about the question. "Trying to think when I last saw you."

Claire looks beyond Helen, out into space. "I reckon it was about… September last year?"

Helen cannot believe it has been that long. "Nooo. It can't be that long ago. It is, what? We are in August now."

Claire agrees with her. "Yep."

Helen is open-mouthed. "Wow."

Claire confirms. "Almost twelve months ago we met. It was before fall."

Helen is surprised. "Wow. I haven't seen you since then. Pardon the pun."

Claire is confused. "How do you mean?"

Helen is surprised that she does not know. "Claire, I was blind."

Claire is open-mouthed. "You're joking."

Helen has a straight face. "Nope. I had a car accident at the end of October. A month after I saw you."

Claire is surprised at what she is hearing. "Helen, I am so sorry. I didn't know. I mean, I knew about the accident, but I thought it was just a knock."

Helen looks down at her coffee. "No. It was the worst time of my life."

Claire holds Helen's hands on the coffee table. "If I had known, I wouldn't have left it till now. How are you now?"

Helen is almost tearful. "I am okay."

Claire hugs her. "Hey, hey, hey. You are past that now. I can't believe you were blind. When did you get your eyesight back?"

Helen composes herself. "It was the first week of June."

Claire asks about the accident. "So, where were you going that night?"

Helen feels better. "I was following Robert. I was on my way home when I had the accident. I followed him to a woman's house and saw him going to bed with her. I only found this out yesterday."

Claire is curious. "How come you only found out yesterday? Did you have amnesia?"

Helen mentions hypnotherapy. "I couldn't remember what happened from the head injury. I saw a shrink yesterday and he helped me to remember. I asked you here because I am curious as to how you knew about Robert's affair."

Claire explains. "I was out with my girlfriends for a few drinks. I spotted Robert at the same bar and started to look for you. I was about to go up to Rob to ask where you were when a girl went up to him. I assumed she went to try to chat him up when saw them starting to kiss each other. I went back to my girlfriends before he could recognise me."

Helen is curious. "What did she look like?"

Claire recalls. "She was a redhead. I only remember because her green dress did not go with her hair."

Helen now knows how Claire knew about Robert cheating on me. "Well, the girl I saw him with had light brown hair. So that confirms that he has had multiple affairs. Even if it is just the two."

Claire also remembers that there was a girl before that. "I remember I came to see you once. This was before the night at the bar. A few months earlier. It was a spur of the moment. I was nearby and had time to kill. So, I drove over and noticed there were two cars in the drive and I naturally assumed one of the cars was yours. I parked up and was about to walk over, and I see this woman coming out of your apartment. At first, I thought you had moved until I saw Robert coming out with her and she unexpectedly planted a kiss on his lips. I could see he was worried about people catching him because he was startled. I could tell that it was mutual as well because he did not push her away. Luckily, I was not noticed."

Helen is now building up a picture. "I guess that night was not a one-off. That is three girls I know now."

Claire looks at Helen's dazed expression. "What will you do now?"

Helen has a blank face. "I will have to confront him."
Helen is too embarrassed to say that she is marrying him tomorrow so she chooses not to say. Luckily, Claire is not invited to the wedding. Only immediate family and neighbours are invited.

The two of them have finished their catch up. Helen walks Claire to her car before walking back to her apartment.

When she gets back a little after three o'clock she packs her things for when she will go over to her parents tonight. She cannot stop herself from crying as she thinks about what Claire said.

When she has finished packing what she needs for tomorrow, she thinks about the letter Harvey wrote and reads it again. Helen cannot believe that she never noticed him until four months ago. She starts to think about what her life would have been like if she met him instead. Helen then questions whether she wants to be in love with Harvey.

Helen knows that she still loves Robert, despite his past. She is not going to tell her parents because of the wedding taking place tomorrow and the embarrassment. Her parents, Florence and Harvey all questioned Robert and Helen was blind to their comments. At the time, she just thought they were talking about his absence. She now realises they were talking about his fidelity.

Robert finally gets home from work and sees Helen sat in the living room. He gives her a kiss before getting changed into some comfortable clothes. He is excited about working his last day before their wedding.

Helen pretends to be excited as well faking a smile. Robert is bouncing about as the realisation of being married tomorrow sinks in.

Eventually Robert sits down and gives her a hug. Helen thinks about what Dr Faye said about children and asks Robert about starting a family. Robert goes quiet and wonders where this comes from.

Helen asks him again. "Do want children?"

Robert stutters. "Huh, huh, huh, I never thought about it."

Helen says. "Well I haven't thought about it either. But one day I would like to have children."

Robert deep down does not want children. "We should enjoy tomorrow and then leave it a year. Enjoy married life and then discuss about starting a family."

Helen starts to question Robert's interest in babies. She remembers in Harvey letter that he wants a family. He is the same age as Robert and in their thirties. They are not twenty anymore. Helen is worried that if Robert is not thinking of kids now, it is likely he never will. Harvey is so sure of his life and Helen is jealous of him.

It is time for Helen to leave for her parents' house. Robert, being enthusiastic still, kisses Helen, reminding her that this time tomorrow they will already be married.

Helen still pretends to be happy, faking a smile and appears to be excited.

When Helen reaches her parents' house, she stays in her car for a while, before going in.

She starts crying again now she realises that Robert does not want children and has been having multiple affairs. She wishes she could phone Harvey for comfort but he made it clear in the letter that he does not want to see her.

She frantically stops herself from crying and hides any signs that she has done so.

When she gets indoors, her parents have champagne on ice in the living room. Her parents do not approve of the wedding but put on a brave face for their daughter's sake.

Helen does not want to go through with the wedding now. She is going to save face because she is too embarrassed to cancel the wedding.

Neither her parents nor Helen do not realise that the other party does not want the wedding to go ahead. All three are faking their happiness about the wedding.

It is Saturday morning and, unsurprisingly, Helen has had a bad night's sleep.

Her mind is racing, thinking about the number of women Robert could have potentially slept with. She feels unclean thinking about the possibility of sexual transmitted diseases passed on by Robert.

She has woken in a safe haven, the family home. She feels secure being with her parents. She wonders if she can live without children. All her friends are married with children except for Claire, as far she knows.

She thinks of Harvey all of a sudden and wonders if he has already met someone. She sees him as a great catch. She thinks it would have been nice still having him in her life.

Helen is too depressed to have breakfast and just lies in

her bed, waiting for the make-up artist and hair stylist to come to the house.

Harvey's family are sat around the table for breakfast. The past couple of weeks have been strange, not seeing Harvey at the table. They talk about him as if he has died.

They each tell stories of what they remember about him in recent times.

Carlton remembers his advice about his date and now he is in a relationship with that girl.

The others moan about Harvey not doing anything with Helen. They all know that he fancies her and she is the cause of him leaving.

Mercedes is the only one who knows that Harvey is in love with Helen.

The time has come now. It is four fifty and the wedding starts at five o'clock. The drive takes about ten minutes. The car has arrived at Helen's parents' house and only her and her dad are at home. Bill helps her daughter in the back of the car. During the journey to the Mountain Gate Country Club, Helen is feeling anxious. She does not know whether to go through with the wedding, this far in. Her dad does not notice that Helen is looking worried.

It is five o'clock and all the guests are sat outside on the grass not far from the golf course. The grass is luscious, green and thick. They started arriving from four o'clock, as per invitation. There is indistinct chatter among the guests sat down anxiously waiting for the bride to arrive.

The ceremony faces the Santa Monica Mountains. Helen and Robert will marry under a canopy. The canopy posts are white with cream fabric draping over the them and on top, like curtains. All one hundred and fifty guests are sat down on white Chiavari chairs with creamy peach ribbons with a bow tied on the back of each chair.

The chairs are laid out to create an aisle for the bride and father to walk down towards the canopy. There are a hundred chairs on either side of the aisle in the middle. The chairs are in rows of ten and ten chairs deep.

The reception is in an atrium with floor to ceiling windows that wrap around three sides of the room. The glass is encased in individual five square feet of black metal frame. The room gives a panoramic view of the Santa Monica Mountains in the distance as well as the emerald fairways.

The sky is blue with the sun starting to set behind the mountains.

Robert is already stood underneath the canopy with the registrar. His parents are sat at the front and his brother is the best man and is stood with him.

Helen's mom is sat at the front, as well as Florence. Helen felt that she should be there as she sees her as family now. Florence looked after Helen for six months.

Harvey's family are sat on the bride's side, half way in, taking up two rows. There are seventeen of them.

I am in the kitchen of my cabin I have been renting out over the past few weeks. I am looking out of the window, staring into space, as I think about Helen's wedding today. I kept a mental note of what day it was. It makes me sad and I wonder if she read my letter.

I can see my neighbour has just come out on to her decking. It looks like she is starting her daily stretches.

I am cooking a stew for dinner, when I notice my cellular is flashing, next to the stove. I keep my cellular on silent.

My cellular shows my brothers number, Xavier. I wonder why he is calling when he should be at the wedding. I eventually answer the cellular, before I hold it between my ear and shoulder, while stirring the pot. Xavier talks first letting me know it is him. He tells me that he and our family are already at the wedding. The service has not begun yet. I try to be vaguely interested while hoping that he gives me a full account of what is happening now. After ten minutes on the phone, he eventually wonders where I am staying now and if I am. He also asks if I have met any new people along the way. I wonder if he means, 'Have you met a new girlfriend.' In which case I tell him that I have met my neighbour, who is doing stretches in front of my kitchen window, a few feet away. I tell him what I know about her so far.

I tell him that my neighbour is a Caucasian Swedish blonde in her early thirties and renting the cabin next door to me. Her name is Erika. I found out that she is here until tomorrow day, much like myself. We have made idle chit chat when we have bumped into each other, when taking out the trash or coming and going.

After Erika and I crossed paths a few times, she eventually recognised me from my books. She happened to be a fan of my work. Now we both make an effort to make conversation whenever we see each other.

From previous conversations and noticing her when she is outside, on her decking, she looks comfortable walking around in just her underwear. She is happy painting her nails with a bra and thong. I have also noticed that for nightwear, she wears skimpy tight silk shorts and a t-shirt that accentuates her breasts.

After I tell Xavier what I know about her, we change conversation about what Lake Tahoe is like.

I am opening kitchen cupboard doors, looking for seasoning, while having our conversation,

"It has been okay. I have lots of fresh air and time to think what I want to do with my life. I could not help but start a new novel. I thought I would base it on my life for a change. But with different names and characters, to make it more interesting. My agent moaned at me to take a break from it all and focus on the television production. Apart from that, nothing of interest."

Xavier is quiet on the phone and checks to make sure no one is listening on the conversation. "So, has this Swedish girl seen much of America so far?"

I am putting seasoning for my beef stew. "She has been touring the top part of America, near Canada and stopped here in Tahoe. She is nice."

Xavier sounds happy for me. "Way to go. Are you going to travel with her?"

I screw my face up in annoyance. 2Nah. I have to be in Atlantic City."

Xavier has frustration on his face. "You said to Mercedes that you were going for a walk about. Maybe New York. So why not go walk about with her? Maybe go back to Sweden to see how it goes.?

I look up to moan at Xavier when I see Erika doing something. "Good Lord."

Xavier is anxious to know what is going on. "What is it? You hurt yourself? Talk to me!"

I get myself together. "The Swedish girl just bent over forward doing her stretches and let's just say, my innocence has gone."

Xavier is getting excited. "What did you see? You know I don't get that much action after two kids."

I see Erika now bending over backwards. "I had no idea a body could do that." As I nearly drop my cellular in the stew.

Xavier can hear Harvey's voice intermittently. "Is everything okay?"

I eventually compose myself. "I am okay. I almost stewed the phone. Erika gave me a peep of her vagina breaking through out of her underwear. There is barely any fabric containing that thing."

Xavier burst into laughter, when his wife hits him. "Ow. Nothing. My wife hit me. I think she is flirting with you. That must be how the Swedish flirt. Christine is giving me filthy looks. I gotta go. Give her one for the guys that are not getting any anymore."

I say. "Yeah. Catch you later. I will be leaving tomorrow ten o'clock so I'll call in a couple of days."

Xavier laughs to himself and hangs up. His wife Christine gives him a filthy dirty look because a wedding is about to start. He tells her it is his brother. She is still not impressed.

Helen and her dad start walking down the aisle with Robert waiting. Helen feels nervous. Bill wishes that something could intervene at this wedding. Her dad is going as slowly as possible and Helen welcomes it. Helen starts thinking about Harvey, wishing that he was at the wedding.

When she gets to Robert, her dad holds her hand and gives it to Robert and then sits down. Her mom looks a bit tearful but for the wrong reasons. The registrar is a man in a white suit and white bow tie. He is black with thin afro hair, almost bald and with slight grey hair. He is a cheery character, always smiling. He thanks everyone for attending and says that he has never seen such a large audience. Some people quietly laugh. The registrar talks about the venue and how long he has been marrying people. He tells everyone about a time when the groom passed out from the heat. The wedding was delayed by half an hour. He happened to pass out when the bride took her veil off. It was quite a day. The audience laugh some more.

Helen cannot help laughing to herself and it helps her to relax her nerves and thoughts after the last couple of days. Helen thinks that the registrar reminds her of the late actor, Robbin Williams. He seems to have the same characteristics.

The registrar says. "This is an important day as two people who dearly love each other are here today to commit to one another."

Helen starts to get the jitters as babies, Robert's infidelity and Harvey interchangeably swim around in her head. Helen tunes out of what the registrar is babbling on about. She looks up at Robert as he smiles to her, judging him. Helen looks at him with judgemental eyes. Helen's thoughts are suddenly interrupted by the registrar asking her if she is ready to start the vows. She nervously smiles and nods at him. The registrar now begins.

The registrar says. "Say these words after me. I do

solemnly declare that I know not any lawful impediment why, I, Robert Swank, may not be joined in matrimony to Helen Simms."

Robert says. "I do solemnly declare that I know not any lawful impediment why, I, Robert Swank, may not be joined in matrimony to Helen Simms." And he smiles at Helen.

The registrar says. "Now Helen. You say I do solemnly declare that I know not any lawful impediment why, I, Helen Simms, may not be joined in matrimony to Robert Swank."

Helen says. "I do solemnly declare that I know not any lawful impediment why, I, Helen Simms, may not be joined in matrimony to Rob… I can't do this. I can't do this."

CHAPTER NINETEEN

We Are the Same

The registrar looks shocked. "That is not what you are supposed to say."

Helen becomes tearful. "I am sorry. I cannot do this. Not after finding out that you have cheated on me at least three times."

Robert looks shocked and nervous. "What. Where did you hear that?"

The registrar does not know where to look. "I have not got to the part of 'If there anyone who feels that they should not be married'."

Helen recalls the car crash. "My accident was a result of following you that night."

Robert looks guilty. "How do you mean?"

Helen mentions about the woman. "I saw you with another woman in the Flair Persian Cuisine."

Robert is embarrassed. "Hey, you must be imagining it. You hit your head hard."

Helen feels patronised. "And I followed you to her house. Opposite Fairburn Elementary School."

Robert looks at the guests and registrar embarrassingly. "I stopped when you had your accident."

The guests all gasp loudly in unison. Then quietly talk among themselves indistinctly. Helen is taken aback to hear the reality of his affairs.

She has had her affirmation and steps away from Robert. She feels embarrassed and rushes into another room out the back. Her mom follows after her.

Helen is tired from crying she has done over the last couple of days. She feels exhausted from the sleepless nights and emotional drain. She has had enough to last a lifetime.

Her mom stands behind her and gets her attention by gently touching the middle of her back. Helen turns around and cries on her shoulder. Her mom is relieved that it is over.

Martha is honest. "Me and your father didn't want you marrying him. We wanted Harvey to help us."

Helen is surprised. "How were you going to do that?"

Martha feels embarrassed. "Getting Harvey to show his feelings. But he refused. Quite right. We were desperate."

Helen is surprised. "It wouldn't have worked. But he still intervened. He got me to see the shrink. That's how I know about the affair. I was following him that night. That is why I had the accident."

Now Martha is surprised. "He must have noticed you. Hence getting engaged when you had the accident."

Helen doesn't think so. "I was very discreet. It would have been guilt. Having an affair while your wife is in a car accident."

Her father now walks in and sees his wife and daughter hugging each other. He hugs them both.

Helen is worried about the guests. "Dad, what do I tell the guests?"

Bill doesn't care. "It is free food and drinks."

Martha says. "So, what do you want to do now?"

Bill says. "The jet is ready fuelled. It can take you as far as the Bahamas. You can take an absence of leave… and figure out what you really want out of life. The world is your oyster, sweet pea."

Helen turns around, with her back to her parents. She thinks long and hard about what she wants to do with the rest of her life. She is single now, after all these years. She then turns to her parents.

Helen is nervous. "I know you are going to be mad with me. But I think I want to go travelling. Clear my head."

Martha smiles. "Whatever you want. Let us deal with this. You slope off."

Bill agrees. "We will make an announcement. Go.

Don't come back until you are ready. Stay in touch."

Helen smiles at her parents. "Thank you. I just need to get my things together and then a lift to the airport. But I should make the announcement. With you two there."

Bill says. "Sure."

Robert is still with the registrar, not knowing what is happening. The guests are still gasping and whispering amongst each other.

Harvey's family are talking among themselves, wondering what is going to happen next.

Helen finally has the courage to come back to the guests, with her parents. She plucks up the courage to tell them what is happening.

Helen's parents stand either side of her and hold her hand for support. "I am afraid there will not be a wedding. I found out very recently that my husband to be is not the man I thought I wanted to be with. There will still be a party as the catering and drinks have already been paid for. So please take this opportunity as a going away party. I have decided to go travelling. I… sorry that this is not what you came here for. It was literally over the last couple of days that I found out about a few things. Thank you for your patience."

Bill quickly says a word. "We fully support our daughter's decision. If you have brought presents, please take them back."

The indistinct chatter of the guests grows lounder. Helen's parents start speaking to the guests, trying to explain what has been happening. Helen stands around, coming to terms with her decision and is struggling to allow her new life to sink in. She is overwhelmed with one minute looking forward to getting married to Robert, to finding out that he had been unfaithful. She has no idea how many years he has been unfaithful. She cannot face his parents because of feeling embarrassed by showing up their son unintentionally.

When she finally came to the realisation of what her vows would mean, she could not fool herself into thinking that everything would be alright. She knows that she eventually wants children and she does not see Robert as a role model for her future children. She starts to envy Harvey for travelling by himself.

While Helen is standing around observing the guests' reaction after her speech, Robert walks up to her and confronts her angrily.

Robert grabs her arm. "You have completely humiliated me. Do you know how much this wedding cost? You are a selfish bitch."

Helen feels threatened and he is starting to hurt her arm. "I didn't make this decision lightly. Please, you are hurting my arm."

Robert does not let go. "If you weren't so busy with your career, coming home late most nights and working most weekends I wouldn't have had to resort to getting comfort from other women."

Helen is close to tears now. "Please, you are hurting me. Let go."

Robert raises his hand at Helen and she can see what he is about to do. She goes to put her arm up to motion to him not to hit her. Just as he is about to strike her across the face, a hand grabs his arm and turns him around. The man then punches him in the face and Robert goes flying across the floor. It is Xavier. The guests go quiet all of sudden and turn to look at the commotion. Bill observes what happened and goes to his daughter to see that she is okay. Helen fell on the grass face down and hit her head, from Robert letting go of her arm.

Helen looks stunned as she feels something dripping from her nose. She touches her forehead and has a cut. She sees a dab of blood on her index finger. She also notices that her nose hurts as well and she has a nosebleed. Everyone looks at Helen and you could hear a pin drop. Everyone looks daggers at Robert as they see what Helen looks like. Xavier and Helen's dad help her up onto a seat. Xavier takes a handkerchief from his pocket and helps Helen to stem her nose bleed. Harvey's other brother and brother-in-law, Chevalier and Montel, come up and ask if they need a hand. Helen feels overwhelmed by Xavier and thanks him. Bill also thanks Xavier and he does not see what the fuss is all about.

Robert's brother and parents look appalled by his behaviour and give their apologies to Helen's parents.

Xavier turns to Helen. "Are you alright? My wife gave me permission to intervene. Normally she would tell me to stay. Lift your head back."

Helen is relieved that he stopped Robert. "Thanks. Ah, is my nose broken?"

Bill and Xavier take a look and Xavier says. "No. It is fine."

Martha tells the guests to go into the atrium for drinks before the sit-down meal. The guests gradually start to go into the atrium, which is to the right of the outdoor ceremony. Eventually the only people outdoors are Helen's parents, Florence and Harvey's family, who want to make sure that Xavier and Montel are alright.

Florence looks at Helen. "You had a lucky escape. I was going to whoop his ass, but Idris Elba here jumped in."

Bill asks her what she wants to do now. "Shall we take you home?"

Helen's nose has stopped bleeding and she stands up. "Yes, Dad. I just want to leave tonight. Will your plane be ready to take me in the next two hours?"

Bill looks at her. "It is ready when you are. I will call the airport to let them know."

Helen asks her dad. "Can you drive me dad back to the house to get my things and then to the airport?"

Bill thinks of the guests. "I need to be here. To take care of the guests."

Xavier offers. "I can do that. Christine, stay here with the kids. I will only be gone an hour."

Helen looks at Christine. "You are lucky to have someone like him. I wish I did."

Christine says. "I know. That is why I love him so

much."

Xavier has his Porsche Macan family car, which is at the wedding venue. He drives Helen to her parents' house to get the things that she was going to take for her honeymoon. Once they have been to her house to collect her suitcase, they go straight to Santa Monica Airport which is a ten-minute drive away. After all the kerfuffle, the time is now close to seven o'clock. Helen cleaned her face up at her parents' house and changed out of her wedding dress, into a pair of jeans and a pullover jumper.

Xavier feels like asking her what she thinks of Harvey but keeps holding back, because of the episode at the wedding venue. Helen is looking out of the window with her back to him. She sheds a tear as she recounts what happened at the outdoor ceremony.

Xavier plucks up the courage to say. "So, where do you plan to go first?"

Helen turns around, apologising for being anti-social. "I have not thought about it. I was thinking perhaps Europe, if there is enough fuel, or South America. I also need to tell my boss that I have quit work."

Xavier nervously says. "Harvey is in Lake Tahoe at the moment. He leaves tomorrow morning at ten. From what I gather, he is finding the travelling good. So, you should enjoy the travelling too."

Helen asks. "Has he met anyone yet?"

Xavier mentions the Swedish girl. "Well, he has met a Swedish girl called Erika. But he seems not to be interested."

Helen feels a jolt of jealously. "Is she pretty?"

Xavier winds her up. "Oh yeah. Legs up to here, blonde. Think she could be a model."

Helen is open-mouthed. "Great."

Xavier is trying not to smirk. "I am kidding. But why would you be bothered, right? You are only just single and about to go travelling for the first time."

Helen frowns at Xavier. "Yeah. When you next speak

to Harvey, can you tell him that I never married Robert. Tell him he was right. And that if he ever wants to call me, he can."

Xavier smiles. "Of course. If you are curious, he is staying in Lincoln Park Place."

Helen does not show any expression. "Cool. Is he happy?"

Xavier is coy. "To be honest, I don't know."

They do not speak the rest of the way to the airport.

Once they arrive, Helen helps Xavier drive to the hanger where her father's air plane is. Xavier stays in the car while Helen gets her bag from the back seat and thanks him for driving her to the airport. She is waited on by the pilot standing by the open door. Helen walks up the steps to be greeted by the pilot who takes her suitcase. Xavier drives off back to the venue as Helen waves him goodbye.

The pilot says. "Welcome. Your father tells me that you are going travelling. The furthest this plane will travel is 1,500 miles. That is as far as the tip of South America. Refuelling in Mexico. We wouldn't be able to fly to Europe."

Helen thinks about South America as a starting point. "South America it is then."

The pilot smiles. "Certainly. We can be there in nine hours, including fuelling time."

Helen takes a seat by the window. She thinks about her life and what she has done up to now. Her head hurts when she goes to rest it against the window, forgetting that she hurt it when she hit the grass. She cannot stop herself from crying again. She is angry for herself feeling upset.

I have been staying in Lake Tahoe for the last two weeks and am finding the fresh air a lot better than L.A. I have learnt to canoe, fish and have been on a boat cruise. I have also been able to continue writing another book about my life but using aliases and different types of characters. It is not a biography of my life but has parts of my life experience as a fictional book.

When I was on the cellular to my brother earlier this afternoon, when Erika was doing her stretches I could see an imprint of her vagina through her white briefs. She knew I was looking at her because she could look back at me through her parted legs, as she bent forward. She smiled at me as I was struggling to hold my cellular before almost dropping it in the cooking pot of stew. She laughed at me trying to compose myself.

The food ended up getting burnt so I decided to order a takeaway to be delivered. I went out to get a bottle of wine from the local shop down the road while I wait for the delivery.

The cabin looks traditional from the outside but inside nice and modern. As you walk inside the front door, is a short hallway that opens out into an open space living area, with a square dining table and chairs. In front of the table and chairs is a wide wooden patio door leading on the wooden porch decking. A study desk is next the double patio doors on the right, facing a window adjacent to the double doors. There is a door to the left of the double doors that leads to a long narrow kitchen, like a galley. The window is on the side of the porch decking.

The decking faces the woodlands and so is totally private with no formal path. The decking has a rectangular glass garden table with six metal chairs round it. It also has a barbecue made out of a barrel.

There is another room which is the living room that has a brown leather sofa bed and a two-seater fabric sofa. This is a room next to the kitchen which is the same width as the length of the kitchen. It is square and a bit poky.

There are two bedrooms upstairs. The main bedroom has an en suite. The second bedroom has a family bathroom to use.

I have been staying in the main bedroom, leaving the second bedroom for my clothes.

I tend to fire up the barbecue, cooking beef, chicken and vegetable skewers for dinner, but it was forecast to rain. Hence why I tried to cook dinner before burning it. I decide to order a Chinese takeaway 'for one' when it is closer to seven thirty. I had no plans to invite Erika over tonight. I felt that I wanted to be alone. The Chinese takeaway shop says it will take about an hour to arrive.

I am at the study desk looking out of the window into the woods. I can just make out the lake through the branches and leaves. I see a fragment of the deep blue water. It suddenly starts to rain, as mentioned by the weather report earlier today.

The sound of the rain starts to send me to sleep while I am writing the final chapter of the novel about my life. The rain is soothing as I hear the drops splash against the trees. It is making me feel drowsy and I want to sleep on the sofa in the living room but I cannot as I am waiting for my takeaway and looking forward to crashing out on the sofa while eating it. Erika is great company as a friend and I will miss our companionship when I head to Atlantic City.

Going back to my book, I am wondering what the ending will be. I do not know whether to end it as a single man or man who finally meets his future wife.

I sit back in the chair and ponder on my life and try to visualise where it will end up when I finally reach New York. I seriously do not see myself meeting anyone in the future. As I ponder, I hear the doorbell ring. I look at the time on my watch and see it is eight o'clock. I am puzzled as the takeaway shop said it will be an hour.

I think it could be Erika wanting to come around for company tonight. I still assume it is the Chinese arriving early. I assume that the Chinese takeaway want to under promise and over deliver.

I go to open the door, then forget I need to get some money. I shout at the door that I am coming and am just getting some money. I see my wallet on the dining table and look for money in it. I get out twenty dollars and then walk to the door to open it. When I open it, I can tell it is not the takeaway man. There is no food bag. I think it is Erika, as my porch light shows an outline of a feminist looking body. However, the person looks soaked through. Erika would not be this wet, walking from her place. I hope it is not a man, as I do not feel comfortable letting a man into my house in case he attacks me. I am confused to why this person has to knock on my door. I can only see a silhouette of the figure because they are not stood directly under the porch light. I notice that the person also has a suitcase with them. I find it hard to close the door on them because my conscious gets the better of me.

I motion for them to come in, wondering if I am making a mistake with my kindness. When the person comes inside, their face comes into view from the indoor light.

I am too shocked to reply. It is Helen and she looks exhausted. I quickly grab hold of her and help her through the short hallway, through the dining room area and into the living room. She falls to the floor and so I make her comfortable. I quickly grab a cushion from the fabric sofa and put it under her head. I notice she has a wound on her forehead and what looks like a nosebleed. I assume she has been mugged or something. I quickly run upstairs to grab a blanket and some spare clothes.

I run up the stairs and frantically look for a top and bottom. Then I run downstairs, so I do not leave her alone for too long. She is just lying on the floor, motionless.

I tell Helen, whether she can hear me or not, that I am going to change her out of her wet clothes. I do not care if I see her naked or not. I just want to get her into dry clothes. Once I change her out of her clothes, I get her a cup of hot tea. The doorbell goes again and this time it is the takeaway. I give the guy twenty dollars, grab the food and slam the door on him. I then go to Helen to make sure she is okay.

I look for cotton balls and get a bowl of water. I sit down next to her and dab her forehead. I also dab her nose to wipe away the dried blood around her mouth.

Helen opens her eyes and looks at me. I lie next to her as I finish wiping her forehead of blood and her nosebleed. I remember how cute her nose is. Despite her forehead and nose, I still find her as attractive as I did when I last saw her in hospital.

Helen does not show any expression. "You're here."

I ask her. "What happened?"

Helen tells me. "I couldn't marry Robert."

I am speechless and am afraid to ask. "What happened?"

Helen puts her hand on my face. "You."

I feel guilty. "Did I do something?"

Helen is still touching my face with the palm of her hand. "You fell in love with me."

I tear up feeling guilty for ruining her marriage. "I am so, so sorry."

Helen quickly says. "No, no, no. You were right. I couldn't marry him. He had been cheating on me."

I ask what exactly happened. "What happened and how did you cut your forehead and get a nosebleed?"

Helen tells me. "Robert tried to hit me but your brother Xavier stopped him and punched him. I fell to the ground and hit my face on the grass. That is how I got a nosebleed and a cut on my forehead."

I am speechless. "I am glad my brother was there. What happened then?"

Helen tells me. "I decided to go travelling. I went in my dad's private jet and was heading for South America. I eventually realised that it was you I wanted."

I do not know what to say. "I… don't know what you mean. I cannot be friends with–"

Helen puts her fingers on my mouth to shut me up. "I also couldn't marry Robert because… I am in love… with… you."

I am open-mouthed and do not know what to say. Helen lifts her head up and hesitates to kiss me. I move forward to make it clear that I want to kiss her. We start to kiss passionately and gently. I almost start to cry as this is all I wanted while I was looking after Helen when she was blind. I savour this moment in case I am dreaming. Helen rolls her body on top of me and we continue to kiss passionately. Her body is so light on top of me and now and again Helen stops to look into my eyes before plunging her lips on to mine. Before I know it, she sits up and takes off the top I put on her, showing her bra and then moves on top of me to kiss me passionately again. I roll her over on to her back and I take my polo shirt off, as she takes her bra off. She then makes me stand up, so she can undo my belt to pull my jeans off.

I feel myself getting an erection and I just want her to play with it. When she pulls my jeans down with my underwear, she notices my partial erection and looks up at me before putting my cock in her mouth. She does not waste any time getting me fully erect. She slides my cock in her mouth slowly, pulling out gently. She uses her tongue to flicker the end of my cock before swallowing it slowly again. The feeling is making me wriggle with the sensitivity at the end of my cock. After a few minutes, she stands up and I help her out of her bottoms and pull her underwear down at the same time. As I do, I kneel down to her vagina and breathe in her scent. She sits on the floor with her legs wide apart and her back against the sofa. I start to lick the walls of her vagina. She gasps quietly as I lick up and down before putting my tongue inside. She puts her hands on the crown of my head as I give her oral. She starts to breathe heavily, enjoying it. I grab her hips and pull her back away from the sofa so only her head is resting on it. This gives me better access to her vagina so I can suck on her clitoris.

I feel Helen starting to tense up, so I stop. I do not want her to cum just yet. Helen looks at me, wondering I have stopped, then she twists us around so my back is against the sofa. Then she sits on top of me and uses her fingers to touch my cock, so she can feed it inside her vagina. She then moves up and down slowly to allow herself to get used to my cock.

Helen says. "We are made for each other. We fit like a glove."

I breathe heavily. "You make me whole."

She continues to move up down my shaft, gradually building up momentum. I feel that she is about to cum and out of nowhere, her body tenses up and suddenly shudders as she tries not to groan loudly as she cums over my cock. I still haven't cum and I move her on her back and put my legs out so her legs are closed and start to push in and out. Helen starts to breathe heavily as she feels the sensation of friction against the sensitive walls to her vagina. The end of my cock is stimulated more by the feeling of the tightness of her vagina. The more my cock becomes sensitive to cuming, the more I speed up my rhythm. As I am about to cum, my body tenses up and I feel myself cuming inside her tight hole and feel her cuming a second time. We both hug each other tightly as we orgasm simultaneously.

We sit on the floor with the blanket around both of us and eat the takeaway I ordered. We both eat like we have not eaten for days. The sex has made us famished. After we eat, we slowly start to talk about what has happened over the last two weeks. I am shocked by what Robert was doing before her car accident and why she had the car accident. I did not realise it was that severe. I tell her that I have been busy doing recreational activities, such as canoeing and coming to terms with being single for the rest of my life. I finally tell her about my book, on my past experiences. I tell her that I was wondering how to end it, till the doorbell rang. Helen asks me what it is about. I tell her it is a fictional story including parts of my life. She asks me what the ending will be. I tell her that I am wondering whether to finish it as being single still or I eventually meet someone and get married.

Helen apologises for not noticing me in school, high school and university. She says that she wishes she had met me instead of Robert. I tell her that it would not have been a great time as I had my own demons to deal with and it would have probably pushed h away. Helen says she knows how I should end my book. I ask her to tell me. She says. "Like this. This moment." I smile and quietly say. "Okay."

Once we finish eating, she plays with my cock to get me in the mood again. We go to the dining area and do not make it past there. She bends over the table and I give her oral again from behind before entering inside her. She groans slightly as I first enter inside and then slowly go in and out. Now and again I pull out and rub my cock against her vagina and just below her belly button and along the crevice of her bum. Then I enter inside her again and keep going until she cums again and I keep going to try to prolong her orgasm. I struggle to cum again and so she makes me stand against the table and she massages my cock in between the palm her hands. She does this until I eventually cum and she smiles almost laughing as she watches my cum flow out and splatter on her face and chin, with some going on the floor. I apologise between heavy breathing but she finds it funny and reassures me it is okay.

It is about nine o'clock the next morning. We did not make it up stairs and ended up sleeping on the sofa bed in the living room. I cannot help smelling Helen's bodily scent and feeling her boobs. She is resting her hand on my belly, almost touching the end of my cock. We are both awake with her head on my chest. She feels warm and her skin is silky smooth. We hear a cellular phone ringing and it is hers. She sits up and tries to remember where she put it and eventually grabs it before lying next to me again. She checks the call and sees it is her dad. She tells me and I wonder what she is going to say.

Helen calls back and her dad picks the phone up. She tells her dad that she ended coming over to see me. Helen looks at me while I can hear indistinct chatter from her dad. She smiles during her dad talking and replies saying that she was with me in Lake Tahoe. She starts to laugh and I am confused. She puts the phone down. She then tells me that her dad is ecstatic that we are now officially boyfriend and girlfriend.

I find it hard to get my head around it. It feels surreal that Helen calls me her boyfriend.

After getting breakfast, we have a shower together, giggling and showing affection to one another. She then helps me to pack my suitcase and she changes into fresh clothes from her suitcase. We then get into my shitty blue Chevy and head to Atlantic City. On the way down, we exchange conversations about lives from elementary school to the present day. We do not realise how much we have in common. The conversation makes the journey go quickly.

I finally find out what it is like to have security and someone wanting to be with me. I never did stay in contact with Olivia and she eventually met someone else and married. She now has two kids.

For Helen and me, well, we are getting there.

We will return in "Spade to Spade."

Turn over for the synopsis of that instalment.

Synopsis

The story continues between Harvey and Helen and this time there is an attempted murder. Harvey's old girlfriend, Olivia, gets involved in a money laundering ring and both Harvey and Helen jump to the rescue. Along the way, they get involved in various capers and eventually solve who carried out the attempted murder.

Printed in Poland
by Amazon Fulfillment
Poland Sp. z o.o., Wrocław